also by larry doyle

i love you, beth cooper

ANTS!

a novel by larry doyle

An Imprint of HarperCollinsPublishers

GO, MUTANTS! Copyright © 2010 by Larry Doyle. All rights reserved. Printed in the United States of America. No part of this book may be used or reproduced in any manner whatsoever without written permission except in the case of brief quotations embodied in critical articles and reviews. For information, address HarperCollins Publishers, 10 East 53rd Street, New York, NY 10022.

HarperCollins books may be purchased for educational, business, or sales promotional use. For information, please write: Special Markets Department, HarperCollins Publishers, 10 East 53rd Street, New York, NY 10022.

FIRST EDITION

Designed by Suet Yee Chong

Library of Congress Cataloging-in-Publication Data has been applied for.

ISBN: 978-0-06-168655-9

10 11 12 13 14   OV/RRD   10 9 8 7 6 5 4 3 2 1

for becky

Through the infinite reaches of
space, the problems of Man seem
trivial and naïve indeed.

—Dr. Minton

I hate all Earthlings.

—James Dean

1

YOUR FLESH will CRAWL

She SCREAMS, as if that will help.

INT. HIGH SCHOOL—HALLWAY—NIGHT

In BLACK AND WHITE, and not art. A hot
smudge of blind whites and ash blacks, this is the sorry
noir of drive-in horrorshows, the dreams of dogs and
monsters.

Enter right, SCREAMING:

THE GIRL, in high distress and heels. She takes
the corner wide, skips and skids into the lockers with
a metallic WALLOP, ricochets and goes SPLAT,
displayed.

In such a lovely and hideous dress.

The Girl CLAWS for traction on the cold waxed floor. Her nails shouldn't SHATTER like that. She could use more zinc in her diet, and less stress.

And here it comes, into the light.

CLOSE ON

THE CREATURE, cranial sac engorged, strange fluids ATHROB, the lobes beneath its diaphanous skull CRACKLING with spidery fire.

Its big cat eyes lume with lust, or thirst, or the first to be followed by the second.

As the Creature reaches for her, its middle digit extends telescopically, and impressively. The tip quivers along her pristine cheek, leaving an inappropriate residue.

She SCREAMS again, her face meant to convey a complex interplay of terror and desire, not coming across at all.

The Creature's features collapse. Its feelings are hurt.

She kicks off her heels, clever girl, and is up on stockings, slipping away, still SCREAMING, night after night after night after night.

She should know by now that nobody's coming.

A bit of a jumble next, an editor's breakfast of SWISH PANS, SMASH CUTS meant to scare and disguise the lack of a usable MASTER:

the Girl's wide eye;

a blur of wall;

the Creature's dripping mouth;

her frenzied rear end;

assorted lights;

some creature part;

a flash of stock lightning;

ending on her pretty, untorn face, eyes darting, seeking, and at last finding

ROOM 51

The Girl struggles with the knob.

The Creature is gangling up on her.

Of course she SCREAMS, a terrible use of her limited time.

The Creature reaches for her with erectile fingers.

The door is jarred loose by narrative imperative, and she exits, SLAMMING.

INT. HIGH SCHOOL—ROOM 51—DAY

The Creature throws open the door. It recoils.

The classroom is filled with human adolescents, taking a test. Their instructor, DR. RAND, glances up from his desk.

DR. RAND

Jim, have you forgotten our exam this morning?

The Creature is horror-struck.

> HUMAN ADOLESCENT MALE
>
> *That's not the <u>only</u> thing he forgot.*

As one, the class looks down.

The Creature looks down.

And sees that it is naked.

The humans LAUGH.

The Creature cannot hide its shortcomings fast or well enough.

The humans GIGGLE MANIACALLY. This blends into a KICKY 12-STRING GUITAR OSTINATO, and they begin to sing:

> HUMAN ADOLESCENTS
> *(in close harmony)*
>
> *It's the end of the summer*
> *We're having a blast*
> *They nuked the oceans*
> *Beaches turnin' to glass . . .*

his lids opened, vertically then horizontally, unveiling eyes many shades bluer than his skin.

J!m Anderson lay in bed contemplating another day, another dolor, as a teenage alien on planet Earth.

Inside the orb at his bedside, Brian Wilson sang:

It's the end of the summer
Here comes a hard rain
They nuked the oceans
The waves are insane

The boy's face wasn't half so monstrous in color. His dusky blue-gray skin muted the ridges and spurs protruding here and there, in patterns beautiful only to mathematicians, and his features were humanoid, if a little more oidy in spots:

his eyes were ultramarine, deep seas of whatever one wished to believe they were deep seas of, and kept in perpetual squint, which reduced their disturbing circumferences and made intimations of a soul;

delicate respiratory slits suggested a vestigial cute nose, and his pouty lips were possibly kissable, if situated on another head, and not periwinkle;

his ears were independently rotational, and highly emotional;

his forehead was quite high, approximately ten inches, and bulging with brains, but even this evoked the slick upswept hairstyle favored by singers and delinquents, without the hair.

A girl with enough imagination might have found him attractive in a rugged, sun-dried sort of way.

The girls at J!m's school did not possess that much imagination.

Not just the end of the summer
Looks like the end of the world

J!m sat at the edge of the bed, the great mass of his head bowing his spine into a posture most adolescent males

5

assumed voluntarily. This kyphosis, though mechanical, neatly expressed his ineffable burden, the worldview he carried on his shoulders.

> *Armageddon's a bummer*
> *Looks like the end of the world*

The singer faded from the orb, replaced by the K-BOM logo, which fissioned, leaving behind a pair of piggy eyes stuck in a slab of pea green fat. *"Shiiii*-nee!" the eyes squealed. "That was an H-Blast from the Past from the Rays, and this is," with maximum reverb, "Marshall the Martian!"

> *In the morning!*

the Martianettes sang, to which the orb jockey appended his catch ejaculation: *"Neep neep!"*

J!m squinted his first hate of the day. With a pass of his hand, the orb muted. The newer models would have automatically skipped the cretin, but there were no newer models in this house. The walls around J!m were paint, not PLEX; the movie posters were physically present, artifacts from another era. The floor below him was fixed, and he would once again have to walk to the bathroom.

He stood.

crk

J!m's nasal slits rippled. His day was about to become fifty percent more self-loathsome.

He was alone, a small comfort. It could have happened later at school, in gym, and that would be fun, or the cafeteria, like last spring, when Sally Fraser screamed and vomited on Hazel Court, triggering a chain regurgitation that got lasagna removed from the lunch menu permanently.

Best to get it over with.

J!m twisted his neck, down and to the right. The seam between his cerebral hemispheres ruptured, revealing his next skin: silvery cyan, bright and shiny, unmissable.

His before skin retracted with a viscous crinkle, peeling back over two glistening humps of cerebrum, blatant beneath the fresh membrane that clung to every nook and sulcus. All his thoughts were on public view, synaptic bursts twinkling across his cranium, the area currently most active being his basal ganglia, or profanity center.

His dead face fell away, leaving one that only wished it was, coated with a clear oil similar to petroleum jelly but highly reflective and thirty times as aromatic. It did not wash, wipe, rub, scrape, scrub or boil off. Gradually the sebum would work into his new skin, darkening and dimming it to the pleathery exterior J!m could almost abide, but until then, J!m would be the Greasy Kid, subject to the customary names and jocularities, offering sweet respite to Bobby Harvey, an oil-producing human who was said to give girls blackheads simply by staring at them.

The molt moved on, shuddering over J!m's sloped shoulders and sloughing off his sinewy arms, crawling down his angular, occasionally pointed, torso, down, down his long, long legs and pooling, in underpants, at his feet.

J!m kicked off his old sleeve. It skittered under the bed.

Shit, J!m thought, meaning himself, and began his morning shuffle, teen beast slouching toward Armageddon, another day strewn with the idiocies and indignities he lived for, the petty evidence that he was right and they were human.

A shame he didn't know he would be dead before the weekend was out. It might have spared him some anguish.

this had been the kitchen of tomorrow, only yesterday. The Plutoluxe decor, guaranteed to last 24,000 years, had oxidized from white to grayish yellow with olive spotting and had recently become unstable, cooking food left out on the counter and causing guests who sat in the chairs to appear in X-ray, a bit awkward. The Cryomagic magnet fridge was ten years old and had gone out of phase, giving foods a tart, cancery taste. And the fusion cooker had developed a wormhole, exchanging entrees across galaxies; a green bean casserole might go in, but out would pop a Giant Berenician Dungdaddy, which is not good hot.

The worst of it was the PLEX nook. The built-in viz was minuscule, and could no longer be turned off or lowered in volume or changed from PIN, and so the kitchen was a constant source of dubious news, delivered by agreeable males and females, always human, ever since Gor from planet Arous, hired for the perceived gravitas of a gargantuan flying brain with eyes, used his program to bend viewers to his evil will, after promising not to.

The current informer, a young man with old sideburns, sat before a mortise of lightning branching from the ground into a night sky. The chyron read: NOCTURNAL DISCHARGE.

"Tonight's PLEX release will be twenty-three teravolts," Tom Snyder intoned, "beginning at one a.m. and continuing for six minutes. While there is no danger from the emission, the President is asking citizens to step up their energy use in this time of excess capacity."

J!m skulked into the kitchen, in his uniform of the day, every day,

> black boots, size 16,
> straight leg Lees, w 19 l 38,
> white T-shirt,

and slumped around a chair.

"In the tightly fought presidential race, Democratic nominee Jack Kennedy today denied that he is having an affair with his running mate."

J!m's mother was at the counter, her tail swishing in a slow, sensuous way that couldn't be helped. More feminine than feline, she filled her silk Capri pants and pink cashmere sweater in an optimal fashion. Her pin-curled hair and short body fur were platinum blond, plush and lustrous.

On the viz, the four-term senator from Massachusetts spoke from the steps of the Rotunda, an unfortunate choice given his own rotundancy, alongside his short-suffering second wife, Judith.

"Governor Baker and I have not been involved in that, uh, way, for a number of years, back when she was an actress, and I was, uh, good-looking."

The reporters laughed, as they always did. Jack Kennedy may have been a political joke but he was a funny one, who might even win this time. A three-time loser, slimly to Nixon in 1960 of the former era and then staggeringly to the President in the elections of two and six EI, Kennedy was four points ahead with less than a fortnight to go, owing to a buffoonish opponent with a scary running mate, and was favored to become the first ex-Catholic president, barring some last-minute surprise, which everyone expected. They would be sufficiently surprised nonetheless.

j!m watched his mother being gorgeous. How had he come out of her?

"And good morning to *you*," Miw teased, her back to him, in that breathy coquette that made J!m cringe, the asthmatic baby voice, because it always came with a little wiggle. No boy wants a sexy mother.

Miw did a little wiggle and went on with her merry business. She pressed a glass against an upper cabinet, dispensing a thick black liquid, grabbed a small plate and turned.

Her eyes were huge and blue, like his, her lips also pillowy, but when she smiled the resemblance vanished.

"Baby!" Her pink nose leather scrunched adorably. She shimmied over in unheeled pumps.

"That's five skins this year! You're getting to be as tall as your father was." She poked his forehead. "*If* you stood up straight."

Already at maximum hunch, J!m slouched his eyes.

"*Baby*," in her lower purr. She sat and petted his greasy arm. "They only tease you because they're . . . ," almost saying *jealous*, ". . . boys. Drink your oil."

She pushed the glass at J!m. He ignored it, but his middle finger, sensing hydrocarbons, dilated at the tip, releasing the Worm, as it was known colloquially. The wet, fleshy tentacle slithered forth, up the side of the glass, and plunged in with a lewd, guttural suck.

Light sweet crude gave J!m natural gas, silent and deadly,

but it was plentiful and practically free, and so long departed that J!m did not have to endure, as he did with animal and plant oils, the psychic aftertaste of how its source had been rudely butchered or brutally harvested. When he was eleven, J!m created a comic book character with his affliction, *The Black Phage*, who solved murders by eating a piece of each victim. He never understood why nobody liked it.

"In Japan, Gojira destroyed six blocks in downtown Tokyo this morning, after becoming displeased with the daily offering. Officials there say the *kaiju* will not be disciplined, in consideration of his long defense of the country, most recently against King Ghidorah, the three-headed space dragon, and Gigan, the giant chicken robot."

The blue worm gurgled and slurped along the bottom of the glass, siphoning up every last C and H, until J!m, newly repulsed with himself, retracted it with a slimy snap.

Miw gazed at her son, her famous empathy failing her, his feelings unfathomable, and the only ones she cared about. Instead, she found herself feeling with Charlie Weston across the street, whose pants wouldn't button. She could have *asked* J!m how he felt. And he would have said nothing. He said nothing all the time.

"Harvest Hop tomorrow night," she tried.

J!m gave her a look of dry amusement, or light contempt, she couldn't tell.

"I hear Marie Rand doesn't have a date."

He smiled or frowned.

"That's what I hear," Miw said. *"Eat."*

Two silver Nixons on his plate. J!m picked one up and flipped it onto his tongue with arguable belligerence.

"Get anemic," her disinterest badly faked. "It's not easy to get coins anyway. You're lucky Mr. Whitley down at the bank likes me."

J!m raised a brow ridge. Miw furrowed back. He tossed in the last half-dollar and started to rise. With one finger to his chest, Miw pushed him down.

She began to sing,

> *Happy birthday to you,*

at her breathiest, *adagio, con expressione*, practically *osceno*, and J!m worried that she was going to dance. She reached under the table, also discomfitting, and brought up an oblong box covered in silver foil.

> *Happy birthday, Jim Anderson . . .*

The boy's name was J!m, but everybody called him Jim, even she.

Miw fanned her fingers at the box. J!m opened it. Inside was the jacket, cloth and cherry red, that J!m had admired, that once, at Mattson's months ago. His mother wrapped it around his shoulders. "Happy birthday to you," she said.

J!m stood. He bent over and kissed her on the forehead. His voice was thin and high.

"I love you, Mom."

And he left.

miw lifted a saucer of milk to her mouth, thoughtfully lapping.

"This is the PLEX Information Network. All the information you need. Brought to you by Memerase. Forget your troubles and sleep, sleep, sleep. . . ."

On the wall was *The Head of Christ*, Warner Sallman's dreamy Jesus, which came with the house. Miw took the print from the wall and turned it over.

The Polaroid attached to the back was old, actual, with a patina that could not be adjusted.

They are posed by a body of water. She's younger, fluffier, in a polka dot kerchief and the thick-rimmed glasses she popularized but never saw a penny from. The bikini is white and fetching but overwhelmed by her belly, buoyant, pinkish and ridiculous. He's wearing those dreadful Bermuda shorts he loved and towers over her, his argentine carapace sparkling in the sun, the glare mercifully obscuring his unfortunate face. His long silver fingers rest on her stomach, the closest he ever came to touching his son.

She did not know why she kept this secret, from J!m, or anyone. It was not illegal, exactly. But when she heard a sound in the hallway, she slammed the head of Christ against the wall so hard He almost judged her.

The sound she heard, a papery creep, was J!m's ex-skin, making for the door. How many times she had told her son not to leave his sheddings lying around, where they could get into trouble, knocking over garbage cans and smothering dogs. Two years ago one of them had made it into Mrs. Porter's house next door and slipped itself on her while she slept. Mrs. Porter awoke thinking that her latest whole body tuck had unravelled and gone to rot. Sheriff Ford was alerted, and Mrs. Porter pressed charges, assault by proxy and more sordid accusations the facts did not support, and fifteen-year-old J!m was required to spend two evenings a month at the

Manhattan Juvenile Education Center, where he learned how to steal cars.

Miw grabbed the molt by the nape. It batted at her weakly as she stripped off the underwear, perfectly good, and fed it into the disinkerator.

It went down kicking, and silently screaming.

2

STALKS
THE
EARTH

their house was imitation cod, built near the end of the last epoch and not upgraded since, save the required PLEX receptor. It was slate blue with white shutters and red door, a color scheme favored by the recently arrived.

J!m stepped outside, squinting, lightly grimacing, getting into character.

From his jeans he extracted a metallic white marble. He slid the alumina sphere apart into two hemis and stuck them on his temples. The right dome flashed once.

"Hey, creatures," K-BOM's morning host prattled around inside J!m's skull, "your favorite Martian will be invading Manhattan High tomorrow moontime to kick off your rhythmic mating ritual. Human females, prepare to be," *basso, con roboto*, "*PROBED*."

J!m yanked up the collar of his new jacket.

"Now here's Bobby and the Zimms!"

Anguished guitar over searing theremin, "Little Red Rebel" was J!m's theme song, though he wasn't little or red and his rebellion had been almost entirely apparel so far. But the music *sounded* like him, and it was what he wanted people to hear when they saw him coming, though only he could hear it.

Bobby Zee rasped,

> *Little Red Rebel,*
> *You're on your own*
> *Little Red Rebel*
> *Got no direction home*

Head down, hands pocketed, J!m crossed his lawn and stepped on the walkway, a futile ritual that made him feel unwanted, which made him feel better. This time the autoped responded, but went backward. He applied forward pressure with the toe of his boot. The walk sped up in reverse.

Fully invalidated, he hopped onto the grass. It warned him to get off, but wouldn't do anything about it.

the leaves were dying spectacularly, their autumnal remains swirling in variously ochered arcs around his boots. J!m crunched them without satisfaction. Tucked into his jacket as far as his big, fat encephalon would permit, he trudged down Maple Street.

He passed another Cape Cod like his, only nicer, a split-level ranch, a cod with a porch, a ranch split the other way, a cod, a ranch, a cod, a cod, each distinguished by quirky mailboxes, of which there were six basic models, four of them chrome and all superfluous, since there hadn't been mail for two years.

The last of the cods had a billboard mounted on the roof, an ebullient housewife dousing her teal living room furniture with a fire hose.

Cleaning's a Blast...

she enthused,

...with Aqualeum!

Homeboards had originated in old Los Angeles, stoking outrage at the cheap commodification of everyday life, which accelerated their spread across the country. Miw looked into one, over J!m's glowerings, and found that they paid a pittance, and that her property was not what they were looking for right now.

Across the street was Gort, the once mighty android, the preserver of intergalactic peace, raking leaves for the widow Benson. J!m gave a low wave, but Gort, who sees everything, didn't see it. The eight-foot metal man trained his visor on the leaf pile, which proved no match for his heat beam. It wasn't an Army tank, but it was something.

Mr. King flew overhead, jetpacking to work, a waste of

hydrogen peroxide and an imminent danger to himself and others, the inconsiderate dolt.

J!m hated this town.

Which was a pity, since he had nowhere else to go.

And it wasn't so horrible, not really, lately.

a typical American town, Manhattan boasted:

> well-kept lawns and clean-nosed citizens;
> a brick and neon Main Street;
> a beach cove pocked with bottomless caves;
> a deep dark forest preserve from which screams
>   could not escape;
> a Dairy Queen;
> forbidden hills up by the old deserted Promethium
>   mine;
> and an evergreen lagoon next to the PLEX plant,
>   a spot favored by young lovers because of the
>   breathtaking sunset always on view, and that
>   unintended pregnancies never seemed to take.

Like any picturesque community located near a heavily guarded military facility, Manhattan had had its share of the unpleasantness, but that was before, and this was after that. They had won, as far as they knew, and the streets were clean.

Most folks liked it here.

J!m, not among them, was unable to articulate why he hated it so much, only that he did. He could not state the paradigm that encompassed all he hated, what rules or measures he used to calculate his hate, why there were things he did not hate, or where this hate had come from, gripping him suddenly and furiously a few years ago. He had been such a happy child, according to his mother.

Three girls were skipping rope in the street. They chanted:

> *He had a big brain*
> *It left a big stain*
> *That looked like chow mein*
> *1, 2, 3, 4, 5, 6, 7*
> *Big Brain didn't go to heaven*
> *7, 6, 5, 4, 3, 2, 1*
> *He went to hell and left a son*

That might have had something to do with it.

j!m turned from maple street to Rose Avenue, which was another thing: this rustic matrix he was imprisoned in, trees crossed with flowers, because nobody wanted to be reminded that not too long ago this was an Army proving ground, built on a hallowed Indian burial site, which had once been an even more sacred sacrificial temple, for different Indians. The less desirable east end had been tar pits, stocked with the bones of Segnosaurs, a slow and unpopular dinosaur.

This subdivision was Arbor Gardens, since they couldn't be bothered to buy a proper thesaurus, and everything about it was unremittingly bucolic.

The lawns were Verigrass, a hybrid of Kentucky Blue and Cytherean Yellow, the only shade of green not found in nature. It resisted weeds, drought, insects, stains and sulfuric acid, and ate chipmunks and the occasional baby.

The trees were cybernetic in no useful way. They grew

naturally but could communicate with the house, which must have seemed a fine idea. Instead, Oak Drive residents were warned of every approaching squirrel, and over on Elm, owners were awakened at all hours by trees fretting that they felt fungal. Last spring, a boy on Whispering Willows Lane reprogrammed all the trees to whisper smutty overtures to passing women. It went unreported for months.

The PLEX transponders were made to look antique, a quality humans associated with nature for unsound reasons. The brass poles, fashioned after nineteenth-century gaslights, were topped with a copper ellipsoid, which, when nightsparking, did not suggest the pastoral so much as the diabolical.

J!m liked those. They reminded him of James Whale's *Frankenstein*, which he loved, as he did most movies that were made before they were all terrible. He called them movies, though they no longer worked that way, while everybody else called them viz regardless of what they were projected onto or plexed from. He watched movies constantly, carefully, desperately. He dreamt in movies, and one day he was going to make them, provided he could get into film school without paying for it. The movies he would make would be savage art, masterworks of light and shadow, vessels of unbearable truth and better than life, which was no better than a B movie in J!m's experience. His movies would be admired and despised, money losers every one, but the people who saw them would be changed, would no longer be able to live among people who hadn't seen them, and after he won his first Oscar, he would marry Marie.

. . .

j!m was giving his acceptance speech, ending with, "I Love You, Marie Rand," and had just rejected that as hackneyed pablum when he arrived at her house. It was five blocks out of his way, his standard route.

J!m tapped the left Bone Dome and the music stopped.

Marie's house was, through no fault of hers, a serious mess, an other-way ranch trashed with fussy contraptions, such as the overprogrammed lawn gnomes that had become sentient and were planning something, or, out back, the twenty-foot above ground pool converted into a Cassegrain reflector, able to pick up broadcasts from Metaluna, chiefly warfarmercials. A holographic picket fence went in and out.

J!m saw only the door.

It opened.

He ducked behind a tree, his back pressed against it.

Dr. Rand appeared, chin up, posture and deportment suggesting a person of greater social stature than a high school science teacher. The pipe was implied.

His eye was drawn to the jacaranda, which had grown two cerebral lobes, clearly visible on either side of its trunk.

"Jim," Dr. Rand said in calm admonishment, "I hope you haven't forgotten our exam this morning?"

J!m remained behind the tree. "No, sir."

Howard Rand, friendly and firm: "No, *Doctor*."

"No, Dr. Rand." J!m upturned his hand and unfurled the middle digit, telescoping it for emphasis.

Dr. Rand climbed into his Rand OmniDynamic MaxiPod Vehicle, a structurally faultless teardrop design that also resembled a slime green turd on wheels, something Reptilicus might deposit after eating a busful of disagreeable schoolchildren. Only three were ever built; the other two were in the backyard.

Once Dr. Rand had backed out, stalled, rolled down the driveway, ground the gears and pooted down the street, J!m turned to peek around—

"Jim!"

She was the girl of his dream, and not that girl at all. Her hair was unflipped, her face unpainted. Her twin set and skirt were plain and pleated, not taffeta and laced. She wore saddle shoes instead of heels, and no tiara. He much preferred this Marie, not least because this one was running toward him, not away.

No screaming homecoming queen, Marie ran like the tomboy she once was, more the boy than J!m, always her idea to climb trees and build forts and eat bugs and stick things up rectums, or cloacae. She could take him in a tussle, and often did, when they were children.

Now she had gone woman, and was coming on fast.

He surrendered to her hug with fear and longing. He was affected the instant she touched him, her hands on his back, over his posterior heart. The curse, a gift from his mother, flooded him with her feelings, the brightness in her uncurdling his brain, spraining it in the process. She blinded him with joy. He was a crude instrument, unlike Miw, and so could only absorb the broad emotional strokes; he could not feel her love, if it was there.

She smelled like soap and strawberries.

J!m didn't know what to do with his hands. He was welcome to touch her, he knew, but afraid what that might unleash. His pants were tight but not secure. He kept his arms out, palms open, in the frisking position. She went on hugging him.

She stretched on tiptoes and rubbed her cheek against his neck. The convulsion along his leg warned that he was seconds from letting his cat out of the bag.

"I love when you have new skin," she said. "It's so soft and cool."

He might have to shove her to the ground.

"Oooo," Marie inhaled. "New car smell!"

That fixed that.

She backed away from him, hooked her arm through his, a maneuver fraught with chastity, and escorted him off her lawn.

The gnomes watched them leave, biding their time.

"so," she chatted, "what's showing at the Skies tonight?"

"Entertainment product."

Her first eyeroll. "People *like* entertainment, Jim! It's not the worst thing."

J!m stopped short of the autoped. Marie stepped on it, and was efficiently transported away from him. He trotted to catch up.

Marie frowned at the walk. "It must think you're a cat or something."

"It knows what I am."

"Well, they should fix it," Marie said. "We've had guest species for more than twenty years; there's no excuse." Her agenda uncovered: "And apropos of that, I'm handing my petition into City Hall today. So, last chance, Mr. *I-don't-sign-things*."

"My name can't be written in three dimensions."

It wasn't that his wit eluded her.

"Don't you want our town to be accessible to everyone? You, of all people."

"I'm not people."

"*Exactly*. When I become president—when you vote for me, Monday, do *not* forget—my first act will be to sit down with Principal Brooks and see what we can do at school, at least. I mean, why shouldn't Kuiper kids be able to take classes with everybody else?"

"They're a gas at room temperature."

Marie pursed her lips. "I don't mind a little gas."

"It melts human flesh."

J!m always thought he was one remark away from a playful slap, a light wrestle, and the inescapable kiss.

Marie, frosted: "We'll have to be creative, then, Jim, won't we? Maybe apply some of our *advanced intelligence* to the problem?"

She started walking on the autoped, leaving J!m behind. He was going to let her go, too, and would have, if he hadn't sprinted after her instead. Marie slowed as he approached and stopped altogether when he rejoined her, but she was still not talking, which was hard for her.

Feeling **Nuked?**

asked the Mannings' homeboard, over a caricature of a human male, ice bag on his head and tiny atomic symbols orbitting his addled brain. The board's slats flipped, showing the same man, alert and ready for work, toasting with a glass of blue liquid.

Thanks, Prussian Blu!

he beamed through stained teeth.

This was the worst possible moment, and J!m seized it.

"Marie," he said, his voice flutier than usual.

She was formal. "Yes, Jim?"

The pose was gone. It was only the boy.

"Going to the . . . event tomorrow night?"

She dropped her snit. "The dance?"

it was a magnificent scream.

Marie toed the walk, startled. J!m might have jumped out of his skin, if he hadn't just done so, and if it wasn't the umpteenth time he had heard that particular scream.

"Do I have your attention?" Sandra Jane Douglas flipped her blond ponytail, her big teeth in gleaming rictus. She bounced toward them.

"Hope I wasn't interrupting," with perky aspersion, "invasion plans or whatever." She raised her palm to J!m in the traditional alien salute. "I come in grease."

J!m looked for shade to step into.

Sandra Jane grabbed Marie, restarting the autoped. "You get that plex about Carol Webster? In-cu-bating!"

A noise, the sound of distaff thunder:

"SANDRA JANE"

Marie stopped; Sandra Jane nudged her to "keep moving."

The front door opened and Sandra Jane's mother, or rather her arm, came out. Allison Douglas had once been a showroom model, for the short-lived Chevy Fissionaire, and so it was an elegant arm, with a delicate wrist and long tapered fingers about the size and shape of a dancer's legs.

Sandra Jane radiated high levels of odium as her mother's arm crossed the yard to her.

Mrs. Douglas's three-foot fingers unfolded. In her palm was an amazingly small man holding a capsule in both hands.

"You forgot your pill, sweetheart."

Without a word, Sandra Jane plucked the pill from her father and turned to escape.

"Hey, how about a kiss from my little girl?"

Sandra Jane huffed, and ducked down furtively, pecking her miniature parent hard on the eyes and knocking him down.

J!m marveled at how much hatred Sandra Jane could muster for a father who adored her, who was alive, who hadn't—

"What are *you* looking at, Butt-Skull?" Sandra Jane goggled her eyes and did fish lips at him, then dragged Marie away. Hearing her front door close, she flicked the pill into the street.

The two girls receded down the avenue, Sandra Jane a good riddance but Marie going, and soon to be altogether gone.

J!m's buttock-shaped cranium sparked, creating a whole new universe. In this one he would not make movies, he would not marry Marie, and he would soon be sucked into this black hole in his chest. He had created hundreds of such dark cosmos over the years, all culminating in his death in multifarious but inaccurate ways. Each of those alternate universes coexisted in his head, along with the many orthogonally bright realities he had constructed, in which he was a pirate, or an alien overlord, or married to Marie, who was president of the United States. He had the neurons to create and store thousands of additional worlds, and the capacity to have more than one active at the same time. For example, even as his last atom tripped over the event horizon in his forebrain, in a posterior section he wore a silver tuxedo and walked down the red carpet with Marie, president of the United States and top lingerie model.

J!m dropped his head into his hands. Filaments of electricity arced to his fingertips, taunting him.

This was the worst of all possible worlds, he realized. It was the one he lived in.

3

MATED TO *WILD* ATOMIC ENERGY!

rock and roll, loud and fast approach- ing, disrupted J!m's reverie of woe. Through splayed fingers he saw the chrome nose cone, leading the electric pink Barris Ballistic, bearing down on him.

J!m didn't move. He knew Russ Ford had no intention of damaging his beloved automobile, and, as predicted, the convertible rimmed the curb and cut away. Russ nuked it down the street and hit the retros when he reached the girls.

Marie pretended not to see him, but Sandra Jane brought the walkway to a halt and pointed her milk glands at the boys. Sandra Jane's mammaries were a fine size, not too large, and she considered them her best feature, which, sadly, they were.

"Russ!" Sandra Jane said, arching her back.

He smiled upon them, a copper god: auburn hair and eyes, a brash of freckles, a thin, mean mouth that could do terrible things to a girl, according to testimonials on Plexmate.

Meanwhile, his buddy Kenneth Morrow was thrusting his pelvis all over the backseat. "Human *fee*-males," the goofy-toothed beanpole screeched, a poor imitation of Marshall the Martian but better than the one he was doing of sexual congress, unless he was rutting with a polytwatted she-boar from Babirusa-8, unlikely on his allowance.

Russ lowered the aud and revved the reactor to a high thrum, extracting a rod while in park, not recommended. He lowered his right eyelid, a seductive move that in his later years would be mistaken for a stroke.

"Which one of you moon maids wants to hop on my atomic rocket?"

Sandra Jane did. Marie demurred. "Someday I'd like to have children," she said. "With forty-six chromosomes."

Sandra Jane secured Marie's wrist and moved toward the Ballistic.

"They wouldn't make them if they weren't safe! Don't be such an Einstein!" She pressed her teeth against Marie's ear, whisper screaming, "*Are you deranged?*"

As they reached the car, Russ looked at Sandra Jane and nodded to the back. "You know Tubesteak."

Yes, she knew Tubesteak.

"Shotgun!" Sandra Jane deployed.

Russ winked and nodded to the back again.

Spread across the seat, Tubesteak had both hands deep in

his pockets, and not in a cool way. Sandra Jane dutifully hiked her skirt and climbed aboard.

Marie chose to use the door. Before getting in, she looked back.

He was standing where she had left him.

"Jim!" she summoned.

"Jeez, Marie," complained Sandra Jane. "It's all *even*."

J!m did not want a ride from Russ Ford. He detested Russ, and Russ more than detested him. They had been at each other for years, from that first noon on the second-grade playground, when Russ called J!m a blue fairy and J!m speculated that Russ was projecting and that those statements Russ made about J!m reflected back upon himself, as if metaphorically J!m were made of an elastic hydrocarbon and Russ were an adhesive. Russ had replied that he was going to pound J!m, then the bell rang. And so it had gone, with Russ crudely taunting J!m, and J!m coming back with cryptic insults, vexing Russ and leading to further threats of violence, unconsummated but cumulative, building tension and testosterone, so that it was inevitable that one day they would have to fight or fornicate, and J!m was in the mood for neither.

Marie motioned for him to hurry up.

J!m hurried up.

The double bubble top did not leave room for him in the front with Marie. There was plenty of room in the back, since Sandra Jane was on Tubesteak's lap, accepting her change in station, but J!m was about as welcome there as the Jovian clap, perhaps a little less so.

He reached for the door. It locked.

"Looking slick there, Scrotar," Russ said.

"Shi-NEE!" Tubesteak parroted, misusing the slang for new, excellent, delicious, drunk, sex, almost anything but reflecting light.

Russ feigned giving J!m the once-over, a fair appraisal. "You gonna grease my seat?"

"Not on our first date."

"What's that supposed to mean?"

The male game bored Marie. "Don't be a pod, Russell."

Russ *yeah-yeah*ed her and released the lock.

J!m wrapped his fingers around the door handle.

Deep in the trunk, the reactor glowed and hummed.

The Ballistic blasted, briefly leaving the ground, jerking J!m off his feet.

On his knees in the street, J!m looked up.

Tubesteak hung over the back, giggling insanely, Sandra Jane braying alongside him, this being the story they would tell their ill-conceived children someday. Marie appeared to be yelling at Russ, who responded with a hard left turn, throwing her against the door.

J!m started to brush himself off, noticed:

His right hand was missing.

Annoying.

tubesteak carried on, giggling even as Sandra Jane inserted her tongue into his mouth and pushed him down on the seat. In front, Marie fumed off to the side. Russ switched on the aud. Behemoth's Mark Bowland sang,

> *You've got the teeth*
> *Of the hydra upon you*

You're dirty sweet
And you're my girl

Outside the Ballistic, J!m's Severed Hand pulled itself onto the door handle. It sprang up, catching the top of the door, and scrambled into the car.

in the middle of the street, outplayed and unhanded, J!m was feeling a certain wretched exhilaration, that all was rightly wrong in his world, when an old-fashioned roar of internal combustion gave him a mild pang of hope. A 1950 Triumph Thunderbird 6T rolled to a stop beside him. Its rider wore immoderately furry black boots, or had ape feet.

Johnny was a cool beast in a black leather jacket with matching face and chest, his head pelt in a carefully tousled ducktail. If he seemed to glow, it was because he did.

He regarded his kneeling friend curiously. "You prayin' or workin'?" he drawled.

"Funny monkey," J!m said, climbing to his feet. "I'd flip you a nickel, *but my goddamn hand just got ripped off.*"

Seeing the stump, Johnny hooted softly. "Grows back, yeah?"

"Well," brandishing his absent hand, "it's an *inconvenience.*"

J!m examined the injury. The wound had sealed and new finger nubs were bubbling on the surface.

"Want me to kiss it?" Johnny asked.

J!m grinned. "I would *love* that."

He jabbed his stump at Johnny's face. Johnny leaned away and fell off his bike.

J!m kept coming.

"Kiss kiss!" Jab, jab.

"*Kiss* it!"

Straddling Johnny: "Just lick it a little!"

Though a foot shorter, Johnny more than twice out-weighed J!m and had perhaps ten times the strength. And yet here was J!m, on top again, one-handed, and Johnny grunting and bobbing submissively. Johnny wasn't afraid of J!m, his fear grimace notwithstanding. Quite the contrary. He was afraid of himself.

It had happened only once, back at the Hospitality Center, when J!m was a baby and Johnny a toddler, and Johnny had ripped both of J!m's arms off playing a game of Let's-See-If-I-Can-Rip-Your-Arms-Off. Baby J!m didn't cry; he laughed while his tiny severed limbs reached out to hug the monkey. Johnny jammed the arms back on, and miraculously they knitted in place, and no one would have been the wiser had Johnny known his left from his right. The arrived-upon solution was to have the radioactive ape boy rip the alien baby's arms off all over again and let new ones grow in. Johnny was thereafter more careful with, and watchful of, his breakable friend.

j!m was rubbing his stump on Johnny's bared teeth when the patrol car arrived. The modified Gaylord coupe bore Manhattan Township's seal, an eagle clutching lightning bolts in one talon and corn stalks in the other, and the motto *To Protect*. The emergency lights flashed and siren wailed until the person in the passenger seat reached over and turned them off.

Swaggering out of the driver's side was Deputy Peg Furry,

rimless glasses and updone hair, the body of a real woman under that uniform, all too real. She wore her Stetson at a dramatic angle and spoke in a folksy northern accent that made her sound both more confident and less right.

"So, whaddya know, whadda we got here?"

Sheriff Nick Ford exited the passenger side, in street clothes, a badge pinned on his jacket. He rubbed his forehead.

Deputy Furry approached the boys, working her hips like a cowboy on a catwalk. "Jim and Johnny, Jim and Johnny, Jim and Johnny," she wound up. "A broken record. Jimmy Anderson and Johnny Love."

Johnny, domesticated: "Ma'am."

The deputy flinched at *ma'am*, but stayed on screed. "Okeydoke, let's do this again: Shouldn't you be in school by now?"

"Shouldn't you be married by now?" J!m asked.

"Smart mouth for a . . . ," Deputy Furry began, before she was joined by her boss, ". . . dumb punk. Maybe you haven't heard—too high frequency or some such—but this town is a No JayDee Zone. That's J, juvenile—"

Sheriff Ford squeezed her elbow, his cue for her to yammer down. He took a long look at these boys, well known to law enforcement, Johnny because he broke whatever laws they had, and J!m because he got caught more often. Johnny was a beyond reform, Army fodder, but J!m unsettled the sheriff. It didn't help that he had feelings for the boy's mother.

The sheriff pointed to the stump. "What happened to your hand?"

"Your son tore it off. Sheriff." J!m had found that being polite to authority figures infuriated them the most.

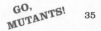

Nick Ford, weary: "You gonna be all right?"

"I've lost worse."

They were trapped in their permanent conversation.

"What're you rebelling against, Jim?"

"Rhetorical questions," J!m answered. "Sir."

Nick Ford was frustrated, halfway toward J!m's goal. "You don't have to be this way, son."

"I'm not your son," flawlessly respectful. "Your son has red hair, and one of my hands. I'd like it back, if you see him."

The sheriff touched J!m's shoulder. J!m felt a sadness coming from him, a sadness deeper and richer than anything J!m had ever felt. This irritated him.

"You know what I'm saying," Nick Ford said. "You don't have to be your father."

"You mean," J!m asked with the least chalance he could, "*superior*?"

The sheriff removed his hand, and his more authentic sorrow, which J!m immediately missed.

Nick Ford glanced down, then returned with his official countenance.

"Go to school."

The sheriff walked to the car. Deputy Furry backed away slowly, keeping the suspects in sight.

"D, delinquent," she continued in strategic retreat. "My eyes, your ass," she warned them, indicating with her finger, repeating the gesture twice, once for each of their hindquarters, before backing into the vehicle.

The cherry top lit. The sheriff killed it. The patrol car peeled out and a moment later slowed down.

Johnny mounted his cycle.

"Thanks for backing me up there, Monkey," J!m said, climbing on back. He wrapped his arms around Johnny's waist, getting that old jolt of inner ape, a primal brew of agony and ecstasy that J!m could feel but not understand.

Johnny kick-started the bike.

"Ain't my war, Freak."

4

TEASING
BECOMES
TORTURE!

that star-spangled banner yet waved, minus the first, thirteenth, thirty-sixth, and forty-fifth stars, over the campus of Manhattan High School. The stars were there, symbolically, the same navy blue as the field, a compromise between legislators who thought they should be removed and those who wanted them in red, a political fight that had gotten churlish without ever making sense. But however many stars and whatever their color, when Lewis Seuss ran that newest Old Glory up the flagpole every morning, somebody saluted. Usually Lewis Seuss. The rest of them were normal teenagers.

Manhattan High was one of the oldest surviving buildings in the area, done in Collegiate Gothic, a majestic, soaring architecture that its occupants associated with cavemen. There was nothing shiny, oblique or curved about it. The three-story brick edifice had a stone façade cast with shields, eagles, arrows and other symbols of higher learning, and a central bell tower that had remained locked ever since Dr. Terwilliker, the old music teacher, had castrated dozens of pupils up there, using the pealing bell to mask their girlish screams, in hopes of creating an unstoppable five-hundred-boy soprano army, his plans becoming vague from there. Either that or the tower was locked because the administration didn't want kids messing with the bell.

The halls of MHS, on this particular morning, were the same as any other morning. Students bustled and loitered, primped and posed. Tony Baker and Joan Staples, intimately intertwined and sharing Bone Domes, swayed down the hall, almost stepping on Bud Beezle, a vampire squidling from Beyond the Deep, causing the startled sophomore to squirt his bioluminescent mucus, at great emotional and metabolic cost. Nine out of ten students were human, and most of the others were humanoid, with enlarged or additional parts or animal attributes, but each somehow alike, as if one could strip away the fur and scales, the ear tips and pig noses, and they would be no different after all.

And then there was Larry Sweeney, a big tub of purple goo in husky-boy clothes.

A protozoan collective capable of taking any shape, Larry had long ago settled into the fat kid mold because it required the least effort, being essentially globular, while maximizing his digestive volume. He wasn't bothered by the taunts, or anything, really. Larry was a happy mass, as transparent emotionally as he was physically.

At the moment there was only one thing on his amorphous mind: a Coco Zoom, the fourth-most delicious snack cake in the galaxy, and the only one currently in his possession.

Larry removed the silvery foil, though that wasn't strictly necessary, from the chocolatey-coated devil's food rocket filled with a creamy fuel of sugared fat and a drop of genuine rocket propellant in every Zoom. He leered at the treat for almost a minute before sticking it into his mouth shape, also unnecessary.

The rocket cake tumbled slowly, lost in inner space, savored by every amoeboid of Larry's being, as he dreamily crooned the Coco Zoom jingle,

> *When the grumbles strike*
> *And hunger looms,*
> *Blast to the rescue*
> *With Coco Zooms!*

which was less lame sung by Titanic Sirens.

Larry was about to begin the dirty version when a hand reached into his head and snatched the cake away.

Tubesteak bit the gloppy pastry in half. "Sorry," he said, cream and Larry dripping off his lips. "Were you eating this?"

"Careful," Larry advised him. "I'm high in fatty acids."

Russ took Larry by the elbow area. "Wanna show you something."

"Fantastic!" Larry said.

the triumph rode past Howland's Farm, a subsidiary of The Carboration, producing corn forty percent higher than an elephant's eye since the year four EI. The proprietarily treated fields abutted the high school and served as an informal smoking and petting area, where, instead of gaining reputations, girls grew mustaches.

The final morning bell tolled as Johnny jumped the curb onto school property, tore up the lawn and narrowly missed the MHS sign, recently converted to viz, and its operator, Lewis Seuss, making the most of it, flashing, scrolling, sliding, flipping, spinning and wiping the morning blurbs:

MANHATTAN VS. SPRINGDALE, SAT., 1 PM

GO, MUTANTS!

HARVEST HOP, SAT., 7 PM

DRINK FIZH!

TODAY'S LUNCH: HOT PROTEIN RODS

Johnny parked the bike in front of the entrance, where no one would touch it, twice. He and J!m dismounted, walked up the steps and through an infrared field that confirmed their identity and tardiness.

larry went along, as he always did, until he saw where Russ and Tubesteak were taking him.

"Hey," he said, "love to hang out with you fellas in the boys' room, but I gotta tell you. I don't smoke. Or excrete."

"That's okay, Goo," Russ said.

"It's Jelly," Larry politely corrected him.

CRUSH THE DUST DEVILS!

demagogued the banner above the entrance hall, a green hand squeezing the life out of a whirling sports demon. It reset, then killed and killed again.

J!m and Johnny dawdled as other students rushed around them, giving Johnny wide berth on account of his reputation and high Geiger count. J!m they shouldered and elbowed and kneed with impunity, even the girls; he was light and squishy, had no talons or stingers or corrosive juices, and so served as a safe outlet for their proactive passive aggression, each blow a penance for the sins of his ancestors and other unrelated individuals.

Johnny's wristplex barked. "We got detention," he noted, erasing the plex. This was J!m's sixth of the year and Johnny's fiftieth, notable in only thirty-nine school days. Johnny also never served his, and since delinquent detentions doubled every semester, he was up to 12,028, which would take sixty school years to retire. Johnny figured they would be easier to do after he was dead.

J!m, rote: "You going to class today?"

Johnny raspberried. He did not put much stock in course work, either; he had only come today because J!m needed a ride, and some characters owed him money. He began two grades ahead of J!m, and for the last five years had been in the same grade, but now he was a junior and holding.

"You'll never graduate."

"I'm here until you go," Johnny said, "then it's the Army for me."

J!m was bemused. "You're gonna join the Army?"

"Who said *join*?"

J!m didn't respond.

"They better send me to Brazil, or the Ozarks, 'cuz I am *not* going to the Pole. That Thing's unkillable."

J!m wasn't listening. He was staring at Marie, smiling back at him, all three of her.

the boys were jolly friends, Jelly in the middle and Russ and Tubesteak on either side, holding him down.

Jelly, apologetic: "I'm just not thirsty."

"Sure you are," Russ said, shoving Jelly's head into the toilet, or, rather, shoving his hand through Jelly's head and into the bowl.

"Sowwy," Jelly snuffled, a fist in his nose.

Russ yanked his hand out, took Jelly by the shirt front and dragged him down.

Jelly's hands and feet shot backward, stretching several feet to grab hold of the outside of the stall.

Tubesteak flushed.

The water sluiced viciously around Jelly's hydrophilic head. Drawn into the whirl, his face twisted around and down.

Jelly's hands and feet let go as his gelatinous mass slid out of his clothes and down the drain with a loud gurgling slurp.

Tubesteak giggled. Russ, too, was pleased.

"I can't believe I didn't think of this before!"

marie's campaign posters were unremarkable, VOTE MARIE, MARIE 4 ALL, MARIE CARES, etc., over an embedded viz of her smiling, politically primitive compared with those of her opponent, Lewis Seuss, declaring LEWIS IS THE KEWLEST and SEUSS FOR YOUTH, showing his intense head, rotating 360 degrees and then transforming into a werewolf, with the disclaimer, FOR ILLUSTRATIVE PURPOSES ONLY; LEWIS SEUSS IS NOT A LYCANTHROPE. All Marie had going for her was her charm and decency and the fact that most of the electorate had not, at one time or other, beaten her up.

J!m gazed at Marie's vizage in a way he couldn't to her face. She was unpretentiously pretty, hair short and black, eyes blue and green, right and left respectively, lips that most human females must purchase. He was most whelmed by her smile, so big, so intense, flagging in one corner near the end of the ten-second loop, and then pushed harder still before starting all over again.

"You gonna or not?" Johnny asked.

J!m walked away from the posters. "I'm gonna."

"If you don't, maybe I'll punch you."

"I said I'm gonna."

"Maybe I'll punch you hard."

The halls were empty; everybody else was in homeroom, sarcastically pledging allegiance and disregarding an announcement that due to a plumbing snafu in the girl's locker room, all female students should schedule mammograms immediately.

"How hard can it be? It's a *dance*," Johnny was saying. "You've seen each other naked."

"We were *five*."

"Savor it. You may never see another one."

"You're a sick monkey." And likely right. There were plenty of girls that J!m could get, the kind attracted to off-species

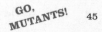

bad boys. Johnny attracted them from out of state. But J!m had never been interested, always thinking that Marie was his girl. They held hands and kissed often, if not succulently, and while the clothes had not come off in a few years (though far more recently than Johnny knew), J!m thought he and Marie were dating, or at least pre-dating, until this morning, when she got in another boy's car.

"How about I do it for you?" Johnny offered. "I'll tell her, *Jim woulda asked you himself, only he is tragically dickless.*"

"I'm asking her," J!m said. "Right after Bio."

"Sure," Johnny said, "you can grow yourself some nuts in a beaker."

the giggle echoed behind them. J!m turned to see Russ and Tubesteak running from the bathroom, beside themselves with malevolent glee.

J!m didn't use public conveniences, in compliance with hazardous waste protocols, and was appalled when he entered the boys' room, how *organic* it smelled: fecal, alkaline, musky, fetid, curdled, Brylcreemy and smoky, from the incineration of three distinct plants. He couldn't fathom why human females would have anything to do with these mammals.

Heaped on the floor of an open stall was a pair of fifty-eight-inch Rolypolyester pants in a gingham pattern. Johnny reached in and fished out an X⁴L Polynesian shirt, the one with the Tiki Goddess that Jelly claimed to have wet humped.

"That's one creature you do not want in the sewers."

A *glurping* came two stalls down.

J!m opened the door. An undifferentiated purple column

rose from the commode, taking shape, head first, filling in eyes, ears, nose, and big mouth.

"Refreshing!"

"Hey, Jell," Johnny said.

"How's the water?" J!m asked. "Meet anybody?"

An idea spurted from Jelly's head, forming a lightbulb. *"Boing!"* he said, head disappearing down the toilet, followed by the bulb.

A few seconds later they heard a woman, possibly Principal Brooks, shriek, with either fright or delight.

Jelly reemerged from the bowl, a grin as wide as the toilet seat.

"Incredible!"

written on the blackboard, in the crabbed
hand of a man unappreciated in his day, mocked
and ostracized by his peers, who were not peers at
all but mental gnats whom he could crush with the
contents of a single neuron in his vastly more sapient
big toe:

Friday, October 27, 10 ex iste
Xenobiology
Dr. Howard Rand
Exam today!

Dr. Rand sat behind an antique wood desk, paging through a plexicon set to A. Z. Rosenbaum's *Show Them All!*, a favorite among misunderstood geniuses and adolescents. Behind him was the skeleton of an aquatic humanoid from the Devonian Age, the last of his race, a splendid specimen that Dr. Rand had harvested personally on an Amazon expedition years ago, over the hysterical objections of irksome locals.

Plastered about the room were hand-drawn charts showing cross-sections of various aliens and mutants Dr. Rand had cross-sected, scribbled with voluminous notes and diatribes. The students sitting nearby were freely referring to them for the test.

J!m was in the back, pretzelled into a chrome and teal desk, its kidney-shaped top tilted acutely into where somebody failing this test might guess his kidneys were. J!m wasn't far along, and wasn't getting any farther; he was watching Marie, sitting up front, going over her answers. He was crafting his next words to her, looking for something friendly that sounded like him, lighthearted yet within his ennui. So far he had: *Dance?*

"Two minutes," Dr. Rand said, looking directly at J!m.

J!m reluctantly returned to the test, an inane exercise in a tiresome subject that J!m would never have any use for unless he decided to direct episodes of *Edward Morbius, Monster Doctor*, which he would not. He knew all of this material anyhow, as he knew everything he had ever heard or seen, along with a lot of drivel his brain came with, including Sumerian, the complete lyrics of Frank Sinatra's *Songs for Young Lovers*, and a post-Newtonian meta-calculus that was only good for guessing the number of jelly beans in a jar. J!m learned so much so fast that he found the process supremely insipid, the

only fascinating aspect being how much worthless information there was out there.

> 2. *What is the main diet of the Venusian*
> *Succubix?*

Baby stuff, much like J!m's new hand. He began to write, his
stubby nascent fingers holding the pen like a dagger, "Myelin
glycopro—"

A thundering crack from the center of his skull discharged
bolts of white through his brain. His craniun flared with a soft
pop, and went dark.

Forty-five seconds he sat there, eyes forward, little fist, all
the lights out.

"One minute."

J!m blinked and looked at his test.

> 2. *What is the main diet of the Venusian*
> *Succubix?*

He was nonplussed to find half the answer written there,
as if written by an infant, and then he saw his tiny hand, and
the morning began to reassemble itself bit by charred bit from
his frazzled synapses, none of it explaining J!m's most pressing
question: *Had he just died for a minute?*

Not quite, or yet.

sqt.

That was external. J!m picked the wet wad of tissue off his
eyelid, and followed it to its source:

Russ, adjacent, impatiently indicating J!m's full-size left
hand, blocking a clear view of his answers.

J!m lifted his hand—momentarily, to swat Russ away—and returned to his test just as a scarlet F manifested on its surface. J!m looked up to see Dr. Rand swiping a finger across his desk with extreme prejudice.

The test fluttered off J!m's plextop, replaced by a soundless adviz for Fizh!, that day's learning partner.

An adolescent human male and female sat in a car in a secluded area. He was earnestly arguing a position that she found unconvincing. He reached between his legs, pausing long enough to raise expectations, and produced a tall bottle of bubbly luminescence. The greenish glow lit up her eyes, which impossibly dilated in response.

The camera craned back, leaving the couple to imbibe indescribable refreshment, or to test the soft drink's rumored effectiveness as a contraceptive.

The product's lazy slogan effervesced into view:

It's
Fizh!

J!m watched, registering another product he would never buy, and waited for the bell to ring.

It did.

Tests minimized off all the PLEX desks, and Dr. Rand announced, "Chapters twelve through sixteen for Monday."

A group groan, sprinkled with whines and one *asshole*.

Dr. Rand, magnanimous: "Just chapters twelve, thirteen and fourteen. Enjoy the dance."

This reminded J!m that there was a dance, and that he was going to ask a girl to it, *that* girl, the one walking out the door.

J!m staggered from his desk, half dragging it down the aisle, and went after Marie.

"Jim?"

J!m kept moving, and so, more forcefully: "Jim, could I see you for a moment?"

Marie slipped into the stream of passing students.

Dr. Rand did not look up from the test papers arrayed on his desk, checking and X-ing, his finger swooping in the air with the metronomic fury of a conductor who would one day be found with a sharpened flute through his neck.

"I expected more from you, Jim."

"I would have expected more from Russell. He was raised right."

Dr. Rand grandly swept the papers into memory. "This isn't about that." He rapped the desktop. The Darwin English Oak reverted to the black gloss of its off state.

"Jim, you've got 6.5 times the brains of any kid in this school, but you're getting straight C's."

"I don't test well."

"That's a load of feces, Jim," Dr. Rand said, pivoting to face him. "Immature feces."

J!m bowed his head in contrition. "You're right, Dr. Rand. I've been suppressing my true intelligence to conceal my plan for world domination." Head up, voice even. "It's unfortunate you found out."

He raised his arm and reached for the teacher's throat, his infantile fingers wriggling slowly.

Dr. Rand, unamused: "This isn't one of your silly movies, Jim."

J!m commenced an evil laugh, and was reaching a gratify-

ing crescendo when his head suddenly effulged, sensational arcs of light fracturing across the whole of his brain. He lost his balance and grabbed the corner of the desk, which emitted a C major chord and restarted.

J!m did not experience pain like humans and other mammals, his body sending discreet advisories on injuries, not wishing to impose, but this was pain, extreme and insistent, and for someone who had never felt such a thing, terrifying.

Dr. Rand found it fascinating.

"Fractal grid," he observed, poking J!m's supple skull, disrupting the grid and causing J!m additional and inestimable pain. "Curious."

The discharges dissipated, a letdown for one of them.

"Jim, after school I'd like you to stop by my lab."

"Your . . . garage?"

With prickly imperiousness: "It may not be as 'shiny' as the one at the university, but it's *uncompromised*."

J!m, senses returning, had one thought.

"Gotta go." And he did.

Dr. Rand sat against the edge of his desk. It changed from oak to Von Braun Gun Metal. He dispassionately smelled the tip of his finger, then sucked on it with intellectual rigor.

6

Their "Growing-up" SHOCKING

lurching into the hallway, j!m miscalculated the corner and slammed into the lockers, wobbled off them and lunged headlong in the direction he knew Marie had gone, clipping and spinning Lewis Seuss, who was unsuccessfully distributing radiation badges inscribed: FOR A HOT TIME, VOTE SEUSS.

"Vader," Lewis muttered, vowing revenge yet again that morning.

J!m was digitigrade, a toe-walker, and wore a prosthetic wedge in his boots to affect a human stride, but at times like these, when he forgot where he was and who he was pretending to be, he ran on his phalanges, torso canted forward, in a kind of manic prance that was quite graceful in slow motion. He forgot to pump his arms, another assimilation, and dangled them in front, limp-wristed. Moving in this manner up to thirty miles per hour, J!m was one scary sissy.

Students waited until he was well past before laughing at him.

J!m downshifted to indifference as he came into view of Room 15, Marie's third period, the room where Marie took Wifely Arts second semester of sophomore year, seventh period.

He could see Marie through the door, facing away, talking earnestly with Sandra Jane, who looked as if she were trying to explain something to a child and proving she should never have children.

J!m signalled to Sandra Jane. A brief eye movement acknowledged, and negated, his existence.

"Marie," J!m said at a volume he calibrated to be heard by her and no one else. She turned and smiled.

J!m leaned forward, and into a bright green raptorial foreleg. The pincer tugged his earlobe, its spiked tibia grazing his throat. A triangular head appeared from above, a woman's face etched in exoskeleton, her antennae twitching impatiently.

"Shoo!" Miss Mantis said.

melia mantis had been teaching Feminine Hygiene at MHS for a dozen years, since the accident. To look at her, her lime hair in shellacked buns on the corners of her head, her prothorax nothing to write home about, it was hard to imagine she had once been Miss Greece, a Jill of the Month, and a promising sex researcher. Had she isolated that pheromone that drives male mantids so wild they don't mind getting their heads bitten off, she'd be Queen of the Earth. Instead she was a nine-foot-tall predatory insect with an enormous caboose, things sometimes turning out differently than one imagines they will.

Miss Mantis loved her girls, though, she often said, while despising them.

"Ladies," she addressed them with a sensuous Grecian hiss. "Shut it up now."

The whispering and tittering came to an abrupt halt.

Miss Mantis clicked across the room and crawled onto the tree trunk that served as her desk. "So," she said, "who are we going to the dance hop tomorrow night?"

After a pause for translation, all the girls raised their hands except Marie. Sandra Jane kicked at her, but Marie shook her head.

"It is time"—Miss Mantis tented her forelegs—"for you ladies to see the sex viz."

There was much unladylike excitement.

Hissssssssssssssss, her spiracles at full blast, brought about order.

"It is not for giggling," Miss Mantis said.

boys were being boyish, denigrating each other's genitalia and reputed genital accomplishments, when Coach blew the whistle and they jogged out of the locker room, spanking and pinching one another's posteriors.

When the last of them had gone, J!m slunk from a bathroom stall wearing his athletic uniform, carrying his street clothes.

STRANGE DESIRES

the title promised, and the dark room tingled with the nervous yearnings of eighteen adolescent human females desirous of desire. Marie alone took notes.

The viz was at least ten years old, judging from the subtly ridiculous hair and clothes, with odd scratches on the image. But what it lacked in contemporary setting, good writing, credible acting, adequate lighting and any camerawork at all, it made up for in being about sex.

In the hallway of a high school much like their own, Molly, a pretty brunette, was talking excitedly to Peggy, an equally pretty blonde.

"And after the dance, we went up to Lookout Point—"

"You went up to Lookout Point with Archy?"

"Sure, silly."

Peggy gasped. "But he's a Cucurachan!"

"It was fun!" Molly said. "But you have to watch out for that second set of arms!"

The two girls laughed.

Molly fainted.

The scene switched to a doctor's office. Molly sat in a gown on an examination table, attended by kindly Dr. Kinsey, whom

Marie recognized from an adviz for Frost Chief, the home head freezer.

Molly was distraught. "How can I be pregnant? We only kissed!"

"Molly," Dr. Kinsey patiently explained, "for your friend Archy, kissing is a form of mating. And now, I'm afraid, he's laid eggs in your brain."

"Oh no!"

Dr. Kinsey placed a reassuring hand on Molly's knee, chuckling softly. "'Oh no' is right." Then, with a pat above the knee: "But that's the risk you girls take when you get into sexual shenanigans with alien species."

Marie stopped writing. She could not understand how identical information could have come from an approved educational viz and Sandra Jane Douglas.

Dr. Kinsey gave Molly a comforting squeeze a few inches higher on the leg and walked over to a file cabinet, a metal device once used to store paper documents. He removed a manila folder, like a plexfolio, only with mass.

"Here, let me show you some disturbing photographs."

The girls in Miss Mantis's class, based on the sounds they were making, did not want to see disturbing photographs, yet could not look away. Especially Marie.

a big red ball caromed off J!m's chest.

"Neck to waist," Coach McCarthy instructed, taking two more balls from Lewis Seuss. "Neck to waist," pegging J!m in the right shoulder and stomach. The boy was his demonstration model of choice, for illegal wrestling holds, clipping, high sticking, and many unsportsmanlike conducts of his own invention. J!m generally took these educational assaults with stoic disdain, but today he appeared *in extremis,* giving Lewis Seuss an insignificant erection.

Seuss's blooming perversion was misguided, however, as J!m was unbothered by the bombardment, or even aware of it, instead preoccupied with a question, raised in his Early Manhood class three years ago, and only now personally relevant:

some of the girls were crying. Some of them were anxiously sketching the disturbing photographs in the viz, impatient for the bell, so they could run to the bathroom and compare what they drew with what was spreading on their thighs. Sandra Jane thought about lunch.

Marie was thinking about what Sandra Jane had told her, and about J!m, and about what kind of person she was, and about *what on earth was that?*

Dr. Kinsey shut the manila folder.

"And that was from *over* the sweater."

"Gee, Dr. Kinsey," Molly said. "I never knew that dating outside my species could be so dangerous."

"Dangerous," the doctor agreed. "And disgusting."

He smiled indulgently at her, since it was her line.

"Oh," Molly said. "But what about these eggs in my brain?"

Dr. Kinsey scribbled on a pad of paper. "I'm writing you a prescription for a DDT inhaler. Two sprays, day and night, for ten days, oughtta take care of those buggers."

He placed the prescription in her palm, and cupped both of his hands around it.

"Thank you, Doctor!"

Dr. Kinsey peered down over his glasses. "Now, what are you going to do the next time an extraterrestrial asks you out?"

Molly was unsure. "Stay home and take care of it myself?"

"Good girl!"

They laughed. She tried to tug her hand away, but he clasped it more firmly, laughing for longer than she did.

The end credit appeared:

**Produced, Written and Directed by
Doris Wishman,
for the U.S. Department of Education and Human Welfare in
cooperation with the Bureau of Alien Affairs.**

The lights came up. Sandra Jane eyebrowed Marie, who, with a small dip of her head, betrayed J!m.

"So," Miss Mantis demanded, "what are the questions?"

The girls had a lot of questions. They did not ask any of them.

"Yes, Miss Mantis, I have a question," Sandra Jane said, in the wholesome voice she found so amusing. "I know it's unhealthy and wrong to"—the word she knew did not go with this persona—"have shenanigans with aliens . . ."

"Yes," Miss Mantis said. "And the mutants. And the robots."

"But does that mean," drawing the trap, "that it's okay to do . . . that with human boys?"

Miss Mantis did not fluster.

"It is tedious," she answered, "but not as bad."

was it normal, this brainstorm, a new and awful stage of J!m's development, another sundry agony? Or was this a portent of his imminent and non-imaginary demise?

J!m did not have the answers, though they were yes and yes, more or less. Sad, perhaps, but not pointless, as human mortality is, for all the howling that attends it, simply dead and that's it. J!m's oblivion would at least be useful, all part of, if not God's plan, something equally divine.

The boy had scarcely faced his doom before sublimating it, eliding it with his other crisis, wondering if he would die before taking Marie to the dance and worrying about leaving Marie a widow with three small children, glossing over a string of high improbabilities in between, thus deserving that red rubber ball smacking him in the brain, knocking some nonsense out of him. It hit him square in the cranium, splattering oil and forming a shallow crater that did not, at first, look like it would rebound.

"That's a penalty," Coach McCarthy said.

The class paid close attention, as if they hadn't learned the rules of dodgeball years ago. Lewis Seuss handed the coach another ball.

"And," the coach emphasized, "I don't want to see any of this":

The ball rocketed toward J!m's groin.

He made no attempt to protect himself.

He would be the last of his kind.

The extinction-level event was averted in Hollywood fashion, at the last microsecond, *balua ex machina*, a black hand snatching the killer elasteroid off the zipper front of J!m's shorts.

Johnny tended to materialize whenever J!m was in trouble, a statistical fluke that would have bothered J!m if he thought about it.

"You missed the first four," J!m said.

Johnny barked affectionately, then directed himself to the coach. He tossed the ball up casually.

"Or *this*."

A red blur grazed Coach McCarthy's crown, fluffing his widow's peak into a cowlick, and hit the wall behind him.

The ball popped.

The coach removed the cliplex at his waist.

"Not dressed for gym, Mr. Love. That's gonna be . . . ," trailing off, "some demerits."

His fingers rattled on the board's surface, closing the class roster and bringing up a photo of Big Mac McCarthy from his bodybuilding days, lifting two twenty-five-pound weights, quite something when done with the nipples.

Johnny strolled off. "See ya at the game, Coach."

"Right," the coach swallowed hard, pressing the board against his stomach. "Let's, uh, hit the showers," twenty minutes before the bell. He added, "You, too, Anderson!"

J!m would not be hitting the showers, and the coach knew it. But he never missed an opportunity to mention:

"Hold on. You have a note from *your mother*."

This made J!m mad at his mother, for some reason.

7

BARE-FISTED HATE!

hot protein rods, hot and proteinaceous, lay in the tray like logs of, one hoped, something not yet digested. A pair of tongs reached in and grabbed two with bureaucratic grace.

The Mole Woman, her slavishness underlined by the smock and hairnet, dropped the rods on the plate and slid it over the grease shield.

"Be serious!" Jelly whined.

The Mole Woman grunted to herself and deposited two more rods on the plate.

Jelly's eyes ballooned to pathetic, Keanian proportions, his voice shrinking into Dickensian waif.

"Please, missus, may I have some more?"

The Mole Woman tossed on four more.

Jelly, husky: "*I love you.*"

The Mole Woman grunted in animus.

J!m was next. The Mole Woman grunted excitedly and beetled over to the deep fryer, pushing aside Ted the Pinhead Mutant, who was useless. She dipped a soup bowl into the sizzling grease, shrieking a little, and hurried back.

"*Anshargal,*" she bowed her head, delivering fragrant oil to the boy king.

"*Gitmalu,*" J!m said. "Thank you, Ninsuna."

Ninsuna looked away, grunting shyly.

j!m wandered across the cafeteria, lost in love and death.

Marie was at the far end, sitting under a MEET THE CANDIDATES banner. Taped to the front of her table was a plain sign: MHS FOR ALL. A gaggle of female juniors gathered around Marie, signing her petition and agreeing with her goals, which sounded *nice.*

Adjacent, Lewis Seuss was pressing one thumb down on the table with the other, undisturbed by a constituency. An elaborate viz played on the poster hanging in front of him, showing a hundred-foot-tall Lewis defending Manhattan High from incoming Ming missiles, catching them and biting the warheads off, a vignette meant to counter his image as a neurasthenic nerd, and not working.

J!m thought he might get in line behind the girls, ask Marie there. As he pondered this, three freshman boys arrived, driving away the junior girls. The boys lined up in front of Marie, rhythmically bumping their crotches against the table edge, saying nothing. They would be awhile.

J!m stumbled. Grease slurped from his bowl, hitting the floor with a fatty hiss.

He looked back. A patent-and-chrome wing tip stuck out conspicuously.

"How was your trip?" Russ asked, running a thumbnail between his teeth.

Tubesteak went into his giggle, cuing the rest of the crew:

Lee "Toad" Hopper, a pocked and mottled goon who earned his nickname long before he resembled it, eating a live toad on a dare in the fifth grade, and every few months after that;

Charles "Ice" Tucker, a near albino psychopath who chewed Freemint lithium gum to keep from feeling bad about being so insane;

Bennie "Bennie" Scott, a glassy-eyed happiness vendor, whose given name worked as both cognomen and marketing tool;

Helen Long and Millie Sidney, known as Hel and Mil, interchangeably;

and Sandra Jane, who had yet to be told her nickname, which was based on an unattractive cut of meat.

They were all laughing, except for Bennie, who thought he was laughing.

J!m could have kept walking, but he never did.

"Bravo," he addressed the head jester. "You can't even see the hand up your ass."

J!m waited for that moment, when Russ's eyes would cross as he deciphered whether he had been insulted. Then J!m walked away, cockily, one step, before slipping on the spilt oil and landing on his tail.

This proved significantly more hilarious, well beyond Russ's circle, first to those with a view and spreading to outlying tables, students standing for a better look at what was so uproarious, and on to the periphery, where some got up *on* the tables, knowing they were laughing at J!m but not knowing why.

Jim's ears folded down and his cheeks burned Bunsen blue, lit from beneath by an amygdalal inferno of humiliation, as he absorbed oil and an object lesson: Why worry about dying sometime in the future—say, tomorrow night—when he was dying every second of his life?

Sitting there until the bell rang did not seem a terrific option, and so he grabbed his tray and got up.

"Now look who greased his seat," Russ said.

It was funny because it was true. J!m's seat was, indeed, greased.

J!m had no rebuttal.

his fellow travelers were waiting for him, Johnny salad picking and Jelly injecting hot protein, acting as if what had happened hadn't.

Rusty ruined it, with her love.

She was Margaret Ford by birth, a twin to Russell in womb only. A giving girl with a lot of girl to give, Rusty had a heart as big as her face, which was quite big, a thousand freckles wide. Her big heart was bleeding for J!m, and her big face was feeling his pain, her freckles throbbing and her jade eyes brimming with co-agony.

"Save it, Rusty," J!m said, "for when he kills me."

Rusty pouted. She really was the best friend an alien could ever have, and a little appreciation would have been nice, or less scorn.

Several yards away, Bennie started laughing.

Johnny put his arm around J!m. "Enslave them," he counselled gravely. "Enslave them all."

J!m shrugged the big hand off his shoulder. Johnny barked in amusement and returned to his caterpillar salad.

the silence was ugly and awkward and would not eventually grow out of it.

Rusty had the least tolerance for conversational lacunae, into which she typically shovelled chipper non sequiturs, but she was in a deep sulk and wasn't saying a single thing until J!m noticed she wasn't saying a single thing and reached out to touch her hand, or smiled at her, or looked at her, or in her general direction. J!m was looking at his tray, ranking this latest ignominy in his lifetime top ten thousand, and would be a while.

A few minutes in, Jelly had a thought and, as was his custom, said it out loud. "Hey, why do they call these 'protein' rods?" indicating the one behind his eye. "Everybody knows they're made from cows."

Rusty's pent elbow shot out, rippling Jelly.

"*May*-be," she redirected her pique, "out of consideration for the"—lowering her voice—"*Bovons.*"

J!m could, but did not, resist. He looked up at Rusty. "Moo."

Rusty was, as intended, aghast. Beside her, Jelly grew a

muzzle, sank his eyes, elevated and elongated his ears. "Merrr-r*ooooooooo*," he lowed.

Rusty indignantly pointed to the other end of the table, where some underclassmen sat, in particular a Cowgirl from Alpha Tauri, looking back with large liquidy orbs.

"You made her cry!"

Jelly, unrepentant: "She always looks like that."

"Aw, she doesn't mind," J!m said. "You don't, do you, Clara?"

Clara swallowed her cud. "Noooooooooo," she simpered, batting those brown betties.

"You boys are so evil," Rusty said, with a flippancy not in her natural repertoire. "I can't believe I'm letting all of you take me to the dance."

This was news to all of them.

Rusty tossed her wild ginger hair like she had seen in an adviz for Chemoste, the gentle tumor remover. "I didn't want you fighting over me."

She chewed her lip.

"Gang date!" Jelly yelled.

Johnny watched a caterpillar cross his knuckles. "Only, Jim asked Marie Rand this morning." He let the larva crawl up his tongue. "Right after Bio."

J!m said nothing.

"It's okay, Rusty," Jelly said. "Johnny and me'd be happy to double-team you!"

He sloshed into her, undulating with unseemly purpose. She pushed back violently, shoving only his shirt and ending elbow-deep inside him.

Jelly's head rolled back in carnal rapture.

"*You taste like bacon, baby.*"

Rusty recoiled, her arms covered with Larry Sweeney. She went berserk, flinging bits of him as far as four tables away. The millijellies instinctively returned to the mother mass, stopping to clean a plate or two along the way.

Rusty was an inexhaustible font of girlish disgust, stringing *eee*'s and *eww*'s and *ayii*'s together into a symphony of revulsion. Jelly did not take it personally, feeling this was a breakthrough of sorts.

J!m knew he shouldn't laugh, but with Johnny pant-hooting and banging on the table, he thought a diverted murmur would be all right.

"And *you*," Rusty turned on him, flicking the last drops of Jelly into his face, "are *not* going to any dance with Marie Rand. She and Sandra Jane Douglas are going with my brother and Tubesteak."

J!m's head tipped forward, the gravity of his universe infinitesimally but catastrophically greater.

"She's going with Russ?"

"Or Tubesteak. I don't know how they divvied them up."

It was obvious, yet inconceivable. In no universe, even the one in which J!m was depantsed in front of the whole school and burst into flaming shame, did Marie end up with Russ. There it all was, happening before him, and he could still not imagine it.

"That Russ Ford's got some big cajones," Johnny said, tilting his head into J!m's view, his play face. "Or *some* cajones."

J!m pushed Johnny aside and made for Marie.

she was talking to steve simpson, president of the Calligraphy Club, who was giving Marie a tour of the osmiridium-tipped pens in his protected pocket. He should be easy to scare off. J!m's jeans alone would do it, and if not, he would have to start breaking nibs.

That foot, this time at pelvic level, interceded. The chrome toe tapped at his fly.

"Who's there?" J!m said.

Russ's eyes crossed. He shook it off.

"I haven't forgotten how you nuked me on that test, Blue Boy."

"And it's been more than an hour."

J!m sidestepped Russ's leg and made it as far as Toad. The scent of wintergreen mood stabilization told J!m his retreat was blocked by Ice. Toad twisted J!m toward Russ, who remained seated, fascinated by his fingernails.

"If I end up on academic probation," he said, "you know who I'm going to blame?"

"Your father's seed, or your mother's egg?"

That one was easy, as J!m knew it would be, and incendiary, more so than J!m predicted.

Russ leapt to his feet, seizing the lapels of J!m's birthday jacket.

"My mother's eggs were normal!"

J!m, coolly: "So rotten sperm, then."

Russ whipped a Zippo from his waistband and held it under J!m's chin.

"What's that, Oily?" he overacted. "Could you speak directly into the microphone?"

Russ flipped the lighter open.

J!m's nictitating membrane slid across his eyes, smarter than J!m himself.

"You won't like the smell," he said.

Behind them, Toad and Ice rose off the ground, to their evident surprise, and flew to the right. Next Johnny grabbed Russ's wrist and, with his lightest squeeze, made the hand spasm and drop the lighter.

"Hey, there," said Johnny, "let's not go and cripple that golden arm of yours right before the game."

Johnny released the wrist but Russ's fingers convulsed a while longer.

The bell rang.

Russ massaged his hand as he marched off, not in retreat, since he had someplace to be, although not in the direction he first marched. His crew marched, and about-faced, behind him. Sandra Jane eyed J!m evenly as she left.

"I bet you woulda burned for a long time."

J!m was about to make a dining suggestion when he saw Johnny waiting to say something.

"Y'know, Freak," Johnny said, "if you don't want to fight, you should stop starting them."

Johnny punched J!m moderately on the shoulder and loped off, vaulting a lunch table and earning another detention.

Rubbing his temporarily broken arm, J!m turned to the candidates' table. Marie was gone. Lewis Seuss remained at his station, showing his teeth to passing students.

Rusty cosied up next to J!m.

"Pick me up at eight?"

Jelly slung his arms around the two, perfusing the space between them.

"Colossal!"

8

ONE NAME
stands out
as the epitome of
EVIL!

"history," the teacher said, "is written by the winners."

The quotation appeared on the blackboard behind him.

"George Orwell."

The blackboard corrected the attribution to UN-KNOWN.

Tom Gray laughed, which teachers at this school did not do. "Uh-oh," he said. "A hole in the PLEX."

There were no holes in the PLEX. Everything was there, with access to all, if one knew where to look, and had appropriate access. But it was fashionable among adolescents, and adults who wanted to be liked by adolescents, to bash the PLEX, upon which every aspect of their lives depended, in ways they would never suspect.

Tom Gray was liked by his adolescents. They liked that he was young, and dressed like they did, and could talk like them without sounding like a Simulant. The females also liked his hair.

"So," the teacher said, a boyish blond lock falling across his forehead, "as you watch this *mandatory* viz today, I want you to keep the words of *Eric Arthur Blair* in mind: 'History is written by the winners.'"

Which was true, as far as it went, but better amended, ". . . by the *most recent* winners."

Tom Gray walked down the aisle, tapping heads. "Everybody," with suspect solemnity, "screw on your thinking caps and crank the bullshit detector up to nine."

The students laughed obligatorily at the light profanity, which Lewis Seuss would have to report forthwith, as much as he liked Mr. Gray as a person.

In the front row, Marie mimed screwing on her thinking cap. J!m again sat several rows behind her, and, again, was doing very little beyond watching her.

Tom Gray waved the lights down. The students put on their 3-D glasses.

The Presidential Seal appeared, stately, staid, and abruptly spun directly at them, the eagle flinging arrows right into their minds' eyes. A couple of students gasped, exhibiting a frightful lack of jadedness.

The President, his jet-black hair slicked back, his mustache well-trimmed, sat behind a desk, fingers tightly interlaced. His presence indicated an occasion; he was not often seen, even on viz, a security measure that extended to the inutterance of his given name, so long in place most of the students didn't know who he was. The precise nature of the security threat that necessitated these precautions was never explained, or questioned.

The President stared at them for several seconds before beginning, "What you are about to see will upset you," in a brisk Texas twang. "It will terrify you. It may make you cry, or puke. But you kids are old enough to know the truth."

The President stopped, stared. As the viz faded to black, his right cheek spasmed.

Out of the blackness came bits of light, resolving into a night sky. Urgent words loomed up to adamant orchestration:

THE STARS OUR ENEMY

j!m festered, watching Marie up there being studious, oblivious to the rift she had torn in the time-space continuum. He turned to Jelly, seated behind him.

"Gimme your plex."

Jelly, in re the viz: "You're missing the bullshit."

J!m grabbed the wristplex and dragged it through Jelly's arm, separating his hand. The fingers twiddled in the air and hightailed it back in place.

With a few gestures, J!m vizzed Marie.

Marie glanced at her wrist, back at J!m. She ducked her head and brought the plex up to her mouth.

J!m's screen was filled with Marie's lips, dark and shadowed, bigger than life, and, in isolation, quite biological.

"Jim?" the lips whispered.

The surge in J!m's hypothalamus shorted his optic nerves, and when his sight came back on, the wristplex was gone.

"After class," Tom Gray said, redirecting J!m to the viz. "You need to see this."

J!m slid down in his desk, his head against the chair back. He closed his eyes.

he did not need to see this. Nobody did. Every student in this class knew what was in it, had known since the fifth grade, its legendary horrors passed along by older siblings and spread on playgrounds and PLEX nodes. And while the earliest reports, that it included scenes of soldiers being eaten by giant mammaries, were later discounted, the overwhelming consensus was that this infamous viz was the most graphic, must-see version of a story they had all heard a thousand times before:

in fairy tales, "The Three Little Pigs and the Big-Brained Wolf" and "Goldilocks and the Three Big-Brained Bears," uninspired adaptations that at least restored the Grimm Brothers' *Sturm und Blut*;

in children's viz, *Magilla Gorilla*, *Mutant Killer*, and *Scoo-*

by's Doo's Mystery Mission, which wasn't much of a mystery, since the villain was always revealed to be a big-brained alien named Hank or Gil;

in literature, Action Comics #242, *The Super-Duel in Space*, with the thinly veiled Brainiac fighting Superman, an invader from space himself, from a planet whose true inhabitants were sulfurous trolls with no power other than the ability to bring any party to an irreversible halt;

in the Next Testament of the Bible, or amongst Adventists, the Book of Demons.

J!m knew the story, by heart and in rhyme, and did not need to see or hear it again. He tried to block out the narrator, the esteemed Shakespearean actor Vic Perrin, going on about what a wonderful world it once was: all nations were at peace, men wore jackets to dinner, there was a country named France, etc.

A low, rolling timpani evinced a change in mood.

The narrator, solemn: "October 3, 1951."

J!m opened one eye.

the film was black-and-white, fuzzy and flickering, like the memory of a childhood dream. People cheered. A man sold peanuts. A child wore a cap.

J!m was not a baseball fan, but he recognized the Polo Grounds.

"America at leisure," the narrator said, "enjoying the national pastime. . . ."

The Giants' number 23 approached the plate.

"Bobby Thomson . . . up there swingin'." The grainy viz was matched to scratchy aud of the Giants' radio announcer,

R. P. Hodges. "One out, last of the ninth. . . . Brooklyn leads it 4–2. . . ."

The narrator interjected, "It would be the shot heard 'round the world."

Dodgers relief pitcher Ralph Branca was on the mound, checking his runners.

"Hartung down the line at third, not taking any chances," called Hodges calmly, believing only the pennant depended on this at-bat. "Lockman with not too big of a lead at second, but he'll be runnin' like the wind if Thomson hits one. . . . Branca throws—"

Thomson swung.

The crowd was on its feet.

"There's a long drive," Hodges's voice rising, verging on unprofessional. "It's gonna be, I believe . . ."

Dodgers left fielder Andy Pafko ran to the wall, watched the ball, sailing—

A bolt of light, a shower of sparks.

The radiant horsehide fell into Pafko's glove.

"Something has—" said Hodges, puzzled, then livid. "That's interference! That's interference!"

Pafko plucked the smoking ember from his glove and held it over his head triumphantly. It was hotter than he anticipated, and he soon dropped it, along with his thumb and forefinger.

"Not an out! No sir!" shouted Hodges, working himself into a lather. "That's a ground-rule double. Hartung and Lockman will score. This is a tie game!"

The crowd remained on its feet, looking up.

Hodges, too: "What *is* that thing?"

The answer wiped across the screen:

A brilliance hovered over the field. The players scattered as it lowered onto the pitcher's mound.

Hodges had lost all comportment. "A silver saucer, big as . . . It's big . . . It's coming, and this blame place is going crazy!"

The saucer's outer energy ring powered down and retracted into the craft, leaving a polyhedral sphere, composed of a lattice of triangular elements too complex for discussion here, and too much for a fellow paid to describe sport.

"This is R.P. Hodges, WMCA-AM, signing off."

At the center of the sphere was an eye-shaped portal. It illuminated, revealing the silhouette of a heart-shaped head, forming a kind of iris.

A large triangular door slid open.

His silvery skin glittered in the sun. He wore an impeccably tailored gray flannel suit.

He raised his palm, and spoke with a proper British accent.

"I come in peace."

"Piece of *this*!" Russ Ford returned the salute, closing his fingers into a fist. His crew laughed, at the gesture more than the wordplay, since none of them were aware there was wordplay.

J!m had not seen his father in a while. Pictures and viz of him were available in the PLEX but restricted to adults who didn't mind visits from the FBI. The reasons for the restrictions were themselves restricted, though most people believed it was because J!m's father possessed a charismatic depravity of such bewitchment that mere exposure to his image or ideas would pervert unsolidified minds. It was only in this controlled academic setting, in which he could be placed in blood-curdling context, that mature teens could look into the face of evil and not run out and form fan clubs.

There was that picture in the kitchen, the one hidden behind Mr. Christ. J!m had long known it was there, but hadn't looked at it since he was twelve, the year he also stopped spending any time with his mother's underwear.

Seeing his father's face now, J!m thought it wasn't nearly as ghastly as he remembered, not remembering that the photo in the kitchen didn't show his father's face.

the viz asked, disingenuously.

"He said he was here to serve us."

Illustrated by old newsreels, infoviz, of J!m's father shaking hands with President Truman, riding in a ticker-tape parade, posing with a towheaded boy and his dog.

"He offered us untold scientific and technological advances . . ."

J!m's father, electricity jumping between his fingers, illuminating his face from below, not his best angle.

". . . if only . . ."

U.S. Army General Walter Ford, his corncob pipe fully erect, leaning against a 31-kiloton Mark IV named Rita, the Fat Lady who sang for Shanghai.

". . . we agreed to destroy our atomic weapons." The image

inverted, black to white, a sustained dominant seventh over-scoring the editorial position of the vizmakers.

Most of the boys and a few of the girls booed the disarmament talk.

Seduction
of the
IGNORANT

"He seduced the weak minds of Hollywood . . ."

J!m's father holding court at Musso and Frank's, seated with Humphrey Bogart, Lauren Bacall, a bald man with sunken eyes—a writer—and, clinging to his father's arm, a young Norma Baker, then an actress.

". . . and the eggheads of Academia."

J!m's father at a blackboard, amazing Dr. B. "Buck" Roberts, a bespectacled iconoclast in an unwarranted lab coat, followed by a shot of J!m's father walking down a hallway, talking to a tiny man with wild white hair.

Predictable derision greeted the Nobel Prize–winning physicist, since dismissed as a treacherous appeaser, the man who gave them the atomic bomb and tried to take it back: Benedict Einstein, Dr. Alienstein, and a few less literate ones.

Jelly put on the old man's face and, with comic retardation, singsang, "*Eiiiiiiinsteiiiiinnnnnn!*"

He knew his audience.

J!m watched his father walk. He was so . . . *upright.*

J!m slouched further into his seat.

An American flag billowed bravely to the foreboding of African drums.

"But when our leaders smelled a rat, the creature showed his true face."

The face of J!m's father floated in smoke, his voice thundering.

"Destroy your weapons or you will be destroyed!"

The class turned toward J!m in uncertain accusation, as if the threat were hereditary.

J!m was elsewhere.

"Creature?" he mumbled.

and here it came, what they all had been waiting for, the fabled gore, the promised horror, the smut of history.

More aged infoviz, of wobbling saucers, bobbing balls of light, jerky cigar-shaped objects . . .

. . . buildings folding like cardboard, bridges collapsing like toothpicks, tanks glowing briefly before vanishing . . .

STREETS OF FRENZY

. . . crowds fleeing, humans screaming, dogs barking, a knocked-over tricycle . . .

This was hugely disappointing, after all these years. Nobody watched anything in black and white anymore except for old people and J!m, and this alleged reality lacked the meaty verisimilitude they had come to expect from watching commercial viz. It was hard to care about a world in peril in which people died without saying anything remotely funny.

NATURE TURNED AGAINST US

The face of J!m's father, up close, laughing at half speed to fiendish effect, and also African drums.

"While his minions attacked from space, the creature unleashed an unholy army of monsters and mutants by land and sea."

ANCIENT BEASTS

These were the nightmares of their youth, the terrible lizards that would stomp into their sleep, uproot their schools and shake them out, gobbling each and every one, no child left behind. Yet in reality, and from the distance of time,

they were ineffective monsters, clumsy lumbering giants unleashing immaterial destruction and repetitive terror: Gojira
destroying Tokyo for the first time; his evil American twin,
Gigantis, doing much the same; their British cousin, Behemoth, knocking down Big Ben; the Dane Reptilicus sliming
Copenhagen; Ogra, a different English dinosaur, knocking
down Big Ben again while looking for her baby, Gorgo, kid-
napped for a London circus, the Brits having learned nothing; an unnamed beast from 20,000 fathoms and a giant
Gila monster wrecking Coney Island and eating promiscuous
teenagers, *et al*.

With each new and less petrifying wave, a palpable fear
began to spread through the class that they were going to be
tested on this.

MONSTROUS VERMIN

A parade of nature's smallest, enlarged: jumbo ants, spi-
ders, leeches, mollusks, *etc*.

The class was unfrightened by the scale and unbothered
by the perversion of the nature, but some of the girls screamed
nonetheless, due to the bugs.

HIDEOUS MUTANTS

A motley assortment of unnaturals, humans crossbred
with other mammals, reptiles and insects, including a brief

shot of a young Miss Mantis, holding something black and sticky in her pincers, like a ball of hair;

and the many and varied atomic mutants, turning incorporeal or interdimensional, extrasensory or cycloptic, growing colossal or shrinking incredibly.

As a young and newly humongous Allison Douglas tore up a Fissionaire showroom, demanding workmen's comp, Sandra Jane lowered her head, pretending to be taking notes. Marie looked up from hers, her thinking cap engaged. She *knew* these mutants, knew them not as evil henchmonsters but as parents and teachers and other low-level service employees, the unfortunate victims of mankind delving into mysteries it wasn't meant to know, unleashing fearsome forces beyond understanding.

What did this have to do with J!m's father?

She was bright, that one.

J!m himself was far beyond excrement detection, and, having run out of expressions of reproach, alternated between scoffing and scowling, more or less randomly.

The rest of the class was listless, surreptitiously checking the PLEX for fresh waste on their peers, so inured were they to a long past apocalypse in which they did not personally die.

A savage and radiant ape livened up the room a bit, leaping out of the viz with lighted eyes, making full use of the dimensional technology. Even Johnny flinched, though his fear was more personal, and confirmed, when the viz ape grabbed a human female, who, Johnny had to admit, was every bit as beautiful as his mother said she once was. She screamed at his father with a vitality Johnny had never seen, and as the ape scampered away with the girl over his shoulder, Johnny got the urge to vault into the viz after her, damn the paradoxes.

Barbara Payton, overcome with a vivid imagining of the savage sweet ravaging that awaited Johnny's mother, sharply inhaled and fell out of her seat, landing in Johnny's lap. He eased her off onto the floor.

"Monkey see, monkey *screw*!" Jelly japed, his comic mugging disrupted when his eyes splashed, leaving in their wake a pair of dice, the only thing Johnny had to throw besides Barbara Payton, which he'd considered. Until that moment, Jelly had not connected the twenty-year-old viz of a radioactive ape with a captive woman and his nineteen-year-old half-human radioactive ape friend. He smiled contritely, and coughed out snake eyes.

CREEPING, OOZING...

A pause, and:

...MURDER

"Ooooh," said Jelly, wishing he had popcorn, picking through the folds of his clothes for anything organic he might have left there, a long shot.

Teenage girls rushed screaming from a ladies' room. The door burst open and a prodigious magenta mass flowed out. Its surface formed a ravenous and familiar face.

A couple of girls glanced in Jelly's direction, revolted and, worse, unimpressed.

Jelly wiped his face clean, and, unable to think of a suitable replacement, sunk the whole mess into his shirt.

IS THIS THE END?

There was strong sentiment in the room for yes, please, and soon.

"We gave our blood, sweat and tears. But in the end, only one thing could stop him. . . ."

Lots of atomic explosions.

"The tiny atom. That which the creature said would destroy us became our savior."

Many more atomic explosions, growing in intensity and annihilistic pop.

This, finally, was the pleasing the crowd had been promised. Russ and his crew pumped fists and cheered as whole space armadas were wiped from the sky and various bêtes noires atomized, along with acceptable swaths of surrounding countryside.

AVENGING JUSTICE

The revelry carried over to the courtroom scene, particularly the image of J!m's father standing in a crystal chamber, awaiting judgment. Composed of a golden isotope of the superactinide element 126, the booth was there to prevent premature execution, but also made J!m's father look like a very dignified bug trapped in amber.

"He was captured, tried and convicted, on nearly thirty million counts of murder."

Tubesteak shouted, "Electrofry him!" which sounded like slang but was just Tubesteak.

Little noticed by most: in the first row of the courtroom gallery, the creature's wife wept, holding the hand of their small bewildered son.

J!m's inner eyelid fluttered.

IT ESCAPES!

"Days before his execution, the cowardly creature made a run for it."

An incandescent ball burst through the atrium of the National Air and Space Museum, showering molten glass onto the Mall. The sphere sprouted its ring and rose into the sky over war-ravaged Washington, D.C.

"But not for long."

Schoolchildren, spotting the enemy craft, cocked fingers and fired, and were jubilant when the saucer took a direct hit, most likely from the atomic tank nearby.

The spaceship flipped end over end, crashing onto the Washington Monument. The energy ring sputtered out, the underlying globe impaled on the obelisk.

"The creature was dead. And peace had come again to our small planet."

Isolated storms raged throughout J!m's brain, in areas associated with anger, denial, depression and, buried there in the back, grief.

In front of him, color had arrived in America, sunny music

playing over contemporary scenes of cheery folks walking bright streets.

"Today, we live in a world of atomic wonders . . ."

J!m rose.

"He had a *name!*"

He jarred desks as he ran from the room. Marie started after him, pausing for permission from Mr. Gray.

On the viz, a businessman ordered from a city street cart.

". . . a world where everyone, even well-behaved aliens and mutants . . ."

The man took a meat-on-a-stick from the Umani vendor, who bore an uncanny resemblance to his bill of fare.

". . . can live in peace and prosperity."

The businessman grinned juicily as he chewed the meat. The Umani grinned back, dryly.

9

MILLIONS ARE ASKING—
What is it?

j!m sat high in the stands, under the VISITORS sign, his usual brood.

He gazed dully across the field at the old announcer's booth, wood and weathered, HOME OF THE MUTANTS peeling green and gold, Manny the Mutant in happy caricature, big overbite and bigger brain. Obsolesced by vizbug coverage and unused for years, the booth remained there because it had been there before.

J!m took a pack of Red Balls from his jacket, tapped one out and flipped it into his mouth.

"What," snatching it away, "are you, goony?"

"I'm not *that* flammable."

Marie sat down next to him. "I don't care what the Surgeon General says. Smoking is bad for you."

"I don't have any lungs."

"You have *six*."

"Yeah?" J!m said. "Was I on the test?"

"I *wish*."

J!m was out of small talk. But it was agreeable, sitting there, being quiet, with Marie.

Marie disagreed.

"I'm sorry about your dad."

"Being evil? Me too."

"You know he couldn't have done half the stuff they said he did."

"Phew."

Marie touched his forearm. He felt that she felt bad for him, and a bit peeved.

"Andee-*ee*-ra." She enunciated the life out of it. "That was his name, right?"

"Something like that."

"Do you miss him?"

J!m thought.

"I never had him."

"I'm really sorry," and she really was.

And yet:

"So," J!m said, "Russell Ford."

"Yikes. No secrets around here." Marie puffed her cheeks, exhaled. "Sandra Jane just wouldn't . . ." her hands moving faster, "and it's not a—it's just a bunch of people going together. *Anyway*, here."

It was a small package, wrapped in exotic brown paper,

hard to find. She placed it in his lap, where it stayed, him looking down at it.

"You have to open it to find out what it is," Marie teased. "Unless you've developed X-ray vision or something."

She pulled her sweater closed.

J!m tore back the paper. There was more paper underneath, a painting on it, a boy in a backward red cap, long black coat, carrying a suitcase, it appeared, into a house of burlesque. An inconveniently placed block of type over the entrance read:

> **This unusual
> book** may shock
> you, will make
> you laugh, and
> may break your
> heart — but **you
> will never forget it.**

J!m didn't understand the title. He thought it might be about baseball.

"A book?"

"You can still get them," Marie said. "I mean, they're not against the law. That one's not in the PLEX, though. I think you'll like it."

J!m was unsure of what to say, touched by the trouble Marie must have gone through to get him this terrible present, but also devastated that she would so blithely betray him by cohorting with Russ, and self-recriminatory that he hadn't asked her this morning, or Wednesday, or last week, when Marie repeatedly brought up the dance walking to school

and he responded with a trenchant critique of adolescent social rituals, the ridiculous inequity of them and vacuity of
anyone who partook in them, which may have led Marie to
believe he did not want to go with her.

And so he said a thing that meant nothing, he thought.

"Coming to the Skies tonight?"

"Yeah. . . ." Marie became fascinated with some air in the
middle distance. "Me . . . and a bunch of people."

The school bell tolled the end of day. Students swarmed
out of the building, in frenzied escape from the dusty maw of
learning, and ran screaming into the weekend.

Marie pushed her hands into her lap.

"I gotta go, Jim. I have a . . . ride."

"Sure," his face obtuse.

Marie circled around and met his eyes directly. She frowned.

"Happy birthday."

She kissed him, for slightly longer than civil, engulfing
him in such pain and pleasure he could not tell which was
which and whether it was his or hers.

Marie ran down the bleachers.

He ran after her, caught her in his arms, whispered something perfect and spun her around, kissing her and her kissing him, the camera flying around them in the scene he was
directing in his head, from a movie set in another universe.

In this one, he put on his domes.

Like a fool, I fell in love with you,

Eric Clapton sang, riffing on a Persian myth, a boy who went
mad when the girl he'd loved all his life was married to an-

other, parallelling the singer's own romantic entanglement, with a moon princess promised to a volcano back home.

> *Layla, they got you on your knees,*
> *Layla, I'm begging, darling, please,*
> *Layla, darling, don't appease your fire gods*

the world was changing. New, freshly beachfront communities were debuting weekly in Florida, collateral opportunity from the repeated nuking of the North Pole to destroy a Thing that, it turned out, ate radiation. Brazil got less prehistoric by the day. In Eurasia, the Ming and the Russians, if they even were still Russians, obliterated one another on an hourly basis, and here in Manhattan, in the stands of a high school football field, childhood ended.

J!m did not like the way things were, but liked even less the ways in which they were changing: his body was going haywire, his girlfriend was dating his archenemy, and his father was an officially sanctioned supervillain. Most frighteningly, he had lost the ability to not care. His hard-earned psychic shell had shattered, his long cool persona stripped away, leaving a dithering fool prancing down hallways and shrieking his feelings on school property.

If he could only make everything stop, and be still, and shut up, for just a few years, it would give him time to think, to make sense of what was happening to him and draft a plan to reverse it, or find a hiding spot. The world never stopped spinning, though, except that one time. Night would follow this day, worse awaiting him in the dark, he knew, because worse always awaited him, like they were chums.

But first, he had detention.

"no sleeping on my time, Mr. Anderson."

J!m was not sleeping, had only closed his eyes so he did not have to watch her watching him. Principal Brooks was a handsome woman, meaning if she were a man she'd be attractive, but she was not, probably, a man.

They were the only ones in her office. J!m had served so many detentions alone he was beginning to think he was the only person besides Johnny who ever did anything wrong. Gloria Castillo used to join them, always paying for something her kooky boyfriend did, but over the summer Ed Byrnes had squashed a family of Ocularians with his car, and now Gloria was in reform school. So it was J!m and Miss Brooks, again.

"I'm resting my eyes."

"No resting those baby blues. I want them looking right at me, mister."

The story on Eve Brooks was that she had been engaged to a soldier before the unpleasantness, and when her fiancé was devoured by a tree that ate women but was bi-curean, she went to work for the CIA, using the nom de guerre Ida Day, where she seduced and tortured hundreds of alien combatants, often at the same time, which led to her career in higher education.

When J!m opened his eyes, Principal Brooks smiled, startling him.

"What are we going to do with you, Jim?"

"Execute me." A half shrug. "Eventually."

The principal got up from her desk and moved to the window in an aberrant way, leading with her lower torso and swinging it arrhythmically from side to side. J!m speculated that her hips were pneumatic, and misfiring.

She ran her finger down the glass and it went dark.

"Do you like being bad, Jim? Being a bad boy?"

She was talking fast and low, a noir patois J!m ordinarily loved, when the femme in question was on screen and about to mess up some other fellow's life.

"Does it make you feel like a man?"

There was no alcohol in the room that J!m could detect, except the residue of four drops of Jean Naté, two behind her ears, one on her sternum, and one somewhere else. J!m also considered an aneurism and menopause.

She sat down on the couch next to him.

"Girls like bad boys, don't they, Jim?" the former fatale husked. "Well, do you want to know what *I* think about bad boys?"

She reached for J!m's right thigh.

This was the most celebrated thigh at Manhattan High, in the entire township, notorious but unmentioned among the female population, tightly denimed with something thick and mesmerizing running down its inner length almost to the knee, something that presently retracted violently and hid between J!m's legs.

She rapped his knee with a fingernail, and turned back into Principal Brooks.

"I think bad boys don't get good girls. Girls like Marie Rand. And they don't get into film school."

She returned to her desk, busying herself with urgent requisitions.

"I don't want to see you in here again, Mr. Anderson."

In agreement, J!m made for the door.

"And, Jim?"

He stopped, knowing it couldn't be that easy.

"Happy birthday."

10

YOUTH
ON THE LOOSE!

the ballistic kept accelerating until it reached Marie's driveway, coming to an abrupt 140-decibel stop, almost dislodging Sandra Jane from Tubesteak's face. Russ bent over to kiss Marie but she moved smoothly out of the car, leaving him with blue lips.

"Eight o'clock," Russ called after her. "Bring that boom."

Marie stilled her hips and walked stiffly to her door, a half wave over her shoulder.

The robognomes let her pass, for it was not yet time for her to become their Courtesan Queen.

As she stepped inside:

"Marie!"

"Hey, Mom," smiling gamely as she entered the kitchen, "guess what—"

"I'm dry," snapped her mother's head, rattling in the pan devised to keep it alive. Dr. Rand did not like it referred to as a pan, or a pie tin, although it was both, untidily constructed with more tubes, wires and lights than could possibly be required.

Marie went to the counter and checked the gauges on the Rand Dynabolic Biopreserver; they were flashing in the normal random pattern.

"Don't just gape at me like a cow."

Marie squeezed the bags of glucose and biopreserver fluid suspended above the contraption.

"Everything seems okay."

Her mother gave her an ugly look, one of the uglier ones. Like most of Manhattan's matrons, Susan Rand had been a great beauty in her youth, but time and decapitation had taken their toll. Years of meanness were gouged into her face, which no amount of cosmetic troweling could ameliorate.

The dutiful daughter lifted a jug of Angry Red and poured affordable burgundy into a glass burette suspended on the opposite side, allowing herself the small indulgence of an almost inaudible sigh.

"Don't you judge me!" her mother said. "Walking around all day on your two legs with your pretty little torso . . ." Mrs. Rand's eyes meandered down her daughter's body, so like her own, as anyone willing to venture into the basement freezer could attest. There was no point trying to reattach it, after seventeen years and several power outages, but Dr. Rand liked to keep it around, for reference.

"I'm sorry, Mom," Marie said, turning the stopcock and releasing a dark red spiral down the tube, roiling into the clear syrup in the pan like a slow rolling storm cloud.

Mrs. Rand smacked her lips.

sandra jane lay on crimson sateen among heart pillows in her fluffy pink room, her upper lip thick with Estroglam depilatory cream, reading the latest node of *Normal Teen*, with interesting articles on "Fitting In Without Sticking Out" and "50 Ways to Keep a Boy," including one involving her index finger that sounded very doable. On the orb, David Cassidy sang:

> *How can I be sure*
> *In a world that's constantly changing?*

Sandra Jane held up her right index finger and mimicked the twisting motion in the aniviz, and was noticing what big hands she had, and deciding that was okay, Tubesteak could take it, when a spritely terrier mix leapt onto her bed, yipping.

"Whoa, Barker!" Mr. Douglas shouted, pulling on the dog's harness, steadying himself atop her. He was almost eleven inches tall, high for him, and a tad much for the dog.

"Something wrong with your finger, sweetie?" Sandra Jane's father asked.

"No," she said, taking cover behind the vizzine.

"We should get going," her father suggested. "Our reservation is in fifteen minutes."

Sandra Jane forced out a baby cough.

"I don't feel so good, Daddy."

A skeptical face loomed up in the missing wall of Sandra Jane's room, which opened out into the underground hangar her mother lived in. Sandra Jane threw frequent fits about this dollhouse arrangement, but it was the only way her mother could get any housekeeping done, and Allison Douglas was as headstrong as her daughter, and ten times larger.

"You don't look sick," Mrs. Douglas said, placing her fingertip on Sandra Jane's forehead and pinning her to the bed. "You feel normal."

"I *am* normal!" Sandra Jane yelled, squirming from under her mother's touch. "I don't want to go with you, okay? I'm going out with my friends!"

"We're going to Tony's . . ." Mr. Douglas hoped to tempt his little girl out from deep inside the blond monstrosity she'd become, but gave away his game by shrinking an inch, squeaking, "*Basghetti and meatbells . . .*"

"*Don't you get it?*" Sandra Jane shouted back. "*I can't be seen with freaks! I'm in high school!*"

"I understand, sweetheart," her father said, disappearing into his suit. "Don't stay out too late, okay?" Half the man he just was, Grant Douglas yanked Barker's reins, turning away.

Mrs. Douglas slowly sank out of view.

four roasted chickens, ten pounds of baked potatoes, a bushel of corn on the cob, a basket of buttermilk biscuits and a five-gallon honey pot were at Larry Sweeney's end of the table.

His mother and father were having soup. They weren't hungry, they always said, and being thin was best at their age, less weight to carry up and down those steps, and when the time came, they could share a coffin if need be. And they did so love to watch their boy absorb.

Larry picked up a chicken, dipped it in the honey pot, and stuck it in his neck. Competing ameboid factions tore the bird apart with brio, but the boy made no outward sign of gratification.

"Are you all right, Larry?" asked his mother. "You're hardly eating."

"And you haven't hit your mouth once," his father said.

Larry cleared the bones from his throat, and looked to his parents with anxious love.

"Mom, Pop," he bibbled softly, "was I adopted?"

Ma Sweeney bit her lip. Pa Sweeney reached across the table and took her paper-thin hand in his.

the red sun fell behind a Martian saucer, remodelled into a four-bedroom, two-and-a-half-bath split-level with a panoramic view of Manhattan from high in the hills, where it had crashed. The à la mode spoil of war was owned, in the sense that nobody would dare remind him that the government officially owned it, by U.S. Army General Walter Ford, on active duty at seventy-one, and was occupied by the former Supreme Commander of Earth Forces, his son the sheriff and his twin grandchildren.

Dinner was served at 1700 sharp.

"You two have your fun tonight," the general was saying, "but Russ, make sure you preserve your precious bodilies for the game."

Russ nodded soberly.

"Let's limit the fluid talk at the table, Dad," Nick Ford said.

"I just don't want him squirting away his competitive advantage," the general said, forking in a pork chop.

The sheriff, redirecting: "Russ, I hear you had a run-in with Jim Anderson this morning."

"Andy's boy?" asked the general.

Russ rubbed his forearm. "It was nothing."

Rusty, through mashed potato: "You *disfigured* him!"

"He was trying to steal my car!" And turning bitterly to his father, "Why are you taking his side?"

The general pushed peas onto his fork. "Deserves what he gets. His father near destroyed the planet."

"*Jim's not like that,*" insisted Rusty, a bit too insistently.

Russ waggled his tongue at her, sliding it from side to side. Rusty crossed her fingers and twisted them, an allusion to a Kaman sex act that paralyzed dozens of overcurious teens every year.

"*The iniquity of the fathers shall be visited upon the sons,*" the general said with a grim chortle. "God said that."

"In this town," the sheriff said, "everybody gets a fair shake. I don't care who they are."

"People are human beings," agreed Rusty, "even if they aren't."

The general coughed into his napkin. "You wouldn't say that, Kitten, if you saw a Venusian Succubix slurp the marrow out of a man's spine."

Russ couldn't believe he missed that one on the test. *"Right."*

Nick Ford put down his fork.

"I think we're done here, Ethyl."

"Rights away, Missah Nick," said EThL, an out-of-warranty nedroid, buzzling in and removing plates, dropping every third one.

Rusty moaned, "Can we *please* get her upgraded?"

the pig stood alone, and if it knew anything about setting or story or ominous orchestration, it would not have kept standing there.

A deep purple tendril entered.

The pig squealed, and was unceremoniously dragged across the field and out of view.

A few feet away, two soldiers were in the bed of an Army truck, throwing pigs, sheep and goats off the back at a rate exceeding the operation's protocols, in an effort to stay ahead of the mammoth gelatinous mass that was devouring everything in their direction.

The crapulous goo had eaten a dozen beloved family pets, seven less-liked pets, a hobo, a bunch of nuns, a sassy waitress and a blowhard who said he wasn't afraid of any grape jelly, all in the eight hours since it had first appeared on the MU campus, another harebrained experiment, folks thought, of those mad scientists working at that Army lab.

"Wait," Larry interrupted his father's evocative tale. "I thought it was unleashed by J!m's dad."

"Is that what they teach you at school?"

"The viz said."

"Well, then I'm sure that's right," his father conceded, before continuing.

The goo chortled as it gobbled down the line of farm animals leading to Bessie, a low-yield device painted black and white in a Holstein pattern, a fresh cow's head mounted on the nose. A large bottle of milk was strapped underneath the payload, a baby calf suckling from it.

The goo splooged forward.

"It ate a baby calf?" asked Larry, distressed and between meals.

"The calf got away," his father said, "if you want."

"Let your father finish the story," his mother said. "We're tired."

From the safety of a hardened underground bunker, General Walter Ford gave the order to Dr. Buck Roberts, who gravely delivered the cow de grâce.

The goo's contented look turned to one of extreme indigestion.

All across Manhattan, families gathered on their lawns, facing east, though they had been warned to stay inside with their windows closed. At the first flash, a few put on sunglasses.

A 15-kiloton fireball bloomed on the horizon, much larger than forecast, or perhaps closer. Children cheered.

Tom and Frances Sweeney watched from their porch with stern sobriety. She held his arm as the hot wind hit them.

splut.

Tom wiped off his cheek, and was about to shake the effluvia into the roses when something made Frances stop him.

Cupped in his palm was a glop of lavender gelatin, bearing an approximation of a baby's face. It began to cry.

Mr. Sweeney finished there. He and the missus sat on a

couch opposite Jelly, hands clasped together, prepared for any questions he might have.

"What happened to it?" Larry asked.

"Well, son," his father said patiently, "we couldn't have children of our own . . ."

"I had so many abortions when I was young," his mother explained.

His father patted the back of his mother's hand.

". . . so we decided to raise you as our own."

"And we raised you to be a good boy."

Larry absorbed the information, losing surface tension as the shock spread to his exterior cells, creating a pooling effect on the carpet.

"Posture, Larry."

"Yes, ma'am."

He pulled himself together.

"it's fascinating," **dr. rand said,** sticking the Rand Autotine Dynatwirl into his spaghetti. The five-pound fork spun laboriously, revolving once a second with a loud *cha-CHUNK*. "This could completely change our understanding of Regulese anatomy, or should I say *architecture*."

He chuckled drolly at his taxonomy gag. At the other end of the needlessly long table, his wife's head mimicked his laugh, minus the self-regard.

Marie, equidistant between them, didn't understand. "You think Jim is a *robot*?"

"If I brought this to the university, they would just call me insane, again." He snorted. "*Narcissistic personality disorder?* I think not."

He hoisted the mechanical fork to his mouth, its autotines dynatwirling, lashing sauce into his eyes, which he pretended wasn't happening.

"Dad . . ."

Marie pointed down, where a roast chicken was slowly moving across the floor.

"Damn you," Dr. Rand cursed the chicken. He stuck it with his fork and lifted it up, exposing a belly swarming with nanoänts, the robots he had so accurately programmed that instead of infiltrating and destroying the colony, they had joined it.

He scraped the cybugs back onto the floor and began stomping them, each snapping like a cap, leaving charred marks on the parquet.

"I . . . gave . . . you . . . *specific* . . . instructions!"

His wife was laughing sincerely now. "Howard," she said, "you're hopeless."

"The ants were getting in *your* tray," he reminded her with increasing volume. "Crawling in *your* wiring. Attracted," he had her, "by the smell of *fermented fruit!*"

"For Godsakes, Howard, you're covered in sauce."

Dr. Rand opened his mouth, closed it and sat down.

Marie shut her eyes, trying to block out the slow seething to her right and hostile bubbling to her left.

The car horn was loud, and welcome.

"That's Russ," Marie said, rising.

Mrs. Rand's dish pivoted toward her daughter.

"You were going to do my hair tonight."

"I don't . . ." and Marie would have remembered *that*. "We didn't . . ."

"Look at me! I'm a skunk!" She was, too, a white forelock

splitting her otherwise black hair like lightning at midnight.

"I think it's pretty," Marie said.

"Sexy," Dr. Rand uttered involuntarily.

Mrs. Rand swivelled back to her husband. "Shouldn't you be out finding me a body?"

"Now, Susan, you know it is not as simple as that."

"For *you*."

"Right," getting defensive. "Let's get your father on this immediately. He's got all those Nobel Prizes . . ."

Marie was already at the door when Russ hit his horn a second time.

"Let's see: Physics, Peace, Biology . . . Oh, wait, *not* Biology. It appears that *your famous father has no biology background whatsoever.*"

The last Marie heard was her mother's testicle-withering cackle, propelling her into Russ's car.

11

TEMPER-HOT TENSIONS...

in quite another part of town, the pits, on a street where chunks of sidewalk floated uneasily on the *terra unfirma* and the lawns were brown and gassy, Arthur Ghroth, a tiny salesman from Planet X, trudged home in a boy's Communion suit, a toy fedora atop his space helmet, his briefcase full of unsold spatulas, whistling and beeping his sad, sad song.

He passed a two-room shotgun shack with no chrome whatsoever, no sign of the past twenty years save a modest state-supplied PLEX receptor. Two of its three windows were broken and boarded, its screen door half off the hinges and descreened, the structure sloping to the rear as it sank slowly into a pocket of tar the developer said was not there, or had been put there by hooligans.

At least Arthur didn't live in the Monkey House, he thought, modulating his tune to only singularly sad.

Johnny was in the commode, raking coconut oil into his hair. He wiped the excess across his chest, rubbing it to a high shine. With the edge of the comb, he freed a thick curl from his pomp and nudged it back and forth on his forehead until it achieved insouciance. He bared his teeth, checking for insects.

The soaring score in the next room told him the planes had arrived. He would have to hurry if he wanted to get out of there.

His mother was propped up on a foldout couch that had never been folded in, wearing that nightdress, her black, gray and white hair a chaos, down to her waist and out beyond her shoulders. She was eating ancient Chinese, mouth over the box, noodles streaming in and out.

Pushed against the bottom edge of the bed was an old bulbous screen made by the Zenith Radio Company, out of business for a decade, after one of its Space Command remotes inadvertently broadcast launch codes, resulting in the sinking of Cuba and that whole foofaraw. A converter orb allowed the tube to receive billions of PLEX viz, though it only ever played one.

King Kong swung from the dirigible mooring mast, swatting at biplanes, as Johnny snuck in and started to roll his cycle out of the house.

His mother patted the bed.

"Sit with me."

"I gotta get to work, Ma."

"Jojo."

Mortally wounded, Kong fell.

Johnny sat with his mother, staying on his side of the bed. His mother slid over, leaning her head on him.

Carl Denham broke through the crowd that gathered around Kong. "Well, Denham," a cop said, "the airplanes got him."

"It wasn't the airplanes. . . ." Johnny's mother mouthed the words along with Denham. "It was Beauty killed the Beast."

The movie music swelled. Johnny's mother beamed at her son and petted his arm. Johnny wanted to return the affection, but couldn't look directly at her, that nightdress so soiled and threadbare, torn in all the wrong places.

"Ma, why don't you wear that new gown I got you?"

"You know, Jojo," she cuddled against him. "I wore this on my *honeymoon*."

"It wasn't a goddamn—"

"Shush!" his mother cut him off. "I raised you better than to blaspheme."

they hummed down route 66 in a black and silver Big Daddy Buzzer, so named because the floor-to-roof split-bubble front gave it the appearance of fly eyes, a resemblance reinforced by the flying buttress tail fins and the sound the electric motor made, causing people it passed to swat at their ears involuntarily. The three-wheeled two-seater was tiny, poky and exceedingly unshiny, but it was all Miw could afford.

"Henry Kissinger returned from Arkansas today with welcome news in the War on Shmoo," Kelly Lange informed on the car's viz screen. "The long-running campaign against the tasty but evil creatures from Cygnus X-3 may be winding down, the National Security Enforcer told PIN."

Miw looked over at her son, crammed into the passenger seat, his knees against the windshield. She didn't need to be an empath to tell something was wrong; she could see, for example, that his hand had been torn off. He hadn't mentioned it, or anything, which is how she knew it must be bad.

"Peace is at hand," intoned Kissinger in his Teutonic bass, resplendent in a golden uniform of his own conception. "The Shmoo will soon all be dead."

Miw turned off the viz.

"Want to talk about it?"

J!m inspected his nearly regenerated fingers. He wanted to talk about all kinds of its: his hand, his head, his heart, his father, the future. But he was punishing his mother, for loving him.

"There's no it," he said.

The air around them ozoned as the Buzzer passed a PLEX pole, picking up an arc. Miw horripilated, her fur on end, making it difficult to take her seriously.

"Well, if there's ever an it . . ."

J!m scratched his knee.

"Problem at school . . . or with a girl . . . or your body, a change or . . ." Cursing her parental impotence: "I wish your father was here."

"Worked out so amazing last time."

His mother's ears went flat.

J!m reached across her and switched on the aud. Peter Gabriel sang,

His is a world alone
No world is his own . . .

dorothy love, Dodie, was a freshman in Christian anthropology at MU when she met Johnny's father, whose presence on campus can be explained very easily, but not at the moment. The 400-pound radioactive ape swept her off her feet, and after a very brief honeymoon in the woods, he caught fire somehow and fell into the Groom Lagoon, where his body was claimed by one of the other things in there. He was therefore not present eight and a half months later for the birth of his son at a top-secret military research facility based at the university. Dodie thought she was having twins, but when the nurses insisted there was only one, she was relieved.

Johnny's mother called him Jojo, after his father's circus name. Other people did not call him Jojo.

Dodie did the best she could to raise Johnny alone, through a series of exotic illnesses, including dental tumors and cancer of the perinoos, a theretofore undiscovered organ thought to regulate love, religion and other gullibilities. She kept getting sick and being miraculously cured; doctors theorized that gestating a radioactive ape had caused the malignancies, which were subsequently treated by Johnny's sleeping beside her every night. He was killing her and keeping her alive.

The settlement from the military lab at the university, which admitted no fault or its existence, had run out long ago, spent on gin and bananas. Dodie had not had a drink in years—Johnny made sure of that—but had gained a few hundred pounds lately and no longer went out, even to her AAA meetings, where she had taken pleasure in lording her abduction over the other women, most of whom had been only probed, and not even in the vagina.

Johnny hated to see her like this, taking up so much of the bed.

"Ma," he said, "you gotta stop. You gotta get out of the house, live a life, maybe . . ." swallowing, ". . . meet someone."

"Oh, Jojo, don't you know?" She took her son's paw and kneaded it with both hands. "Your father ruined me for other men."

Johnny did not broach this subject often, and this was why.

"He ruined my," gravidly, "heart."

Johnny gently groomed his mother's hair. He plucked something, nibbled it. He would be here until she fell asleep; he might as well make a meal of it.

harked the celestial-themed marquee, promoting to-night's double feature,

I WAS A TEENAGE MUTANT
AND
THE SCREAMING BIKINI

They hadn't spoken in a while.

Miw pushed in the steering column, bringing the Buzzer to a stop in front of the drive-in entrance. She turned to her son, guiding his chin to look at her.

"That was not your father," she said. "The one they talk about."

"And have all those visuals of."

"Don't believe your eyes."

There was so much she could tell him, but could not tell him, for his own good, and more than that. Perhaps there would come a time, and a place, but this was neither. She took another approach.

"You're *my* son, too, you know."

J!m's brain was quicker than his heart.

"That's colossal," he said. "I'm half monster and half pussy."

Miw's whiskers trembled.

She slapped him.

The scratches across J!m's cheek welled with indigo blood. It didn't hurt.

He knew *this* would:

"Blow 'em away at work, Mom."

The passenger bubble popped and J!m stepped out. The vehicle rotated 180 degrees and buzzed off, kicking a dry cloud around his feet.

He started to raise his hand to call for his mother, but she wouldn't have heard him anyhow.

12

Back Seat DATING

"surrender, earthling," j!m said, **the sil-**
ver emperor's robe adding alien menace, undercut
by the glitter-ball antennae bopping about his head.

He aimed his raygun and fired.

A red laser beam hit the young soldier in the
eye. It swept across his iris.

The soldier, identified as Pfc. Roy Haskell, sat
in his car with his date, a local thirteen-year-old
named Dolly or Lolly.

"Warning," J!m recited, "this program may
cause heart tremor, night sweats and demented
dreams. Free nitroglycerin tablets with every large
popcorn. Watch the Skies!"

The Ford Atmos pulled away from the ticket booth, headed for a spot on the periphery of the lot, but not across state lines.

J!m drooped, his glitter balls dangling glumly.

"Jimmy!"

A brawny hand smacked J!m on the back, whipping his balls into his eyes.

"What's the gate?" boomed Bill Schloss, who boomed everything, a remnant from his days as busker for the side-show attraction Trudie's Bigg Topp—ENTRANCE RESTRICTED TO SERIOUS STUDENTS OF MEDICAL ANOMALIES.

"Forty-nine."

Schloss chomped his unlit cigar, squinted, his whole face crinkling. His skin was crispy brown, his hair ermine white, his nose, his chest, his arms, everything about him big. He was what J!m imagined a movie producer to be, which Schloss had been, as well as writer, director and sometime co-star of such arty fare as *Nudie Trudie*, the western *Nudie Trudie Rides a Horse* and science-fiction epic *Trudie, Queen of the Nude Planet*, left unfinished when he lost Trudie in the divorce. Now all he had was this drive-in, and six girlfriends.

"Early still," Schloss satisfied himself.

"I think this terrifying costume is scaring off customers," J!m said.

Schloss was not a coddler.

"Jimmy," he said, *entre nous* and to anyone within fifty feet, "you want to be in the business? Well, this is the *show* of the business." He swatted the glitter balls sideways, whacking J!m's ears. "I gotta zoom. You good?"

"Stellar."

Shouting as he strode off: "Customer."

J!m glanced wearily, then panicked. He reached for the glitter balls, but it was too late.

Russ hummed up in the Ballistic, Marie beside him, with Sandra Jane and Tubesteak in the back, well into the evening's festivities.

"Hey," Russ said, "it's Vagittarius from the planet Uranus."

Tubesteak found this inordinately rib-tickling, so much so that he took his hands out of Sandra Jane in order to slap his thighs.

Marie looked embarrassed for J!m, or to know him, or so J!m thought, when it was quite the opposite.

"C'mon," taunted Russ, "do your speech."

"Surrender, Earthling," J!m said flatly, fingering his ray gun, the setting that toggled between SCAN and STUN.

from the road it looked like a concrete bunker, partially hidden by trees, unmarked but for a small and typically unlit fluorescent sign:

She

It was a bar by license, but in hiring practice it became an intergalactic smorgasbord of xenosexual delights, females of fancy species serving drinks and offering cultural exchange to human males seeking some strange.

Stepping inside was like entering another world, or several other worlds, all jumbled together by no coherent design, as if somebody had plastered heaps of native artifacts from assorted civilizations on the walls, thinking their difference made them all alike, which is what someone did.

Onstage a tired combo played an unenthusiastic cover of a recent popular song, a middle-aged man singing:

> *Well, I'm your Venus,*
> *I'm your fire at your desire.*

In cages suspended from the asbestos ceiling, She Beasts thrashed about, though not to the music.

Miw was in the back, putting on her cat face.

"Kid didn't mean it, Miw," said her colleague Lilitu, a Venusian Succubix of indeterminate age, lightly freckled with a ruby poodle cut and carnelian eyes. "He's just a boy," she rasped. "Boys will be boys."

She was one, to be talking about other people's children.

"And speaking of, boys will *pay* to be boys, Miw; you could triple your take-home, two minutes in a private pod . . ."

Miw winced. Film school was expensive, but—

"That fur ain't mink, sister."

"I know, Lil."

"And besides, it's fun," she cracked, coughed. "They're so afraid I'm gonna suck out their spine. But that's extra."

Mickey Mansfield, aged beefcake, drew back the curtain to the dressing area.

"Persia, Desiree," he called them by *nom*, "they're not here for the drinks."

Lilitu slinked up to Mickey, tracing a crimson talon down his neck. "Hey, Mickey," she husked, "can I sing tonight?"

Mickey said no before she finished speaking.

Lilitu, wheedling: "When can I sing, Mickey?"

"When I'm dead."

As Mickey left, Lilitu's eyes glowed red.

the night was immense, a billion trillion stars out there and all of them out tonight. To the west was Regulus, his paternal home, among the brightest but still 500 million million miles away; an inch above it, μ Leonis, his mother's system, faint and twice as far. The stars were old news, packets of light sent from the distant past, but watching the skies was decidedly more entertaining than what was showing at the drive-in, and less heartbreaking than what was transpiring in the Ballistic thirty feet away.

His attention shifted to the screen, where the Mutant Teen had come home from having killed a local kid. He wanted to turn himself in, but his Domineering Mother wanted to move to another town, like they always did when he killed a local kid.

"Dad . . . answer her," the Mutant Teen appealed to his Ineffectual Father. "Aren't you going to stand up for me?"

He was not. The Mutant Teen yelled, "Dad?" and leapt at his Ineffectual Father. He began choking him with his mutant crab claw hand.

"Stop it!" his Domineering Mother screamed. "You'll kill him! Tony! Do you want to kill your father?"

J!m could not believe that the man who directed *In a Lonely Place* and *Johnny Guitar* had done this. *I Was a Teenage Mutant* was cinematic sausage, ground up with perfunctory spices in amounts inoffensive to every palate and extruded for mass ingestion. To think that this was the film Nicholas Ray had been trying to make since before J!m was born, when it was *Blind Run*. (Only the late addition of mutation had gotten it made; no studio wanted a movie about a teenager who

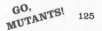

malfunctioned for no good reason.) The project had been so long aborning that the Ineffectual Father was played by the actor Ray had originally wanted for the lead, an exciting young performer from the early days of broadcast viz who saw his career cut short when he was conscripted for the Martian Conflict, which bled into the Giant Ant Problem and the Pod Situation. By the time he got out, James Dean was thirty and barely able to play teenagers. He became best known as Dr. Phil Brewer, the rakish rapist on *General Hospital*, and this piece of work wasn't going to change that.

J!m leaned against the cinderblock, smoking a Red Ball, looking at the stars, the screen, anywhere but the Ballistic, right in front of him, where he could not have missed Russ reaching over and pulling Marie to him.

J!m tossed the cigarette and turned away, suddenly wishing he had hugged his mother goodbye.

marie, nestled uncomfortably in Russ's arm, shifted her shoulders up and down, which worked for him as well.

"Hey, you grew boobs over the summer."

"What a lovely compliment."

Russ, suspicious: "They are . . . *boobs*, right?"

Marie disarmed Russ and slid back onto her side.

"So," she said, resetting to cordial, "why'd you break up with Carol Webster?"

"She got fat."

Tubesteak added from the back, "She had to go to the Home for Unwed Fat Girls."

Sandra Jane perched in his lap, befriending him with her

buttocks. "Tell me, Tubesteak," wiggle, wiggle, "why do they call you Tubesteak?"

"*I love me some tubesteak!*" Tubesteak said.

"Oh," Sandra Jane said.

She readjusted her skirt, causing J!m's Severed Hand, which had been diligently crawling up her leg, to lose its grip and fall to the floor.

the bar was lousy with kiwanis, bused in from Springdale, where they had destroyed all their female aliens years ago and were regretting it now. They arrived polite and up-standing but, unaccustomed to freely available intoxicants and exotic creatures who, after a few intoxicants, also appeared to be freely available, they became feisty, and Mickey had to knock a few of them out. It was another Friday night.

Miw was run off her feet. High traffic in and out of the private pods left her one of the few servers on the floor, besides that poor dear from Alpha Fuglii, who never got asked to a pod but was as friendly as could be. Miw navigated the tables, past a Bovon topping off a gentleman's white Russian, past yet another Kiwani explaining that the organization's name was an old Indian saying meaning "We have a good time," crossing Lilitu, who was helping a satisfied, trembling customer back to his table, and arriving at the miserable little table commanded by Dr. Howard Rand.

"Herd of brainless, soulless robots," he proclaimed, though not to her.

Miw deposited the Red Spot (a Jupitini with cranberry over dry ice) and dropped the baby voice.

"That's three, Doctor. You're not going to stand on the table and give us all an anatomy lesson again?"

"Sit, sit," bobbing his head in time. "Sit."

"I'll have to order a drink."

Dr. Rand swayed in agreement, and Miw sat, gesturing to Nyah, the Devil Girl from Mars, who sneered. Miw wasn't going to drink what she brought in any event.

"What's on your mind, Howard?"

"Why do you wear that degrading outfit?"

She employees wore their native costumes, provided they were skimpy enough, but Leonine females wore nothing at all, which clashed with the liquor license, so Miw had concocted an indigenish cat suit of black leather teddy, gloves and a whip. She wasn't proud of it.

"Tips," she answered. "Anything else?"

Dr. Rand began to sob. "I don't know what to do, Miw," correcting, "*Persia*."

"Ohhhh," her empathy getting the best of her, "what's wrong, baby?"

In a whisper of despair: "*I'm supposed to be out finding her a body.*"

"We're all using ours here."

"No, no, no," he kept shaking his head. "Has to be human. And fresh. How can—? Does she really expect me to—"

He closed his eyes and listed forward, and Miw thought, hoped, he had passed out. He sighed dramatically. He sighed twice more, the second one woefully and the third one for oxygen.

"It was my fault."

Nyah brusqued by, dropping off milk in a champagne flute. Funny girl.

"It was all my fault," Dr. Rand teed her up again.

"No, Howard," Miw consoled. "No, Howard. It was your quick thinking that saved Susan's head. And the baby."

"She wanted to have Marie at the hospital. *I* insisted on saving money by doing it at the lab.

"Oh, Miw. Miw, Miw." Dr. Rand grasped Miw's hand, petting the back of it.

"I have to charge you for that, too," she said.

another many-splendored thing was developing at the drive-in, unbeknownst to one of the participants, a love that dared not speak its name, for fear of injury, a love forbidden, if she got wind of it. Jelly would have to be subtle and shrewd to pull it off, or perhaps devious would suffice.

They sat in the cab of his parents' primitive Ford pick-up, an off-the-PLEX model that required dead dinosaurs to run. Jelly was behind the wheel, a jumbo popcorn in his lap. Rusty was affixed to the passenger door.

"Popcorn?" Jelly asked, extending his lap to her.

She did not like the way the kernels were agitating in the tub, emptying from the inside. "No, thanks."

Jelly rested his arm on the seat back, coming within two feet of his target.

"Yeah," he said, "so it turns out I'm the Godless Spawn of Science Run Amok," already turning the central trauma of his life into date bait. "I was not a good boy." His arm began oozing in her direction. "According to history, I was a very *bad* boy . . ."

"I thought Johnny was coming," Rusty said, cracking open her door.

johnny was already there, had ridden past them, going by several empty spaces to the very end of the row, where an older model Edsel was parked.

Johnny climbed into the backseat, as per the arrangement.

"You're late," her face hidden in the shadow of an extravagant hat.

Johnny shrugged and started to get out of the car.

She grabbed him by the fur. Soft and low, growing in intensity and pitch, she began:

"*Oo oo oo-oo-oo oo-oo-OO-OO-OO-OO!*"

She threw her head back with a final pant-hoot, her hat coming off, her bun undone.

Deputy Peg Furry came at him with an open mouth.

"look at me now, dad!" the Teenage Mutant shouted from the roof of the planetarium. The police fired. The Teenage Mutant dropped the grenade and blew the dome to kingdom come.

That would be the way to go, J!m thought, *a blaze of glory*, not felled by a headache.

He would not be so lucky. Not tonight.

J!m tied his apron and went inside to prepare for the onslaught.

13

In NAKED SCREAMING TERROR!

the cob ran through the corn, panting, beams of light incinerating the stalks in its wake. The husk broke out of the field and found itself on a country road, alone.

A hum, from above.

The saucers were everywhere.

The first blast shucked it, to its risible distress.

Tubesteak giggled at the nude vegetable, giving up on the clasp of Sandra Jane's brassiere, after spending the last seven minutes grappling with it.

A barrage of lasers hit the cob, turning cartoon

kernels into live-action popcorn, soon spilling to the edges of the screen.

Resigned to having to do everything, Sandra Jane reached back to unclasp her bra; the hooks felt tiny, and when she undid them, the straps flew apart as if relieved of a great burden. Sandra Jane made a note to start throwing up again.

Onscreen, a jaunty jingle animated a parade of refreshments, eagerly marching to their consumption.

> *Oh, we're salty and we're sweet*
> *We're your favorite kind of treat*
> *Whatever your tummy wishes,*
> *We're willing and delicious*
> *So go to the concessions . . .*
> *. . . and purchase us to eat!*

Tubesteak hummed along while Sandra Jane licked the back of his teeth. She came up for air, chugged from a flask, spat the liquid into Tubesteak's mouth and went after it, passing the pint to the front.

Russ offered the bottle to Marie first, wiping the rim with his sleeve, twin courtesies he rarely accorded girls already in his car.

"Hip Rocket?"

Marie, dryly: "What year?"

Russ poured several ounces of the fortified mixed berry beverage into his open mouth, gargled, and swallowed.

"Tuesday."

That was a little witty, Marie conceded, a tactical error, because here he came.

"Are you going to kiss me?"

"You gonna stop me?"

She didn't stop him, choosing rather to discourage him through passive resistance, which worked as well as one might expect.

J!m's Severed Hand, meanwhile, had crawled to the front. It grabbed on to the gearshift and swung up onto the seat.

Russ slobbered in the general area of Marie's mouth while she waited for him to finish. She felt fingers on her knee, light and soon gone, so did nothing about it.

J!m's Severed Hand detected squalene, a natural hydrocarbon found in sharks and sexually aroused human females, whether they wanted to be or not. The hand turned in the direction of the lubricant, raised its index finger, and unleashed the worm.

Marie got a peculiar look on her face. She pushed Russ off her and scooted away, flushed. The hand fell to the floor and scrambled under the seat.

"Could you get me a Coke?" asked Marie, flustered, and flummoxed at finding herself flustered.

Russ was not thrilled, but "Yeah, okay. C'mon, Tubesteak."

Tubesteak looked up from between Sandra Jane's breasts.

"Hey, I'm *mating*."

"Coke with a Dopa-Blast?" Russ asked Marie.

"Just a Coke, please."

Russ hopped out of the Ballistic, followed by Tubesteak, slamming a fist into his groin.

Russ snapped his fingers as they passed the adjacent

TurboFlite. Toad and Ice piled out, joined by Bennie after a synaptic delay.

"Get me a Fizh!" Mil barked.

"Squared!" yipped Hel.

sandra jane rooted around in her purse, looking for a new face, having rubbed the last one off on Tubesteak's pants. She also had chilled advice for her friend.

"Stop playing hard-to-get, Marie."

"Oh?"

"Because you're not that much to get." Sandra Jane touched the BeeKist wand to her mouth, swarming the tissue with apitoxin-releasing nanomites. "Don't ruin this. It's our chance to move up, join the human race."

"I am human."

"Act like it." Her facial labia swelled to a lovely, septic red. She couldn't feel them, but that had its advantages.

"marie would like a coke."

Russ said the word "Marie" like he owned it. He winked and added, "To rinse out her mouth."

Behind J!m's head,

3...
    2...
        1...
            Fizh!

the bottle detonated into the insatiable face of Marilyn Briggs, the model turned actress in one of the few recent films J!m could stomach, *The Last Picture Show.*

"I would think so," J!m said. He placed a cup under the AutoJerk, dispensing the brown syrup, water and spritz of liquid carbon dioxide, and slid the frosty, fizzy soda across the counter.

"Would she like a Euthanex with that?"

Russ grabbed the cup and headed for the exit. His crew, who had accessorized their jackets with bottles and snacks, and in Bennie's case exclusively chocolate, followed.

"Adding larceny to your portfolio?" J!m asked.

Russ turned back.

"What're you gonna do? Viz my dad?"

J!m reached for the com.

several teens in their late twenties were gathered around a beach bonfire, listening to a Prefab Teen Idol tell his spooky story, delivered with the sunny dysphonia he brought to every line.

"And *they* say the creature's still *out* there . . ." his face lit by flames that eerily mimicked a Roscolux #2002 gel, ". . . out *there* combing the beaches for *promiscuous* teenagers!"

"That's-a some scary sheep!" a floppy-eared furry alien whimpered.

"You *don't* have anything to *worry* about, Moondog!" the Idol quipped. "You're *the* opposite of promiscuous. *Ugly!*"

"I *bite* you!" Moondog snarled, for the twenty-first time onscreen, not counting the thousands on the street, at restaurants, and, on three occasions, at a urinal. Moondog Barkley, né Tazhi Spai, was a Kuôn from the Sirius system; a classically trained woofer on his home planet, he was studying with Lee Strasberg at the Actors Studio and trying without success to get his version of *Othello* off the ground.

The Idol pushed Moondog to the sand, which segued into the Kuôn's tail-chasing bit, classic but xenologically incorrect.

It was time for the Buxom Virgin's thesis statement, a variation of which she did in every one of these.

"Good thing *I'm* not promiscuous!"

The Idol made his scary face (his happy face plus eyebrows) and said, in a southern-fried Transylvanian accent, "We shall see about that."

He reached for her career.

The Virgin did her scream.

As the horned Idol chased the vestigial Virgin down a moonlit beach onscreen, the real show was behind the audience, five teenagers marching out of the Snack Bunker holding a struggling alien over their heads.

jelly concentrated, each of his collective yet selfish cells acting in concert toward a singular goal: the copping of a feel off Rusty Ford. Jelly had no brain per se but was in essence all brain, a shared consciousness programmed for desire. He had an appetite for consumption, of food, of entertainment, of everything, voraciously absorbing the culture that surrounded him and becoming it, only louder. In other words, he was extremely teenaged.

And so it was natural if unnatural to find him acting casual over on his side of the truck while his arm oozed along the seat behind Rusty's head. His hand flowed over her shoulder, slowly, slowly, down the strap of her dress until, Jelly whistling, his fingers drizzled into her cleavage.

Without a word or look, Rusty plucked Jelly from her person and splattered him against the passenger window.

"Ow," Jelly said, unharmed but wounded.

Rusty's response was terrifically coarse but drowned out by the riotous yells of five boys passing the pickup, holding something over their heads.

"It would be my pleasure," Jelly answered her challenge, "if you'll watch."

russ and his crew carried j!m to the area under the screen where a corroded slide was all that remained of a playground that once provided fun and tetanus for unwanted children whose parents had locked them out of the car.

Above them, the Virgin had caught her bikini top on a piece of driftwood, somehow.

J!m was thrashing wildly, but there were five of them, and one would've done, even Bennie. J!m was lean and well muscled but mysteriously lacked tensile strength. He wasn't a weakling, simply weak.

The audience, fixated on the exciting plot development the Virgin had left dangling on the driftwood, paid no heed, except for Marie.

"Russ!" She stood up in the Ballistic. "Leave him alone! C'mon!" Then, desperate:

"It's his *birthday*!"

Marie was so mature that she sometimes acted like she had no idea what teenagers were.

"Spankings!" Russ shouted.

The boys grabbed at J!m's clothes.

"Let's see what he's been hiding in Gym!" said Tubesteak, pawing J!m's jeans with impious zeal.

"Birthday suit!" Toad yelled. He wrenched the sleeve of J!m's new jacket, separating it at the shoulder in a profusion of batting.

J!m made a noise. It was high and pure, otherworldly, a sound not heard on this planet in millions of years. His whole head vibrated with it, his brain dimly lit from a fire deep within. His mouth remained closed throughout.

The cry, or call, diverted the assembled from the entertainment product onscreen, and once they saw that J!m Anderson was about to lose his jeans, all eyes migrated downward.

"you're tearing him apart!" Rusty squalled, standing outside the truck, stomping and carrying on, more wrought than if she herself were being stripped in front of everyone, appreciably more.

Jelly's mouth extruded out the passenger window. "Yeah!"

Rusty punched the mouth back into the cab and activated her wristplex.

"Stupid, evil brother."

Nick Ford sat in the dark, watching an old vizcom, a daffy redhead swamped by a confectionary assembly line. He was not laughing.

A photo of Rusty appeared in the lower right-hand corner. How much she looked like her mother.

He flipped his daughter onto the main screen. He had never seen her so upset, and he had seen her upset nearly every day of her life. He reached for his gun.

"Dad!" she cried, mascara runnelling her nose. "Russ is pantsing Jim Anderson! Hurry!"

Sheriff Ford put down his gun, got up to get his jacket. The screen returned to the daffy redhead, cramming chocolates into her mouth and down her blouse. He used to think she was so funny, when he loved her.

the topless virgin ran at camera, hands full, unwatched.

J!m's jacket and boots were off, T-shirt asunder, and Tubesteak was all over the jeans, deeply invested in them, had them around J!m's hips, about to expose the inner right thigh that struck terror into the hearts of men, and something else in the somewhere else of women.

"Stop . . . *stop it!*" Marie was up there, trying to pry 850 pounds of boy off J!m. A space opened and there he was, writhing, contorted, haunted. He saw her. His expression slid from agony to betrayal to contempt all in the time it took for Ice's elbow to slam into Marie's face—an accident, he shrugged later.

"Marie!" J!m yelled.

ever the professional, even postcoital, Deputy Furry settled accounts. "Okeydoke, there's a hundred," she fingered her plexpad. "And a little extra, for hooting like I like."

"Thank ya very much," Johnny mumbled.

"Next time don't be late. I did half your work for you before you got here."

Johnny wished he could vomit to get the taste out of his mouth.

"Exit the vehicle, Love Monkey."

A horn blast directed their attention through the windshield. From so far way, Johnny could faintly make out five boys, horsing around, with something blue.

His nape bristled, and glowed.

mil and hel got out of the Turboflite to cheer on their boyfriends' molestation of a classmate from a better vantage. The timing was propitious, or tragic, depending on how one felt about Mil and Hel, for they were well out of the car when a big green hairy thing landed on the cockpit, shattering it and getting glass in their panties.

Johnny bounded on, crumpling hoods and roofs, growing in luminescence, until he reached the front, where Russ and the boys huddled around J!m, admiring their handiwork. Johnny grabbed the back of Tubesteak's waistband and flung him twenty feet, to where the merry-go-round used to be, which would have been highly comical, him spinning around and around to calliope music instead of eating gravel, only diverting. Johnny tossed Toad and Ice less far, as they were needed for the game tomorrow. Russ ran off, and Bennie remained, eating a SuperNuga bar. Johnny turned him around, and he wandered off.

j!m crouched, naked.

On the beach above, the Virgin stopped flopping and looked down, seemingly at J!m. She opened her mouth and

spun out to slashing violins, inadequate to wring fear from the flashed insert of a prop skeleton in a bikini, but worked for the horror proceeding below.

The first set of headlights blinded J!m.

One after another, across the lot, high beams elucidated his bright and shining plight, scored by a chorus of car horns.

J!m backed away. His hearts pounded, his ears flattened, autonomic signs associated with . . .

He reached behind him, but too late.

A long, hairless and previously unseen tail shot up from the base of his spine. He cowered, hands in front, fingers splayed. He froze.

His shadow, writ large on the screen, was that of a terrified, deformed cat.

Sandra Jane shrieked, with equal glee and disillusionment:

"He's got no dick!"

It was true. There was nothing there, as only Marie had known, and never told.

Moondog arrived on the scene and gawked down, again, it seemed, at J!m. His eyes popped from their sockets, against the advice of his physician, and his ears stuck straight up, done with wires.

"Yipe-yipe-yipes!"

. . .

johnny was dispatching bennie when he heard Sandra Jane and saw what everybody was laughing at. He leapt in
front of J!m and encased him in fur.

"I got you," Johnny said. "I got you."

Rusty rushed to gather in J!m's clothes, possessively, charg-
ing at Marie when she tried to help.

Deputy Furry sauntered onto the scene, hair spilling from
her Stetson and shirt tail sticking out, her swagger a little
stiffer.

"Show's over!" she shouted, patting her gun. "We all saw
it! We *all* saw it!"

lightning struck the sky.

The Monster hurried down the steps to meet his Bride.
She looked sensational, for a corporation of dead body parts,
if a trifle standoffish.

"Friend?" the Monster asked, a gentleman.

This was why J!m worked here. Bill Schloss owned two
Super Simplex carbon-arc projectors and thousands of 35mm
prints the studios had planned to incinerate after transferring
them to plexcode. Schloss was not a preservationist; he spliced
new titles onto the old films and showed them at the bottom
of double bills to save money. This one he called *She-Mate.*

Every night after the patrons left, and before his mother
got off work, J!m watched another of the movies they didn't
make anymore: *Casablanca*, *The Best Years of Our Lives*,
Marty, shown to the teenagers of Manhattan as *Tropical Tri-
angle*, *Man with the Iron Hand* and *Heavy Lust*. Tonight, feeling sorry for himself, he had gone with a Frankenstein.

The built-to-order Bride shrieked at the Monster's offer of friendship, sussing out his full intentions.

Three more bolts, originating from a single source on the ground, struck upward, an exciting feature of the PLEX, that it could not be turned off, necessitating these releases from time to time. No one ever asked what would happen if they did not occur.

J!m patrolled the berms with a Vapo stick, zapping cups and wrappers and butts and prophylactics and vomitus and fresh mammal scat, probably not from a 150-pound dog. Teenagers were the vilest creatures on the planet, and that included the Cûlusi, who couldn't help being giant anuses, since that was all they were.

No one had remembered anything when Sheriff Ford arrived. Rusty was all for her brother's arrest by her father but less keen on Johnny facing multiple counts of criminal destruction, and so blamed her hysterics on the viz, which she mistook for reality. Marie's nose was bloodied but unbroken, so J!m had nothing to add. Deputy Furry had arrived only seconds before the sheriff, she reported.

But they had all seen it, and were laughing about it still, at Googie's over fried carbohydrates, snickering into their pillows as they fell asleep. J!m could hear them.

The Bride continued to react poorly to her prospective groom, hissing at him, and he took it badly.

"She hate me," the Monster said. "Like others."

"Huh," J!m said.

The reverse lightning struck in sixes, then nines. The air tingled with anions.

J!m felt dizzy, fissile, his head splitting, his febrile mind sparking in answer to every strike. The pain was greater but cleaner than before, pure and intent.

He looked up.

Tendrils of light spread across the night, branching dendritically to the stars, connecting them in a matrix shimmering with meaning, with the feeling of meaning. The inscrutable static mirrored in J!m's brain, confounding and debilitating him. He fell to his knees.

"What?!"

"We belong dead," the Monster said, not the answer J!m was looking for, but a solid one. The Monster pulled the conveniently placed self-destruct lever and the tower collapsed with explosive precision.

The monster was dead, until next time.

Behind the screen the sky quieted, the nocturnal emission completed, the night again a random and meaningless array of stars.

J!m heard a buzz. Miw was more than an hour early. He should have wondered who called her, who knew where she worked, but he didn't.

His mother ran to where he knelt. She held him, which he hadn't allowed in years, and for the moment could not imagine why.

14

A gash of white across the black . . .

. . . silent, and then THUNDEROUS.

EXT. HIGH SCHOOL—NIGHT

The approaching storm silhouettes the building, dark
but for the Bell Tower.

INT. BELL TOWER

The laboratory is splendidly diabolical, more gorgeous
than it has any right to be, German Expressionism in
the service of mass-market hysteria.

THE CREATURE lies on a platform, naked and dead.

Human adolescents gather around the body. A BLOND FEMALE lifts the Creature's long, limp tail. She drops it, disappointed.

THE DOCTOR, his operating gown spotless, his hair precise, his mind not as tidy, lectures his students.

> THE DOCTOR
>
> *Tonight I shall take dead flesh and endow it with life!*

The LIGHTNING is well timed.

> THE DOCTOR
>
> *And this will be on the test!*

The Creature's fiancée, a DARK-HAIRED FEMALE of uncommon sense and grace, is hesitant.

> DARK-HAIRED FEMALE
>
> *Are you sure he's dead? I think he's breathing. . . .*

She places her hand on the Creature's chest; the doctor snatches it away.

> THE DOCTOR
>
> *Crazy, am I? We'll see whether I'm crazy or not!*

He turns to his assistant, a hideous HUMP OF GOO.

THE DOCTOR

Larry! Begin!

The Hump jigs over to an immense iron wheel.

HUMP OF GOO

Yes, Dr. Rand! Yes, yes!

The Hump turns the wheel. The platform rises.

The machinery HUMS. Dials jump.

*Copper spheres SHIMMER with current. Voltaic arcs DANCE
in a glass apparatus.*

*The body is lifted to the sky. There is an EXPLOSION OF
LIGHT.*

The Doctor motions to the Hump. He turns the wheel back.

The platform lowers.

The observers look upon the Doctor's genius.

The Creature is a burnt, SMOLDERING cinder.

THE DOCTOR

*Everybody sit down and open your books
to chapter twelve.*

. . .

j!m woke in a fever chill, his face beaded with liquid.

> *Starry, starry night*
> *Paint your palette blue and gray*

Don McLean sang from the orb, his paean to Van Gogh, an artist J!m identified with and hoped to emulate, in particular the dying-penniless-and-insane part. When he was ten, J!m twice cut off his left ear, fruitlessly.

He lay on his back, arms folded across his abdomen, not yet noticing he had wrapped himself in the sheet as he slept, nor that he had been leaking oil, staining the shroud a bluish black, his body in gravure.

vice president reagan was having trouble reconciling his campaign promise to eliminate evil alien influences at home and abroad with the recent report that his wife was an alien, and from all indications an evil one.

"How long have you known," pressed PLEX correspondent Helen Thomas, "that Mrs. Reagan was a Fùlóng, a race dedicated to the destruction of men?"

"Well, let me tell you," the vice president replied in the amiable bumble for which he was somewhat beloved. "My wife is a good Republican. She has a coat, and a cloth dog."

"How could you *not* know? *Look* at her."

"Now, there, Helen. Nancy is a beautiful woman, or whatever she is."

Miw had known Nancy when she was Si-Tchun, and

everyone knew *what* she was, except poor Ron. She had liked Ron well enough, before he jumped on the aliens-in-Hollywood bandwagon, which had seemed so silly at first. She had known them all: Norma Baker, whom she met at Romanoff's and had adored until she came sniffing around her husband; Jack Kennedy, who sniffed her when he ran out of human blondes on the West Coast; even the President, a studio mogul at the time, who dated Miw's sister Sakhmet until her untimely, and unsolved, demise, then put the make on Miw at the funeral.

That was a world ago.

Miw heard rapid footsteps coming down the stairs. She picked up her mending.

J!m, in the black overcoat his father had worn, the coat the boy had slept in on and off until the age of ten, hurried toward the door. His mother interceded.

"I sewed your . . ." She offered up the red jacket, like new and never the same again.

"Need . . . warmer," transparent, a four-year-old's first lie. "For the game."

J!m held one arm tight across the coat, not enough to conceal the bulge. Miw lifted a lapel and out spilled greasy black disgrace.

the sheet was piled on the table between them.

Miw had started and stopped seven times. "There's no reason to be . . ." Eight. "Every boy . . ." She was so good at this with other men, which J!m was, very nearly, but she was not good at this with him.

"Jim," his mother came up with, "your body is changing."

"Yeah," J!m answered her, a small offering, "from bad to weird." He would never admit it, but last night his mother had gotten inside him again and he couldn't keep her out, for the time being.

"Growing up *is* weird," his mother agreed. "It doesn't stop being weird."

J!m volunteered: "I'm getting these headaches."

Miw's measured response was belied by the prick of her ears. "That's pretty common for a boy your age. I'm sure it's . . ." she trailed off. She was not sure. Miw had an idea where J!m was going, providing he would mature as his father had, no certainty that. He had his mother's eyes, her lips, her tail, and his father's brain, his skin, his finger, and who knew whose what inside.

"Maybe you should talk to Dr. Rand," she offered. "He's a man," hedging, "and he's studied you."

"Maybe he'll submerge me in ice water again, or cut off my toes to see if they grow back."

"They *did* grow back," in tepid defense, and moving on. "Dance is tonight. You talk to Marie?"

"Check the PLEX, Mom. Marie and Russ Ford are like *this*." He formed a circle with thumb and middle finger, raised the forefinger of the other. He couldn't bring himself to gesture completion.

Miw so wanted to say one thing that would make her son feel better, or less bad.

"I know it doesn't feel like it now, but trust me: there is someone, somewhere on this planet, or another planet . . ."

"Or another universe, another time and space . . ." J!m squeezed his mother's hand. "I know what I am, Mom."

"You are *not* getting away with that," her frisky reprimand.

"You know, your father was . . . he was not conventionally handsome, and *he* could have had Norma Baker!"

"She's a moon cow!"

"She's your *governor*. And our next vice president, hopefully. And she wasn't always"—catching his eye—"but *you* know that."

Which reminded her:

"Film school. I've been thinking, and we could—"

J!m got up. He bent over, an inch from her nose.

"Dad did a lot better than Marilyn Monroe."

A kiss, and exit.

Miw sat, lost in that, only too late, seeing her hand in the oily sheet. She swiftly withdrew and licked her soiled paw, another mistake, sending her screeching to the sink.

Later, when she picked the sheet up with a pair of tongs, it fell to pieces.

15

THE RAGING VIOLENCE OF A MADDENED APE...

perfect football weather: cold, unpleasant and unsuitable for anything else.

J!m was there, under the VISITORS sign, hiding under his father's long black coat. He had considered not coming at all, after last night. But then the teenagers would have won.

Besides, Johnny was playing.

J!m had attended every one of Johnny's games and bouts, just as Johnny had sat through hundreds of films in dead languages and two colors. It had been so since they were children, unalike but seldom apart, their friendship a special blend of their essential differences: J!m would build an empire of blocks and Johnny would destroy it; J!m would want to play chess with a real set and Johnny would steal one. They had become less inseparable only recently, Johnny going out at night without saying where and J!m no longer exposing Johnny to art he couldn't appreciate. J!m thought he was the one who was growing up, but Johnny already had.

Though sitting in the opposite stands, safe from direct peer oppression, J!m was far from invisible. The real visitors were from Springdale, a town with only one alien (whose identity shifted with local sentiment, currently Doc Jaffe, who wore a space beanie on weekends and knew things no human could). Uncomfortable with strangeness in their midst, the Springdalers had allotted J!m his own row and the two above and below. He was, consequently, easy to spot, as a spot, black flotsam in a sea of bleacher.

the mutants warmed up, hitting the four-man blocking sled. Johnny made a cursory run at it, sending the half-ton contraption tumbling into the end zone.

Downfield the Dust Devils discussed this, formulating strategies ranging from forfeiting to letting the second string play. Ultimately their breeding prevailed, and it was decided to "get the monkey." Wilbanks Smith, a defensive tackle known for his bow ties and wandering elbow, volunteered to take Johnny out on the first play. The other players, who didn't much like Wilbanks Smith, agreed.

On the sidelines, Mil and Hel led the cheerleading squad

for the first time as co-captains since Carol Webster left school to lose her Russ Ford weight.

> *Hey, hey, mighty Mutants*
> *We're gold and green*
> *And mighty mean*
> *Get out of our way*
> *We got hot D-N-A!*

(whereupon they touched their steaming behinds)
Yessssssssssssssssss.

Dancing randomly beside them was Manny the Mutant, Lewis Seuss in a dingy green rubber suit that smelled like teen spittle, steeped in the accumulated desperation of every social maladroit who had attended MHS since 1955. Lewis could not see or hear well in the big-brain headpiece, and was gyrating spastically a half beat behind.

> *Go, Mutants!*

the cheerleaders chanted as the Mutant wagged his rear, showcasing the costume's newest feature, a length of garden hose dangling from the coccyx.

> *Go, go, go . . . Mutants!*

jelly, stripped to the waist, held aloft two cans of paint.

"Gold and Green!" he yelled, dumping both cans into his head, his body aswirl with school pride.

One row down, Marie looked across the field at J!m. She felt horrible about last night, sad that it happened, upset she had not been able to stop it, and frustrated that J!m wouldn't talk to her afterward. She couldn't understand why he was so angry with her, beyond the obvious, and that didn't justify discarding everything, did it, after all hadn't she given him every opportunity, what right did he have, and fine, she was mad at him, too.

"Why does he do that," asked Sandra Jane, "always sit over there?"

"It amuses him."

"That's, like, *treason.*"

"He's a dick," opined Tubesteak, who, upon hearing what he'd said, rejoined himself, "*Only he doesn't have one. A dick.*"

"He's worse than his dad," Sandra Jane said. "He shot Nixon, you know."

"He did not," said Marie, once again. "That was John Hershell Glenn."

"*After* he was captured by aliens in space and programmed to do it—and under *whose* orders?" countered Sandra Jane. "It's so facto."

"Jim's father wasn't even alive when that happened."

"You're so *educated,*" Sandra Jane sniffed.

"Sandy's right," Tubesteak gallanted to her side. "He was implemented. It was in the PLEX."

Sandra Jane rewarded him by squeezing his leg, her fingers wrapping all the way around.

Tubesteak looked down. "You got big hands."

She rhythmically inched up his thigh. "You know what they say about a girl with big hands . . ."

Growing fearful: "She's a dude?"

Marie was glad to be out of that debate, but unable to surrender the last word. "You can't believe everything in the PLEX," she said.

They were already in each other's mouths and did not care to rebut her.

one couldn't believe everything one read in the PLEX, or saw, or heard, or felt (with the appropriate helmet, gloves or genital attachment). Little in the PLEX corresponded with anything else there, and much of it was not simply in conflict but multiply mutually exclusive, diametrically opposed along n dimensions, contradictory beyond the comprehension of binary mammalian brains, except for dogs, who utterly fumbled their opportunity 15,000 years ago.

On the matter of J!m's father the PLEX was especially discrepant, a great galaxy of nodes offering competitive truths:

that he had died when his ship crashed into the Washington Monument, as history recorded it;

that he survived the crash and was living on a Greek island with Nixon and the thawed head of Walt Disney, subsisting on government air drops of fresh Mouseketeers;

that he survived the crash and was living on different islands with different people who were supposedly dead, in one variation Paul McCartney, who had been replaced on the Silvers by a pod, explaining one of their lesser hits,

> *Scrambled eggs*
> *I would like some scrambled eggs*
> *Oh, I would like*
> *Three scrambled eg-eggs;*

that he escaped in his ship, that another ship was built and crashed as a cover-up, and that he was on his home planet planning a second Earth invasion to take place on 10/10/10 EI, a couple of weeks ago but on schedule to have happened through time-travel technology that the government has had all along and was using to steal the ancestral wealth of certain individuals;

that he never left, his ship was crashed by joy-riding teen-agers, and he was working with the President aboard the *Flying White House*, an H-8 Hercules space jet in perennial orbit around the globe;

that he never left and was working with the President and the reanimated head of Nikola Tesla in a secret underground installation, the *Flying White House* story a transparent fake;

that it was all a hoax, perpetrated by the government and executed by Hollywood, that there were never any invading aliens or atomic mutants, the whole thing fabricated to sell color viz screens;

and innumerable other variations and disputations, pos-iting co-conspirators ranging from the Freemasons to the Bildenbergs to the Bohemians to the flooring industry, though curiously none linking anything to the Army's Research and Development group at the university.

The government did not control the PLEX, it was often announced, even though it began as a military project and remained under the protection of the United States Armed Forces. The reality was similar: the government did not *choose* to exercise control of the PLEX. They had learned, as Stalin had not, that the truth could not be destroyed, but could be lost amongst lies.

It was also helpful to know what everyone thought.

So the PLEX was a discordant confabulation, incompre-
hensible in toto to any human but natural for J!m, who could
hold as many contradictions *in cogno* as he cared to, which
was many. In J!m's inner realities his father was dead and
wasn't, Marie was his and someone else's, his mother was
Mary and Magdalene, he was a deadly serious filmmaker and
a seriously dead teenager, each alternatively true and immu-
table in some universe.

Which is not to say that he did not have a rooting interest.

the dust devils' coach walked onto the field, beckoning
Coach McCarthy. They met on the fifty-yard line.

"We're not playing a goddamn ape," the Devils' coach said.

"He's half human."

"I don't care if he's half my nut sack."

"Look, Reverend," Coach McCarthy said. "There's nothing in the rules against it."

"It's not right," the Reverend Coach Wesley Swift said, citing, "*And you shall not lie with any beast and defile yourself with
it*—Leviticus 18:23."

"We're not screwing here, Wes. It's football."

The Devils' coach didn't see the distinction.

"they're willing to forfeit," Coach McCarthy said.

The Mutants were fine with this.

"I thought we came here to play," said Russ Ford.

The players also were fine with that.

"Should we," the coach asked, "take a vote?"

Johnny grasped the sides of his helmet as if to lift it off

his head but instead pulled laterally, snapping it in half. He dumped the pieces in the coach's hands as he left.

"Tell me how it comes out."

"Christ, Johnny," the coach said. "These are custom made."

vizbugs hovered over the field, flitting about in an apparently chaotic pattern that was in fact precisely chaotic, creating a real-time four-dimensional image of the action that could be observed from any angle or distance or point in time by any viewer in the stands, or at home, or in Japan, where American High School Football was the second-most-watched programming behind *Meishi Shishi*, a variety show hosted by a toilet. This game wasn't that important; they all had vizbugs now, as did most public events and nonevents. The winged robocams were ubiquitous but unseen; they looked like flies and even died like flies when swatted, going dormant until disposed of. They were a quite useful technology.

manhattan high won the toss and chose to receive.

Jesus Christ Christian kicked off. The crowd roared.

The Mutants scrambled.

The crowd hushed, revealing another roar.

Charles "Ice" Tucker, number 9, signalled for a fair catch, not knowing Johnny was behind him, coming on fast, and on his motorcycle.

Johnny, number 43, plucked the football out of the air, clotheslining Ice for no sports-related purpose, and sped downfield, ripping up the turf.

The Devils ran like hell, with the exception of number 72, the tackle Wilbanks Smith, who was a man of his word if nothing else. He charged Johnny and the Triumph, throwing his lucky left elbow into the monkey's jaw, fracturing his own radius, ulna and humerus, dislocating his shoulder and bloodying Johnny's lip but not with Johnny's blood.

Johnny tore through the end zone, spiking the ball. It bounced very high.

Rusty, seated between her father and grandfather, leapt up and yelled, "Touchdown!" though she knew full well it wasn't. Jelly heard her and jumped up as well, woozily, the lead-based school colors mixed to a glittery pea soup and churning in his core.

"Goo, Mutants!" he *urped*.

Tubesteak tilted his head back to address Jelly.

"Shut up, you fat clow—"

It was an inopportune time to be saying the word *clown*.

Marie missed the shower of golden green. She had left to talk to J!m, who saw her coming and was gone when she got there. A mile down the road he reconsidered and walked back. But by the time he arrived the Mutants were down by twenty-one, and Marie had gone with Sandra Jane to get Tubesteak's stomach pumped.

16

WHAT CAUSES THE UNBELIEVABLE TO HAPPEN ?

"body of christ."

"Amen."

"Body of Christ."

"Amen."

Father Egan stopped when he got to J!m. He looked into the face of this boy he loved but was unhappy to see here again. And whom he could not refuse.

He presented the Host as a challenge.

"Body of Christ?"

"Thanks," J!m said.

The church was three-quarters empty, average for a Saturday-evening Mass.

Faith had been in crisis for two decades since that day on the Polo Grounds. For the planet's religious adherents, someone descending from the heavens who was not their particular god was problematic. That there followed a large assortment of such someones, from throughout the galaxy and beyond, most with reasonable claims to superiority over humans, and few sharing their godly likeness, contradicted the books humans deferred to on such matters. It made them feel a lot less special.

People responded to the Revelation in dramatic fashion, although inconsistently. A large majority took the refutation of their eternal faith as a godsend, freeing them forever from its strictures, and for a couple of years there was a worldwide pork shortage and a ten thousand percent increase in urinary tract infections. Most never returned to the fold, after finding that the hole in their souls that God had filled wasn't actually there.

The remaining faithful dealt with their cognitive dissonance in a number of ways. The first was to kill all the incongruent beings they could, and not just the ones who were trying to carbonize or eat them, but expressly those who claimed moral superiority, coming in peace and all other manner of devilish trickery. This righteous slaughter ultimately proved unsustainable, and the theological questions remained.

Some adapted. The Unitarians changed their name to the Cosmotarians and expanded their refreshments; Reform Jews retroactively added another dozen tribes. Roman Catholics, seldom living in the same century as everyone else, issued the *Dei Verbum*, containing this passage:

13. In Sacred Scripture, therefore, while the truth and holiness of God always remain intact, the words of God, expressed in human language, have been made like human discourse, as His word was made for other beings spread amongst the stars in their languages, and their holy texts hold Divine truth for them, but for the Martians, who are wicked.

(from chapter III: "Sacred Scripture, Its Inspiration and Divine Interpretation")

Two years of the Second Vatican Council were consumed debating solely this, and the rest on allowing guitars in church, forcing the what-to-do-about-women question to be bumped to the next council in a hundred years. The Church's shocking recognition of the present day provoked an extra Reformation, splintering off the Real Catholic Church, the Church of the Human God, and the Holy Name of White Jesus.

Other faiths dealt with the new reality in keeping with their practices. Conservative Christians declared the aliens demons, sent to tempt them into awesome sin, while radical Muslims threw them in with all the other infidels. The Hindus worshipped the aliens, who bore uncanny resemblances to their gods, and the Buddhists remained, as they had for millennia, completely cool about everything.

In 1962 AI, with the unpleasantness dying down, the enormity of it sank in. The world, reality itself, had changed, and needed to be recognized. Officially, the *aetas ignara* was brought to an end, and the era after that began. Some Christian denominations stubbornly clung to the old Gregorian scheme, but no one cared what they did.

• • •

j!m was the last to leave the church. He liked to sit in the near dark, smelling the vaporized paraffin and embedded incense of the pews, browsing the stained-glass windows and deciding which Station of the Cross he was at. Today it was easy:

X. Jesus is Stripped of His Garments

Next up:

XI. Jesus is Nailed to the Cross

The summer before high school, J!m had come to believe that he was the Antichrist, based on things that were yelled at him. While this harmonized with his thirteen-year-old sense of self-importance, J!m had not wanted the job, which he equated with being the villain in somebody else's movie. He wouldn't have minded being the second coming of Christ, but the painting in the kitchen made that fantasy unsustainable.

He had first sought counsel at Christ the Avenging Baptist, an unfortunate choice, as the Reverend Harold Powell had insisted on baptizing the boy and was disinclined to let him resurface, keeping him under for a full five minutes before giving up and declaring him unsalvageable.

The boy trudged, soaking wet, across the street to St. John's, where Father Egan took one look at him, muttered "Goddamn Harry" and invited J!m in.

The priest made short work of the boy's metaphysical dilemma—"Anybody who's worried about being the Antichrist ain't the Antichrist"—and asked if he played gin rummy. J!m didn't, so Father Egan taught him. J!m lost the first hand and none after that.

The father had lived a colorful life, and had the stories and face to prove it. A boxer in his youth, he looked as if he had been beaten so badly so often that the swelling never went down. He had an elephantine lump of a nose, rosacean and pustular, save for the tip, which was missing, attributed to frostbite in Tibet, occasionally to leprosy in Nepal. His tales of his days as a mercenary and a missionary, often overlapping, enthralled J!m, reminding him of classic movies, sometimes quite specifically. J!m didn't mind that the stories often digressed into parable and catechism.

J!m began attending Mass, drawn to the costumes and props, in particular the ciborium, the golden chalice that held the Jesus pieces, and the paten, the silver plate the altar boy placed under the communicant's chin to prevent God from falling to the ground. One day J!m went up to receive communion himself, a gross impropriety, but Father Egan indulged him, perhaps hoping the irresistible paste wafer would convert him. Lately J!m had been going to confession as well, mostly divulging the sins of others.

Rising from the pew, J!m walked up to the altar, a venial, ran his finger along the top as he passed, mortal, and poked his head into the sacristy, not an official sin but also not done.

"Father . . ."

"Jimmy!" The priest was out of his vestments, in a sweat-stained sleeveless T-shirt and gray trousers so threadbare that his ample seat shone beatifically, giving the impression that his arse had a halo. He was rinsing the chalice at the sacrarium, a gilded sink that went straight into the earth, ensuring that any excess savior did not go into the sewers, where it might breed with the locals, and nobody wanted to pray to a Giant Rat Jesus.

"I can do that," J!m offered, eager to get his hands on the magic cup.

"Do you offer to do surgery, too? Sit."

J!m obeyed. Father Egan pulled up a chair and sat facing him, their knees touching.

"Listen, buddy. You can't take communion anymore."

Though they had discussed this before, as recently as six months ago, J!m took fresh offense.

"So much for *Dei Vermin*," J!m said.

"*Verbum*, meaning the Word, wiseass," their tatty repartee. "Look, we got rules here. And one of the rules of the Catholic Church is, if you want to take Communion, you gotta be Catholic."

"When'd you start caring about rules?"

"When some old biddy—Mrs. Porter, I bet—reported it to Bishop Retardo, that's when."

"Well, just tell Bishop Retardo—"

"*You* don't call him Retardo."

"—tell the bishop I'm Catholic."

"I ain't lying to a bishop. About this."

"No lie. I'll *be* Catholic. Wave your wand."

"Jimmy, Jimmy," laughing, "do you remember when we discussed transubstantiation?"

"*The permanence and adorableness of the Eucharist.*"

"That the consecrated Host doesn't *represent* the body of Christ; it *is* the body of Christ. Do you remember what you said?"

"I had doubts."

"You said, 'I'm sorry, Father, but that is horseshit.'"

"I may have."

"Here's the thing, Jimmy: if you want to be a Catholic, you have to buy that horseshit. And a lot more."

J!m didn't know what to say. He liked Jesus well enough, a little too nonjudgmental for his tastes, but the rest of the canon, the archangelic insemination, the miracle fish, the zombie Christ, yeah, that was horseshit. On the other hand, there was no one he could talk to like he did with Father Egan, not Johnny, not his mother, not Marie lately, and maybe never again.

"But Father—"

"Barry."

The priest saw terror in the boy's eyes. He softened.

"Son, I know you're searching. But the answers we got ain't to the questions you're asking. You're gonna have to look elsewhere."

J!m, with extreme unction: "*Where?*"

"Up there," Barry pointed, "out there," and, thirdly, to J!m's chest, "in there." The priest made a face. "What do *I* know? I'm just a potato-eater."

He rapped J!m's leg. "What's with the get-up?"

J!m wore a shirt with buttons, a tie and a tweed jacket, three levels higher dressed than he got for church.

"You got a date tonight?"

"I'm sharing one."

Frowning: "You didn't ask her."

"I was going to."

"You're a jerk." Father Egan knew more than he could divulge, and so he phrased his next statement carefully: "She loves you, you know."

"So she says," J!m answered morosely.

He got up.

"Can I still come to confession?"

"We can talk."

"In the booth?"

"We'll have coffee and I'll turn the other way."

17

Explosive Drama...
Set to Rock 'N Roll Tempo!

the mhs billboard zoomed, cross-dissolved,
etc.,

MANHATTAN 6 SPRINGDALE 51

EAT AT GOOGIE'S!

HARVEST HOP TONIGHT!

DANCE, MUTANTS, DANCE!

as Johnny and J!m rolled by, the last to arrive.
Johnny had been late to J!m's house, every last Saturday of the month being his mother's bath night,

and this one becoming crevice intensive. Miw delayed them further, insisting on shooting viz of the two boys looking so cute, like they were going to court.

Johnny parked in the back, where they agreed to meet Jelly and Rusty, rejecting Rusty's proposal that they all pick her up at her house like a real date, arguing that they did not want to. Instead, Jelly had shown up at the door in a green and orange checkered jacket and asked if his fiancée was ready. The general invited Jelly to sit, and proceeded in his affable manner to comment on how much Jelly reminded him of a situation he thought he had taken care of.

"Hey," Johnny said, dismounting the bike.

"Yeah," said J!m.

"I never woulda . . . if I'da known, I wouldn't of called you 'dickless.'"

Johnny had been calling J!m dickless for almost a decade, so often and so variedly that J!m hadn't connected it with his actual lack of dick, and didn't see the point of discussing it, ever. But the dickless thing had been bothering Johnny since last night, for more than one reason.

"No way," Johnny said, "if I'da known you didn't have a dick."

"You're all heart."

Johnny was hoping he wouldn't have to say what he meant.

"You coulda told me."

"And tell me, Monkey: How would that conversation go?"

"Gosh, I'm sorry," said Johnny. "Let me rephrase that: Go automate."

"Now you're rubbing it in."

• • •

rusty toppled out of the pickup, protoplasmic goo all over her white tunic dress.

"If you *ever* do that again, I'm going to make you *eat* it!"

Jelly flowed out of the cab.

"I *am* scrumptious."

Rusty slammed the door, cutting him off and in half. Seeing J!m and Johnny, she transformed into the innocent but available humanoid female from an idyllic planet that her toga was meant to convey. She sashayed over, the gold cincture bisecting her voluptuaries quite nicely, a sensual look that would have worked better if she had lowered her voice an octave and several decibels.

"Johnny! You were colossal today! After you left, Russ got sacked, like, eight times! So, you quitting the team?"

"Nah," Johnny shrugged. "I like knocking people down."

J!m cleared his throat, indicating Rusty's tunic, where the Jelly stains had migrated into two camps, bilaterally symmetrical on her upper torso, forming puffy purple mounds that much improved the dress but perhaps overadvertised Rusty's availability.

"Get the hell off me!" Rusty screamed.

The goobies blurbled gaily as they dripped off and returned to sender.

"neep neep, you hairless monkeys!"

Marshall the Martian was squat, fairly hairless and, for this low-paying appearance, costumed only from the shoulders up:

his face and head grease-painted baby-poop green;

black rubber tentacles sprung limply from his neck;

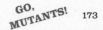

and a tiny silver cape safety-pinned to the shoulders of a cheap suit.

Anything more than that, he wanted carfare.

"Neep neep!" shouted Tubesteak back, feeling he had made a celebrity friend. He looked to Sandra Jane for affirmation, again failing to note how amazing her dress was or how strenuously her breasts were trying to escape it.

"Take off that stupid hat," Sandra Jane said.

Tubesteak grabbed the porkpie he had chosen to offset his green sharkskin jacket and cocked it at her.

"That's my *personality*, baby!"

Marshall waited out the parroting of the devoted, the *neep neep*'s and *Prepare to be probed!*'s and *Die, puny Earthling!*'s, all fully trademarked and printed on twelve thousand T-shirts sitting unsold in his garage, and went into his basic package.

"Are you ready to gyrate in a grotesque simulation of biological reproduction?!"

They were.

"Inoculators and incubators, collide your appendages for"—he demonstrated hand clapping for those new to the custom—"Chromium!"

Chromium, a quartet of slumming rhythm-and-blues musicians, launched into a serviceable version of a Davie Jones tune. The Martian exited, pursuing check.

Warm orange and amber spots swept the gym, traversing the center circle, where Russ was holding half-court. Toad and Ice arrived with drinks for the girls. Marie tasted hers, gave it back. It was pure grain alcohol, possibly sweetened with cough syrup. Sandra Jane sent Tubesteak for a second one.

I'm the Space Invader
I'll be a Rock-'n'-Rollin' Bitch for You

on cue j!m entered, Rusty attached, Jelly at his heels, and Johnny eventually, through an arch of overgrown Indian corn, leading into an elaborate harvest tableau, the centerpiece of which was the Mutant costume stuffed with straw, wearing overalls and crucified.

"It is finished," J!m said.

"We just got here," said Rusty.

J!m looked out into the darkened gym and saw the reflected whites of a hundred female eyes, angled down, betrayed and bewildered, unable to accept that the monster in his pants was simply monstrous. Brackish laughter erupted in pockets around the room, the schadenfreude of average boys.

J!m stepped back and into Johnny. "This'll pass," Johnny nudged him forward. "By Monday it'll be something else."

That wasn't reassuring.

this whole evening was a mistake, Marie thought, sipping more cleverly spiked punch. She had nothing in common with Russ beyond a basic genetic blueprint, and she wasn't even positive about that, and had only agreed to this setup because Sandra Jane had talked her into it, and because J!m hadn't asked her, after thirty-two excruciatingly obvious openings, and she got miffed. Yes, Russ had looks, and a swell car, and would never make her feel shallow. And there was comfort in being part of the social mainstream for once, in being . . . *normal.*

GO, MUTANTS! 175

So why did it feel so wrong?

"Your boyfriend's here," Sandra Jane said, wagging her pinkie toward the gym entrance.

He had worn a tie!

"I guess not 'boy,' though, huh? *Itfriend*."

Marie handed Sandra Jane her drink, taking care to make the spillage seem accidental, and went to J!m.

as she got closer, J!m got the feeling that he had met this girl before, but she was not Marie. She looked strange and familiar, in that dress, with that hair, those heels, that face, not pretty but something else, dreamy and unreal: beautiful.

And all for Russell Ford.

J!m's souring expression slowed Marie but didn't stop her.

"I'm so glad you came," she said, and in a show of good faith: "And you brought Rusty!"

"We couldn't afford separate girls," Johnny said.

Jelly, loudly: "It's a gang date!"

"Stop saying that!" Rusty kicked him, the fourth time they had touched.

J!m smiled, and Marie relaxed.

"How's your date?" he asked. "Are you popular yet?"

Marie had misjudged the situation.

"Excuse me."

She pushed past J!m and rushed out the gym door.

Russ trotted up.

"What did you say to her, Missing Link?"

He followed Marie, with a passing attack at Johnny: "Coulda used you on the field today."

The rest of Russ's pack and their dates followed.

J!m looked around.

"This could be all right."

a strangled sob echoed down the darkened hallway, more aching with each iteration. It spooked Marie, who didn't recognize the cry as her own.

She heard footsteps and began to run.

Russ appeared in the hall behind her.

"Yo, . . ." and then remembering, "Marie!"

Marie turned, lost control of her heels and fell. She curled into a taffeta ball against the lockers.

Russ knelt beside her, ran a callused fingertip along the track of her tear.

"What did that blue bastard say?"

"Nothing." Marie sniffed strongly, inhaling her hurt, not wanting Russ to have it. "We're just . . . It's complicated."

Russ had a limited repertoire for dealing with upset girls, beyond not calling again. But he hadn't closed this one yet, and had to come up with something. Borrowing from another heuristic, he rubbed her back.

"If you want," he said, "I can beat the shit out of him. Or whatever comes out."

The back rub had moved to the side back and was circling around to the front back.

Marie twisted away, saying, "No, thank you," to his generous offer and what he was doing.

The launch sequence had been activated and there was no turning back. Russ opened his mouth.

"Hey!"

It was Tubesteak, et al.

"Wait for us!"

Marie was the only one who found that disquieting.

The group joined Russ and Marie, encircling them, too close for Marie, not part of the set but trapped inside it. Russ got to his feet and, tipped off by a look from Hel or Mil, offered to help Marie up. She took his hand, unaware that in doing so she had agreed to genital manipulation, at the very least.

The circle tightened and Marie feared a Paniscan Frisk, which required eight different kinds of genitalia, but such technicalities never stopped teenage boys when it came to sex.

The closing of ranks involved another sort of foreplay, however.

"Anyone in the mood," said Bennie, disclosing a long, untidily constructed peach cylinder veined with rose, "for a mind ride?"

Tubesteak, after the Dick Moon hit: *Let's Go Triffin'!*"

Triff, a space weed long cultivated for its oil despite its habit of killing and eating humans, was banned once it was discovered that smoking the petals produced pleasurable sensations in the brain.

"You're smoking triffid?" asked Marie, alarmed to be in such close proximity to illegality.

"Wake up, Marie," Sandra Jane said. "It's *tomorrow*."

"That stuff causes brain damage!"

Bennie rolled his eyes as he lit the triff, his pupils never coming down.

"Sorry, brain."

• • •

johnny, rusty and jelly sipped unadulterated, unentertaining punch. They hadn't made it more than fifteen feet into the gym, remaining in the light of the entrance. They weren't at the dance. They were witnessing it.

J!m paced in a small mental box he had created, trying to astroglide into the universe in which he had not said that to Marie, the one in which she kissed him and he turned into a prince.

Rusty fidgeted her hips. "Anyone care to ask me to dance?"

"Wanna dance?" Jelly asked.

"Anyone?" asked Rusty.

J!m walked away. Johnny looked straight ahead. Rusty flushed, her freckles aflame.

> *I have only one-a burnin' desire,*
> *Let me stand next to your fire!*

sang Jimi Marshall, the clean-cut and conked lead singer and guitarist of Chromium as well as King Kasuals, their R&B combo, and Foxy Lady, their wedding band. The song was an original. They weren't paid to play originals.

The dancing few struggled to keep up with music that had more rhythm than their limbs were calibrated for. The rest waited for a song they could Bikini to without dislocating something.

Johnny pulped his cup and tossed it into Jelly.

"I am so sick of high school," he said.

"It's been six years," Jelly commiserated.

Chromium finished their number. No one applauded.

"You're too kind," mumbled Jimi. "This next one . . ." He shielded his eyes. "Johnny?"

Jimi urged his friend to the stage. Johnny waved him off.

"Everybody," Jimi shouted into the mike, "how about a hand for my favorite half-breed, Johnny Love!"

The crowd, confused, nevertheless clapped. Rusty prodded Johnny forward. He balked; this was not something he did here, for them.

And yet he was moving toward the stage. He looked down and saw a plasmatic carpet conveying him across the floor.

"*Heeeeere's Johnny!*" the carpet bellowed.

The spread Jelly deposited Johnny at the riser. He surrendered, and stepped onto the stage.

Rusty watched, rapt. Next to her, Jelly's clothes rose from a puddle, rejoining her. As Johnny strapped on a guitar, Rusty clutched her hands to her chest. Jelly illustrated her, spurting purple hearts out of his head.

With an aside, Johnny propelled the band into big and meaty rock and roll. He took the mike and snarled:

> *Honey, you know what I want*
> *Baby, you got what I need*
> *Come a little closer*
> *Just a little closer*
> *You gotta feed*
> *The Beast in Me*

Jelly held out his hand to Rusty. She had no choice, really.

j!m roamed the halls, not looking for Marie and with no idea what he was going to say to her when he found her.

Something stupid, he guessed.

Around the corner, next to the girl's lavatory, smoking a Chesterfield, the vice president's brand, was a middle-aged man who had been major-market, Cleveland to New York, a friend to the Silvers and Bobby Zee and the Presley Brothers, until, through no fault of his own, a law nobody obeyed, he was banished to this godforsaken small town teeming with freaks, reduced to a gimmick act, which wasn't working.

"Neep neep," Marshall said to J!m, exhaling smoke.

"Yeah," J!m said.

Close up, the Martian was unconvincing, the makeup gloppy and smeared on his collar, the tentacles cracked and rotting, the silver cape made of tinfoil. He had an explanation.

"Somebody's gotta play the clown, right?"

"Right."

J!m kept walking. The Martian took a puff.

"Screw you, mutant."

johnny got going, had forgotten he was in high school, was in a basement in the city or a shack along the highway, three a.m., where they didn't care what you were, as long as you weren't a white boy and could sing.

He sang:

> *The Beast in Me*
> *The Beast in Me*
> *You bring out*
> *The Beast in Me*

Dancers did the circumscribed contortions, unacquainted with the tune but moved by it, the beat pumping like the fornication girls dreamt of and boys aspired to. Rusty gyrated with her eyes closed, all the better to not see her dance partner, who was duplicating every dance move he'd ever seen, simultaneously.

> *The Beast in Me*
> *The Beast in Me*
> *Please release*
> *The Beast in Me*

toad had mil or hel pressed against the lockers, next to Ice with the other one. A few feet down, Tubesteak was the one with his back to the lockers, Sandra Jane pressed against him, most of his ear in her mouth, to no discernable effect. Tubesteak's mind was clearly elsewhere. When her dependable conchal whirl failed to elicit a response, Sandra Jane sucked hard, popping his eardrum. He was unmoved. Sandra Jane undocked and looked to see what he found more fun than her tongue.

Across the hallway, Russ had Marie against the wall, under her own campaign poster, GO 4 RAND. He was wetting her face in a manner she did not find intoxicating, the drying saliva smelling like sour milk and making her forehead itch, and yet she allowed it, the behavior of an insecure teenage girl, not herself.

Tubesteak was enjoying it a great deal more than she was, evidently.

"You wanna *watch*," Sandra Jane said, her hand spanning his pelvic region, "or you wanna *do*?"

"Watch," Tubesteak answered, nudging her aside for a better view.

Russ cupped Marie's breast outside her dress, squeezing and twisting to assess what sort of brassiere he was dealing with. Marie might have allowed even this, had she not seen Tubesteak envying her, Sandra Jane working his torso.

Marie pinched Russ's pinkie and leveraged it to detach his hand, holding it away from her like a dead Manos.

"This yours?"

Russ, however, had two hands.

"C'mon, baby," going in with the left. "I'm gonna explode."

She pushed him away.

"I'd better stand back."

Russ became instantly and irretrievably furious, something Marie hadn't seen coming but which didn't faze anybody else in the group.

"I *thought*," he swept a hand across his apostles, "you wanted to be a part of this!"

J!m stepped out of the shadows.

"I guess she doesn't."

the second verse kicked harder, faster and more to the groin than the first.

> *Baby, I swear this is love*
> *Honey, I ain't just in lust*

After a sweaty start in which he'd tried to do the Monkey, Hully Gully and Charleston all at once, ending up with four arms, six legs and no head, Jelly stopped trying to show off and became quite impressive. He was a resonant mass, and when he let the beat pulse through him, jiggling to the rhythm, he certainly could dance, for a fat boy.

> *I ain't actin' funny*
> *This ain't tactics, honey*
> *That's just the Beast*
> *The Beast in Me*

j!m stood his ground.

"Walk away. Nobody gets hurt."

The first punch came across his left cheek.

"I don't like that plan," Russ said.

Toad had J!m's arms pinned, keeping him upright. The others were rivetted; they had never seen Russ hit J!m before. There had been countless promises of violence, but none kept; this marked a milestone in Russ's psychopathic development, and everybody was excited, Tubesteak visibly, to Sarah Jane's great irritation.

"Ah, violence," J!m said. "Clever."

"Then you'll find this"—Russ searched for the trump word—"*cleverer.*"

"Russell, *please*," Marie implored, with no better result than the first eleven times.

"One sec." Russ rabbit-punched J!m's brain. His hyperelastic cranium swung back and forth. This amused a majority of the humans there.

Russ raised his fists for more cleverness. Marie grabbed his arms and tried to drag him away.

"C'mon, Russ. Don't . . ." She lowered her voice in a go at sultry. "Come over here. I'll—"

Russ swung Marie into the lockers. She dropped to the floor, next to Bennie, gratified for the company.

"You fell down."

Wobba wobba wobba. Russ pummeled J!m's head like a speed bag. *Wobba wobba wobba wobba.*

"Look at me," Russ said, "I'm Cassius Clay!"

Wobba wobba wobba wobba wobba.

"Float like a butterfly, sting like a bee!" shouted Tubesteak in a plantation dialect. This galled Russ, who was about to say it, and could at least do a respectable impression of the champ.

Wobba wobba wobba wobba wobba wobba.

J!m's brain began sparking, not from the exterior input, which was harmless and somewhat stimulating, but from a torrid inner storm of speculative fiction, little bangs of universe creation, including ones in which:

through a newly discovered ability, J!m hit Russ with a mega-mindblast that propelled him backward at fantastic speed, impaling Tubesteak;

the authorities arrived and carted Russ off to an internment camp for creeps;

after J!m's heat vision roasted Russ, J!m broke off an arm, took a big juicy bite, remarked "tastes like chicken," and Marie gently admonished him with a pat on the rear;

an escaped Gorgon snipped Russ's head off;

a small atomic device lodged in Russ's colon went boom.

So fevered was J!m's revengineering that the ugly thoughts spilled out of his head, frenzied current scurrying atop his skull, weaving an electric toupee that did not flatter him.

Wobba wob—

Russ pulled back his fist, crawling with fibrils of light. "Tickles."

He sensed someone behind him.

"Marie," he said, according her a cordiality she no longer deserved, "don't make me—"

A bristly black claw grabbed him from behind. Russ was in the grips of a hideous Man-Fly!

johnny wailed:

> *The Beast in Me*
> *The Beast in Me*
> *You bring out*
> *The Beast in Me.*

Jelly tossed Rusty around: a Swingout into a Shoulder Throw, Piggy Back Flip into Double Sugar, Frog Jump and one of his own invention, the Jelly Roll, a modified spin in which the female spins all the way inside her partner. Rusty looked disconcerted at first to be enveloped in Jelly, but caught the spirit and performed a few moves, wearing him like a suit, before he spun her out and into a Princess Dip.

> *The Beast in Me*
> *The Beast in Me*
> *Here it comes*
> *The Beast in Me.*

Johnny hooted, and the crowd howled in return.

. . .

his enormous maxillary palps clacked fiercely, his labella gushing and spluttering, making very little sense.

"You're drooling on me, Al," Russ said, swatting at the Man-Fly, who flitted away in his blue jumpsuit, a victim of his instincts. "Buzz off." Russ raised his hand again and the mutant janitor buzzed off.

"Now," Russ said, returning to his victim. "Where were we?"

"You were making an aggressive display to assert your alpha status, which you are driven to maintain because of a crippling lack of self-esteem, stemming from your early abandonment by a mother who never loved you," J!m said, tired of being wry.

Russ looked around for something sharp with which to express his displeasure.

"What are we having here?"

Miss Mantis buttoned her blouse as she entered the light, Al Delambre a safe distance behind her.

"Nothing, ma'am," said Russ. "I was just punching Jim."

"Do not lie to me!" her antennae vibrant. "I can smell your sex!" She lectured Marie and Sandra Jane. "And are you silly and stupid? These boys will never earn good livings! They will give you worthless babies!"

"Come!" She clicked at Hel and Mil, though she had long ago dismissed them as subprime.

On her way out, Marie presented to J!m the same brutal smile he had attacked her with earlier.

"If I need your help," she said, "I'll scream."

Russ yelled after her.

"Nice knowing you, Marie!"

Miss Mantis's head ratcheted around without her body moving. "Don't make me bite your head off!" She licked her chitinous lips.

Russ scoffed, going in the opposite direction. He pointed at J!m, fixing him with a look that said, *I'm pointing at you.*

"Later, masturbator."

johnny was soaked, his face and chest trickling with transuranic perspiration, grinding to a hot and slow climax.

> *Honey, I know what you want*
> *Baby, I got what you need*
> *Come a little closer*
> *Give a little whisper . . .*

Rusty leaned in, drenched in Jelly, and sang, *sotto con fuoco:*

> *I wanna feel*
> *The Beast in Me*

She lapped the sweat off Johnny's cheek. Johnny laughed. Jelly licked the other side, his tongue the size of a flapjack. Johnny liked that less.

18

CHARGED WITH MILLION-VOLT EXCITEMENT!

robby took his floor-waxing as seriously
as he took protecting eccentric scientists and befriending underparented boys, which was very seriously. He was a robot.

The rotary brushes retrofitted to his foot pads
whirred gravely, so that on Monday the boys and
girls who attended gym would never know fun had
been had there; every trace of diversion would be
waxed away, and the athletics program could oper-
ate unimpeded. It was not as glamorous as appearing on *Gilligan's Planet* and *The Addams Phylum*
after returning from Altair IV, but it was what he
had been reprogrammed to do, and would do, unless it conflicted with his prime directive.

o

J!m picked up a cob of Indian corn and heaved it. It went wide of the mark, but the Hypersan gravity can drew it in, whisking it into another dimension, thereby dumping it on Old Man Mxyzptlk's lawn, who was damned tired of this and might accelerate entropy for a couple of days to see how we liked it.

Everybody had gone to Googie's. J!m begged off, knowing Russ would be there, and his imagination was sore. He had stayed to help Al, figuring he would one day need a recommendation for a sanitation job. He liked Al. J!m had never gotten his story; Al had told it to him several times, but he had never gotten it. He'd heard that Al was from Canada, but that didn't fully explain it.

"I'm gonna zoom, Mr. Delambre," J!m called to Al, who was high on the wall, retching digestives on some stubborn tape residue.

The Man-Fly spluttered pleasantly, making the "in peace" salute with his human hand.

"Yeah," J!m said.

the billboard twinkled, zippered, etc.,

DRIVE SAFE!

DON'T MATE!

PLEXURE™ YOURSELF INSTEAD!

IT'S CLEAN AND EFFICIENT!

as J!m walked past, pulling his tweed jacket tight around him. The nights were getting colder, and darker.

He activated his domes.

"We're deep into the night," a smoky female voice whispered in his head, "and from this point on, all sense of time will cease to exist, only space, and the sensory, that which we feel and experience becomes the manifestation of all of the cosmic waves of the universe. The sound pours in the brain and pushes all barriers to the outer limits of perception, and we are in space and we are above, and beyond."

J!m swooned from the beautiful idiocy of it, this cosmic nonsense lost souls embraced upon the death of their god, the notion that the universe, a math equation, would embrace them more warmly than a deity they had built for that very purpose.

"Come, fly with me, Alison Steele, the Nightbird," in her soothing mesmer. "We begin this night with an early Halloween treat; from White Trash, here's Edgar and Johnny Winter's 'Frankenstein.'"

J!m had never heard the instrumental but immediately liked it, the heavy, lumbering beat suiting his mood, the frenetic synthesizer lead mirroring his mental state.

There were no streetlamps along this stretch of road, next to the cornfield. The light from the waning moon filtered through the towering stalks, the silhouettes forming black bars, a prison extending into the night, if one were inclined to think that way, which J!m was.

Halloween in three days. That was a lively night at the Anderson house, though wasteful, since they didn't eat eggs or use toilet paper. And only 194 more nights before he graduated. If they were all like the last two, and in all probability would be much wor—

It hit him first in the left lobe, buckling his right leg. He fell onto his side and a second blast erupted on the right, causing the opposite limbs to spasm. His entire head lit up, and everything was moving, his right leg and arm scrabbling in the dirt, spinning his body around, his left limbs out and shaking all about. The music in his domes, a muscular fugue of evil insanity, was an ideal accompaniment. The seizure seemed to be taking orders from the drum line, crescendoing with the percussion solo and trailing off thereafter.

J!m managed to stand. A night breeze almost knocked him down again, setting off a paroxysm of chills. He shivered uncontrollably; he felt wet, and wrong.

A harsh light struck him from above.

He shrank away, shielding himself from the incoming lumens.

Two bluish beams, a series of small red lights flashing between them, began to descend, and approach.

J!m tapped off his domes.

The low crunch of gravel told him this was not his father's spacecraft, come to take him home to assume his rightful place on the Regulese throne, with his pick of queens from throughout the galaxy.

It was an Earth vehicle rolling down the hill.

The car stopped fifteen feet from J!m, idling with a cold, slow thrum. A chorus of spectral voices ended in the only words J!m could make out, *shut up, dipshit*, and then it was quiet, and dark.

Russ Ford's head appeared, floating several feet in the air, lit from below.

"It's later."

. . .

they had not gone to Googie's. Halfway there, an idea had fallen into Russ's head, much like it had occurred to him a few days earlier to start dating Marie, after not noticing her for seventeen years. This evening's plan had arrived fully formed, a vision of such brilliance that Russ assumed it must be his own.

For two hours he and his gang had been parked on that hill, with no music or conversation. The only excitement had come when Bennie said there was a disembodied hand crawling on the floor, prompting the others to toss out the Zoomers he had distributed.

Russ wanted everything to be perfect, and it had been, up until he turned off the Ballistic and Tubesteak found it necessary to comment on how perfectly it was all going. Yet the light trick, placing his wristplex under his chin and turning on the torch function, had been superbly effective, and Russ was still relishing the look on J!m's face, frozen in terror, when J!m disappeared into the cornfield.

"After him?" Tubesteak asked, stepping on Russ's next line.

"Sure," Russ grumbled.

j!m hurtled through the corn, which, stiffened with human bone genome and emboldened by anabolics, was unyielding, the truculent crop batting J!m to and fro down the rows. Disoriented, he tumbled and spun, away, he hoped, from Russ and his thugs.

Shafts of light stabbed at him from all directions, combining with binaural cues, woops and giggles, to tell J!m he was surrounded.

Humans were an inferior species in numerous respects—playing well with others, cleaning up after themselves—but they were unparallelled at hunting down other animals.

J!m ran into a solid object, its alabaster face and rat eyes underlined with ghoulish illumination.

"Boo," Ice said.

J!m staggered back, cracking the spines of a couple of corn stalks, which cursed him, and fell at the feet of Toad, also holding a wristplex under his chin, his facial craters taking on lunar scale.

A glance to either side confirmed Russ and Tubesteak, lit from underneath as agreed, Tubesteak grinning against orders.

"I apologize," J!m said, getting up. "I am *truly* sorry."

J!m had never apologized before. This made Russ uneasy about what was going to happen next. It contravened the Uniform Code of Bully Conduct:

XVII B. *Spontaneous Contrition*

> (1) Should it apologize or cry "uncle" or otherwise express regret for whatever it did to enrage you, whether during a beating or prior to one, you are to:
>
> > (a) Consider the sincerity of the admission, taking into account shrillness of voice and copiousness of tears, and
> >
> > (b) If the apology is deemed sincere, offer it an opportunity to save itself, either through
> >
> > > (i) financial restitution.
> > > (ii) continued grovelling.

(iii) fulfillment of other conditions,
determined at your sole discretion
but not to include felonious acts or
sexual favors. (cf. Appendix O, Prison
Exceptions)

(c) If the apology is deemed insincere,
or excessively babyish, you may proceed
with the beating

(i) at the current level, or
(ii) with renewed vigor, to teach it a
lesson about being a lying pussy.

Russ saw himself awash in paperwork.

J!m, deeply penitent: "I didn't know this was a private circle jerk. As you were." He walked away, almost two steps this time, before Toad grabbed him and drove him to his knees.

So *XVII.B.1.c.ii* it would be.

"What's it gonna take," Russ said, his anger refreshed, "to teach you some manners? A good beating? A *great* beating?"

"A *best* beating!" Tubesteak chimed in.

Russ had a whole speech, dependent on rhythm and momentum and building to a well-chosen cri de coeur, now ruined.

"Let's just kill him," suggested Ice, snapping his obviously spent antipsychotic gum. "It's not illegal."

This was an intriguing interpretation of the case law, and if this were Mississippi, a conservative reading. Before the one-stop genocide could be debated on the merits, Bennie staggered into the circle, wristplex under his chin, unlit and in transmit mode, sending viz of his neck to his personal business node, *The Happy Stop.*

"A beating will do," Russ decided, feeling chivalrous.

Toad lifted J!m to his feet. Russ got in close.

"Now," reprising his earlier witticism, "where were we?"

"That thing I said about your mother," paraphrased J!m, "abandoning, never loving you, thus explaining your deep-seated yet entirely justified feelings of inferiority."

Amply reminded, Russ prepared to proceed with the beating with renewed vigor, when his eyes were drawn to a prospective humiliation he could not pass up.

He turned his torch on J!m's abdomen. The shirt was soaked blue-black, seeping up from the waist.

"You piss yourself, Anderson?"

Oh, how they laughed, never tiring of Russ's observational humor, laughing at J!m for the fifth or sixth time that weekend, as if they were doing it for the very first time, instead of the last.

"How can he piss?" Tubesteak bon motted. "*He's got no dick!*"

The laughter died.

"Don't talk anymore," Russ said.

J!m saw his opportunity and wrested himself away from Toad, who effortlessly wrested him back. J!m thrashed, the dark secretions spraying off his head and into Russ's face and mouth. The droplets boiled on his skin.

Tubesteak, squeaky: "I don't think that's piss!"

Russ spat out the silver nitrate. He gritted his blue and corroding teeth and threw a punch to J!m's gut. J!m's head responded with a concussive wave that knocked Russ to the ground and broke Toad's nose.

Every synapse in J!m's brain fired at once, invoking a million billion memories, several not his, the pyrotechnics scored through a cognitive quirk with Tchaikovsky's 1812 Festival Overture, Op. 49. Wild current encircled his head, swarmed down his neck and crazed along his torso and to his extremities, consuming his clothes.

Russ shouted to his crew for support and saw the last of Tubesteak disappearing into the corn. He faced J!m, unable to turn away from the burning and shining light.

J!m raised his arms, hands open, his face to the sky.

"Dad?"

"Listen," Russ said, stepping back. "I didn't mean to set you off. I'm gonna—"

The electric tempest whirled away from J!m with tremendous force, curlicues of light crisscrossing Russ a thousand times as they threw him deep into the corn.

And then, complicating matters, J!m burst into flames.

He burned brightly for several seconds, flared, and fell over.

About a half hour later, he extinguished.

IT'S INTERMISSION TIME, *Folks!*

THE NEXT
FEATURE WILL
START IN JUST A
FEW MINUTES

And Now...

ON WITH
THE SHOW

19

DEATH and DESIRE!

OPEN ON

Black.

Not noir or vérité, not the luxuriant gloss of the classics nor the sooty murk of the bottom of the bill. There is only one true black, and it can't be filmed.

This black.

FADE TO BLACK

· · ·

from the air, it was divine, a vast mandala carved out of the corn, Fibonacci spirals and Platonic solids woven with a golden string, of greater beauty and complexity than one of those Martian crap circles. The only blemish was a tiny black smear at the bottom.

A Gaylord coupe pulled up underneath it.

The sheriff and deputy stepped out. Left in the backseat was Tubesteak, who had struggled with his duality as a loyal flunky and a natural snitch before coming to a thrilling solution: ratting out his friends in secret.

It did not look like a burnt body. The remains were charred but intact, each of its reaching fingers articulated, its upturned eye sockets unsunken, the anguish on its face exquisitely detailed. It was as if J!m had been cast by Rodin, the missing black Jesus from *The Gates of Hell*.

"Crispy critter there," Deputy Furry said.

"He was a boy," the sheriff said.

"Boy," the deputy repeated, skeptical.

Nick Ford crouched next to the carcass. It smelled wrong, absent the cupric acridity of boiled blood or sulfurous stench of burnt hair; of course J!m *had* no hair, and his blood could have been chocolate sauce for all the sheriff knew. What concerned Nick was what he *did* smell: plastic and gasoline.

"Napalm." There were canisters of it in his basement, which his father used to facilitate weeding.

He couldn't believe his son was capable of this, but he couldn't disbelieve it either.

The rumble of a motorcycle cut off further supposition, followed by the crack and thresh of falling stalks and the arrival of Johnny at the crime scene. He leapt off his bike and knelt next to the body.

"Freak."

He cupped his hand under the head.

"That's evidence," Peg Furry said.

Had the sheriff not been there, Johnny would have torn the deputy's heart from her chest, bitten off half, and shoved the rest up or down one or more orifices.

Instead he roared, from the half that could not speak, ancient and ferocious.

He picked J!m up.

The deputy went for her gun.

"Peg," the sheriff said.

J!m's outstretched arms proved awkward, but Johnny solved it, carrying his cruciform friend over his shoulder in the traditional arrangement. He mounted the bike, nodded to the sheriff and left.

"That's tampering, Sheriff," Furry said. "You've gone and lost chain of custody there. Why in God's holy name would you let him take it?"

"*It,*" the sheriff said, "was his friend."

And, yes, he was aware it was evidence, too.

j!m didn't fit on his bed. His arms stuck out, and with his body stiffened to his full height, his feet hung over, too.

Marie, Jelly and Johnny milled around, feeling rightly useless.

At the bedside, Dr. Rand studied the blackened boy. He rapped on the fire-hardened chest, *shave-and-a-haircut*, and took as significant that he did not hear *two-bits* back.

"Anthracite," he concluded, incorrectly. "What did Dr. Bennell say?"

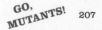

"That he's dead," Miw sniffled in the corner, needing two walls to remain upright.

"I'll see what I can do." The science teacher unlatched his tackle box and pulled out a hammer. He considered it, and put it back.

"what I don't understand," said Sheriff Ford, in uniform and on duty, in his own living room, in his own goddamn chair, "is, what were you doing in the cornfield in the first place?"

"You think this is *my* fault?" Russ's hair and eyebrows were gone, his head and upper chest etched with a web of fine second-degree burns. He was slathered with Vaseline, slick and pinguid, a delicious irony if J!m weren't dead.

Rusty sat at the other end of the couch, medium-keening, her grandfather behind her, patting her head.

"If you ask me," the general said, jawing his pipe, "our boy has done a service to his community."

Russ, protesting too much: "I didn't do dink!"

"Like he burst *himself* into flames!" Rusty lost it, yet again. "Why would he *do* that?"

"*I don't know,*" Russ whined. "He's a *creature.*"

EThL, programmed to attend to that very cry, motored up behind Russ, extracted the pillow from behind his head and fluffed it. As the consequent cloud of feathers settled into Russ's gooey scalp, Rusty felt a teensy bit better.

the professionals had come and gone. Handsome Dr. Ben Bennell had stayed only a minute or two, using the word *dead* seven times, but offered to come by that evening if there was anything he could do, or any other evening. A weeping Father Egan performed the Anointing of the Sick, despite the disqualifying factors of J!m's not being Catholic and no longer sick; later, he said a prayer for the boy at Mass, the first time a priest had been heckled in that church since they'd added perfume to the holy water to keep Mrs. Porter from guzzling it. Sheriff Ford also came by to express his genuine sorrow and disingenuous avowal to uncover what had happened.

And so it was all up to the mad scientist.

Miw had not called Dr. Rand; he had assumed an urgent invitation based on his nonexistent relationship with Miw. Also, J!m had always been his favorite specimen. Miw didn't hold out much hope. She had heard rumors that Howard had fooled with the primal forces of nature during his days with the RAD Group at the university, but also that his results had ranged from poor to apocalyptic.

Miw knew only one person who could bring back the dead, and they had killed him.

But she hoped.

Dr. Rand had what appeared to be a grade school microscope strapped to his head, and was hovering over the body making scientific sounds.

Marie watched her father with low expectations, conditioned by her mother's lifelong harangue on his inability to grow or fetch her a body, along with all the pets that had gone into their garage for repairs and never come out.

On J!m's bedside table was the book she had given him.

It fell open to the first page. J!m had underlined a passage at the very bottom:

> he'd bought it with his own money. It killed me. Now he's out in Hollywood, D.B., being a prostitute. _If there's one thing I hate, it's the movies. Don't even mention them to me._

"You dummy," Marie said, closing the book.

Dr. Rand lifted off his Rand Zoomatic Portoscope. He ran a fingertip along J!m's forehead and studied it intensely. He licked it, confirming his hypothesis.

"Based on the carbon signature," he pronounced, "it appears as if Jim here has been incinerated."

A short interval later he thoughtfully added, "Sorry."

Miw crumpled and Johnny caught her. Jelly went to give Marie a hug, but she escaped it; he pivoted and embraced Johnny from behind, reaching all the way around to include Miw.

Marie sat at J!m's side. She touched his cheek, bent over and kissed him.

She turned to the others. Her lips were black.

She might have said how much she loved him, or what a bastard he was for dying in the middle of a quarrel. She knew a lot of applicable poetry.

"He," she said, and ran from the room.

Dr. Rand should have waited a few more minutes before saying, "Miw, if it's all right, I'd like to take this," meaning J!m, "back to the lab."

Miw wasn't certain she had heard that correctly.

"All my power tools are there," Dr. Rand elaborated.

She had.

"You want to cut him open?!"

"Perhaps," pronounced Dr. Rand, "from what I learn, we can prevent this tragedy from reoccurring."

"To who?" Miw screamed, to be forgiven the grammatical lapse. *"He was the only one!"*

"So," said Dr. Rand, "no?"

it was almost not a sound at all.

s.

An individual fizz, liminal, and yet to Miw it was deafening.

A ray of light emanated from J!m's lips, and multiplied, stippling across his mouth, shooting from his eyes, everywhere, a thousand points hissing in high harmony, singing a body celestial.

Miw and Johnny were transfixed. Dr. Rand observed from an increasing distance.

"He's gonna blow!" Jelly yelled, duck-and-covering.

The beams shut off. The smooth hard surface of the body was riven with fissures.

"The core is still burning," Dr. Rand said, stepping back into the room. "Obviously."

Jim's right hand slowly closed, crumbling its carbon shell.

"He's alive," Miw wished.

J!m sat up, arms outstretched. The dark chrysalis fell away in hexagonal shards.

"He's alive!" Miw kissed Johnny, and kissed him again. *"He's alive!"*

"As I suspected," said Dr. Rand, leaning in for his kiss.

Miw pounced on the bed, on J!m, *baby-baby*ing him, all over him, blackening her fur as she squeezed him.

"So hard," she said. "Like your father."

His skin was a cool silver, armored in a shining carapace; his brain bobbed regally in a diamond skull.

"He's mutated into his adult form," Dr. Rand said. "Obviously."

Johnny was crying, a little bit, but able to maintain male camaraderie.

"Ain't puberty a bitch?" he joked.

J!m looked around the room, wafting into consciousness. His voice was twelve notes lower than before, fuller and more mellifluous.

"Where's Marie?" he asked.

"She left," Johnny said flatly.

Jelly pulled his head out of his anal region.

"Astounding!"

the mood was grim at the Ford household. First Rusty outright accused Russ of murdering J!m, because J!m was too pure and Russ couldn't stand it. Russ maintained that J!m attacked him, and that Rusty was defending J!m because she'd wanted him bad, only she could never have had him, since J!m had no *him* to have. The twins swapped obscenities while the general mused, what with aliens attacking humans and the local constabulary doing nothing to stop it, if maybe it wasn't time for the Army to step in, prompting the sheriff to counter that the last time the Army stepped in, it had resulted in tens of millions of deaths and the loss of four U.S. states and seven countries. The general took this personally, and thanked the Lord that the sheriff's sainted mother wasn't around to hear this, and the sheriff said no, she was in Chicago and had far more unsaintly things to say about the general, provoking the general into bringing up the twins' mother. The twins stopped bickering, wanting to hear this, at which time EThL mistook Russ's feathered head for that night's supper and tried to pluck it, which required a hard shutdown.

Sheriff Ford's wristplex rumbled. He read it twice.

"It appears that Dr. Rand has . . ." easing into his chair. "Jim Anderson is alive. He's going to be fine. Good news."

Rusty whimpered with joy. Russ just whimpered.

"How is that good news?!" he moaned, his grandfather dismantling the robotic claw clamped to his head.

black liquid swirled down the drain. J!m waited as the water went gray and then clear, unsure when the shower was over. He did not know the protocol; his previous greasiness precluded human ablutions. He was oil-free now, though, and filthy, this black powder in every crevice, of which there were millions more, his whole surface encrusted with carbon nanocrystals, harder than ordinary diamonds and a bother to clean.

The water got cold and he got out.

He stood before the mirror, which he hadn't done in years, admiring himself, which he had never done. He was like a five-year-old boy after a bath, posing and preening and finding no flaws, only his own fabulous self.

J!m had not liked dying (and he *had* died, a fully off state required for his transmogrification, so there'll be no carping about that). The preceding pain was intolerable, and preferable to the moment when all feeling ceased and his last lucid thought was of nonexistence. After that there had been nothing, not Heaven nor presumptive Hell, nor even the sense of nothing, until he was resurrected, or reincarnated, or re-booted. The experience had taken all the fun out of entertaining his own death.

And yet, he couldn't argue with the results.

He was nearly seven feet tall, half a foot over last night, and daunting, his shoulders broad and sharp, his posture martial. The soft ridges and bumps of his larval self were glimmering blades and spurs, the rest of his skin a glittering lattice of the highest mathematics, playing in the light, stylish paisley waves gyring across the surface. And being silver was far superior to baby blue.

His mother was right. What standing up straight and eating your Nixons could do, along with a little immolation.

His gorgeous exodermis was not merely cosmetic. His limbs were angular and reengineered, responding crisply to instructions. His head was streamlined, his old soft buttocky skull an adamantine heart, imperial rather than scrotal, and held high; he couldn't feel its weight at all. His tail was coiled tightly against his lower back, not lolling around creating a disturbance.

J!m clenched his fist, encountering something queer: strength. He rapped his knuckles on the wall and went through the plasterboard, kicking up gypsum.

"You okay in there?" called Miw, from the hallway.

"Yeah, Mom."

"Go to sleep. You've got school tomorrow."

So: everything and nothing had changed.

J!m slipped on underpants and got on the bed. He picked up the book from his night table, finding his place, about a third of the way through.

Then she *really* started to cry, and the next thing I knew, I was kissing her all over— *anywhere*—her eyes, her *nose,* her forehead, her eyebrows and all, her *ears*—her whole face except her mouth and all. She sort of wouldn't let me get to her mouth. Anyway, it was the closest we ever got to necking. After a while, she got up and went in and put on this red and white sweater she had, that knocked me out, and we went to a goddam movie.

That kid is messed up, J!m thought.

"Lights out!" his mother yelled.

J!m put down the book and shut the lamp off.

"*Thank* you."

"Love you, Mom."

"Go to sleep."

J!m pulled his knees up to his chest.

The moonlight felt sweet.

He laughed when he realized: he did not dread tomorrow.

20

TEENAGER *or* TERRIFYING BEAST?

INT. SHOWER—NIGHT

White HISSING from above.

THE CREATURE tilts its head back, letting the hot water cascade down its face.

A FIGURE behind the milky shower curtain.

The Creature, unsuspecting, massages its neck.

A hand RIPS back the curtain.

MUSIC: SLASHING VIOLINS

It's only THE GIRL, wearing a sly smile.

The Creature lowers its gaze, to her bare shoulders, to:

HER BREASTS, crowned with two pairs of dark plump lips.

NIPPLE LIPS

Jim?

The Creature is overcome with very strange desire.

The mammary lips part fully, flashing row upon row of slavering fangs.

The Creature opens its mouth to scream.

MUSIC: SLASHING AND SLASHING VIOLINS

INTERCUT ravenous biting, impotent thrashing, etc., edited into artful horror.

The Creature slides down the tile, grabbing the shower curtain as it goes.

Water laced with black fluid circles the drain.

j!m's eye, sapphire in a silver setting, slid open.

He awoke, discombobulated, unsure how far back went the dream.

He smelled smoke.

His sheets were singed, and there were scorch marks on the wall behind him.

We're just a hunk,
a hunka burnin' love

the presley brothers sang, in conjoined harmony.

J!m stepped into the cool blue day. His red jacket, extremely square across his shoulders, ended a little above his waist. His jeans were tight and damp, stretched to their denim limits.

Just a hunk
A hunka burnin' love . . .

The twins faded away, and into the jabber jockey: "Elvis and Jesse, still shaking that pelvis after all these years. . . ."

As J!m neared the autoped, it began moving, hesitating in a shy, servile way. J!m noted the change but walked alongside.

"Hey, and what the hunka burning *what* was that on Saturday night?"

The infocast had mentioned the incident as well, characterizing it as "an alleged alien attack" that was "under investigation."

"But, listen, creatures," the jockey taking it down to nearly conversational level. "Us aliens aren't *all* flaming spaceholes. Take it from Marshall the Martian and . . . the Silvers."

John, Paul, George and Norman, their females and celebrity friends, all chanted:

She got
Pink skin, brown skin,
Gray skin, green skin,

GO,
MUTANTS!   219

Earth skin, fur skin,
Gold skin, Mole skin . . .

Then Lennon, in tremulous falsetto:

Skin is skin
Is what it is
Skin it is

The sunlight tingled on J!m's face, a ridiculous feeling his old self would have mocked as shallow and dangerous, facile commodified emotion replacing true sensation (which was always pain), another sign of the creeping puppyfication of the populace.

And yet: it tingled.

And put a bounce in his step. An actual bounce, a springing up and down as he walked, as if gravity had loosened and time had quickened. My, what the J!m of Friday would have had to say about this Monday-morning J!m, tingling and prancing without a care in the world, while the world around him rushed to its conclusion.

He had the same problems he had last week, and a couple more; his overthoughts zinged and zanged around his brain, in and out of alternate futures, as usual but more cleanly than before, without the muddy buzz that made them so mad and saddening. His mind was energized and expanding, not torqued into tighter and tighter circles. He remained confused but not confounded.

He felt . . .

. . . *lighter* . . .

was exactly the right word.

The beautiful people chanted:

> *He got*
> *Toes and fingers*
> *Claws and stingers*
> *Wrists and ankles*
> *Writhin' tentacles*

Tazhi Spai, sans the Moondog dialect, howled achingly:

> *Parts are parts*
> *Are what they are,*
> *Only parts*

A heavy-browed, snouted female looked out from a home-board, sporting an unlikely brunette flip.

Is she ... or isn't she?

the copy read.

Only her hairologist knows for sure!

He would apologize to Marie, for whatever, and try to arrange a truce with Russ, perhaps easier now that J!m could crush him.

Everybody sang:

> *All people are people*
> *From below or from above*
> *All beings are people*
> *And all people need lo—*

Severe static, then: "He's out there."

J!m took off his domes to examine them.

He heard the frightened woman again. "He doesn't look dead," the voice originating midway between his ears.

J!m deduced, nearly correctly, that he was acting as a PLEX receptor. He searched for its source.

"He's right in front of my house!"

Mrs. Van Buren was peeking out from behind her front room curtains, talking on a com.

"My God, he looks exactly like his—"

She saw J!m seeing her.

"No," she gasped, ducking out of his view before hanging up on his head.

The music resumed.

> *All creatures are people*
> *And all people need love . . .*

J!m stared into his hand, at the two white hemispheres lying there.

"do you want to see it again?" Sheriff Ford asked.

She didn't but assented. They were in the kitchen, which Miw had already apologized for, and for the unstoppable PLEX Information Network, currently doing a segment on Halloween costume sales as a predictor of the following week's presidential election. A last-minute uptick in Gojira costumes was seen as favoring the Democrats.

The sheriff replayed the viz, dim and unsteady. It started as Bennie Scott blundered through the corn, thinking he was turning his torch on, a muffled Charles Tucker saying, "Let's just kill him. It's not illegal."

Sheriff Ford sighed, again. Miw, again, reacted as if they were about to kill her son.

The camera, with Bennie, entered the clearing as Russ Ford said, "A beating will do." The sheriff blinked methodically.

Miw watched, distraught, as Lee Hopper yanked J!m up for his beating, though she knew how it would come out.

"Now, where were we?"

"That thing I said about your mother, abandoning, never loving you. . . ."

The sheriff and the mother both looked away.

Next was the mistaken-urine sequence, which they both would have rather zoomed through, followed by Russ being splattered by J!m's metamorphic fuel, and the abdominal punch.

J!m's retaliatory pulse knocked out the wristplex temporarily, and the next visuals were, from several feet away, of bolts shooting from J!m's fingers, a cyclone of light picking Russ up and hurling him into the dark, and more corn as Bennie ran.

Sheriff Ford thumbed off the viz. "It's hard to say . . ." he began. "The boys were up to no good, and I can't excuse what they did, but from what Dr. Rand told me, that this event was part of Jim's, uh, maturation, then they didn't do it—although, obviously, J!m did nothing wrong, and Russ was clearly, he's always been . . ."

Miw took his hand, gratis.

"I'm sorry about your son," she said.

Nick squeezed her fingers, and she felt all his regret.

"A boy needs a mother," he said.

"And a father," she said.

There were two ways this conversation could have gone, and while one would have led to a far more comical situation, with J!m and Russ bunking together, and Rusty dealing with steplust, and the general making hilariously inappropriate remarks, and EThL the nedroid dispensing sassy folk wisdom, it went the other way.

"Have you ever thought about," Miw asked, "talking to her?"

"Do you really think she'd"—almost hopeful, but—"The last time I saw her . . ." His leg trembled in memory.

"Maybe you're right," Miw said.

They continued to hold hands, which was darling but wholly inappropriate.

"And in other news, Republican vice presidential candidate Phyllis Schlafly challenged Senator John Kennedy, the Democratic presidential contender, to prove he is a natural human and not an Illuminati, the primeval race of reptilian shape-shifters that have allegedly controlled mankind's destiny and promoted sodomy for centuries. Speaking from the Smoking Hole of Houston . . ."

the music in j!m's head went in and out for a minute before ceasing altogether. He couldn't decide if this new brain feature would prove useful or damnable, when the answer, of course, was both. "With great power comes great responsibility," as the philosopher-poet Stanley Leiber once wrote.

J!m reached Marie's house and astonished himself by not hiding. He felt only minor discomfort as he approached her door, even though he had not obsessively practiced what he was going to say, reasoning it was never what he ended up saying anyhow.

He lifted the Rand Dynasonic Electroknocker and the opening herald from Wagner's *Walkürenritt* played, at operatic volume but variable speed.

"Jim!" said Dr. Rand, wearing a bathrobe over his suit and tie. "So you're functioning in your new chassis. Any anomalies to report?"

"I'm here for Marie."

"She left an hour ago," Dr. Rand crushed him cheerfully. "Practicing her big speech, the election, you know."

J!m had forgotten.

"Though heaven knows why she's trying so hard. She's a shoo-in. That Lewis Seuss is a Poindexter, as you kids say."

"We don't say that."

Mrs. Rand called from inside: "Come back here and finish what you started!"

"See you in class," Dr. Rand said, shutting the door.

21

VICIOUS AND VENOMOUS!

"you're like a rock," gushed rusty, hanging off J!m like an ornament, or rather wearing him like one, parading down the hallway showing her boy bauble off.

"He's made of *diamonds*," Jelly said, trying to keep close on Rusty's other side, even as she drifted over, steering him into the wall.

"Something like diamonds," J!m said, with the caveat, "according to Dr. Rand."

Jelly saw the water fountain coming and, in lieu of going around, went through, acquiring three pieces of chewing gum and a string of saliva laced with citrus, possibly orange juice.

Rusty ogled J!m. "Have you gotten *taller*?"

"And *dreamier*?" aped Johnny, a few feet behind.

"*Jealous?*"

They approached a knot of girls, in deep and heated chitter. Rusty adopted an air of recent sexual satisfaction and show-coughed.

Kathleen Hughes saw them first and managed to gasp "It!" alerting the others, who swallowed screams and scattered in as many directions leading away from J!m as possible. Julie Adams went down in the melee and crawled frantically all the way to the stairwell, making tiny animal sounds.

Johnny barked sarcastically. "I guess they're just shy."

"Christ," J!m said, regarding a separate but related matter.

Two of Marie's three campaign posters were torn down the middle, glitching the viz, her face halves twitching like a potato with too much swine chromo. The remaining VOTE MARIE was altered with a red marker, adding workmanlike horns, dripping razor teeth and spiral eyes. VOTE had been struck, and below MARIE was scrawled EATS CREETURE. The penmanship was atrocious.

Things were less better than J!m had thought.

Rusty, publicly appalled: "Who would do something like this?"

"Someone who can't spell *creature*," Johnny said.

Jelly whispered, "It could be *anybody!*"

the auditorium was packed, because attendance was mandatory, these school elections being a vital civics lesson in democracy and how little it mattered who was elected.

Principal Brooks had pre-admonished the crowd to behave

like citizens, perhaps not the best word choice. Marie, who had agreed to go first when it appeared as if Lewis Seuss would connipt if he had to go first, approached the podium. Behind her, Lewis revelled in his spazz gambit, while in front there was enough murmuring that the principal had to stand up and stare very hard.

Marie opened with general pleasantries and a joke no one knew was a joke so it couldn't be said to have failed, and launched into a plethora of unnecessary details.

"My first act as president will be to meet with Principal Brooks to ensure that Manhattan High's bathrooms are accessible to all of our students, regardless of their eliminatory organs—"

"Hey! Eliminate *my* organ!"

Tubesteak sat back, proud of constructing a comeback out of words he had heard. Russ was beside him, his face glistening grimly.

"That's detention, Morrow," said Principal Brooks.

Marie, shaken, swiped her finger at the vizprompt, scrolling ahead in her speech.

"And I believe we should add more extraterrestrial choices to the lunch menu, like traditional Kanamit Shaved Skin Soup . . ."

This proposal proved unpopular.

". . . or Bovonian Cud Nuggets."

Clara Cowley excitedly clopped her hooves together, until she heard all the groans and boos.

Marie nervously scanned the vizprompt. Her next topic: "Alien Arts Curriculum."

Out of the dark came a voice, disguised but definitely Russ.

"Freak Meat."

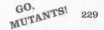

Marie had not heard that term, an indelicate variant of *Creature Crone* and *Space Wench*, in quite some time, and never applied to herself. She had once defended Russ's sister from that very slur, saying it was offensive to both women and nonhumans and that Rusty should be proud of her diverse friendships, which was easy to argue in the abstract.

Laughter mixed with jeers throughout the auditorium, an odd cacophony that highlighted the cruelty of each.

"Thank you," Marie whispered, swiftly returning to her chair.

Lewis Seuss geeked to the podium like the arrogant twit he was.

"My name is Lewis Seuss," he proclaimed, "and I am a human being!"

The crowd cheered, given what they wanted: an affirmation of their fragile superiority.

J!m, Johnny, Rusty and Jelly sat in the top row, with successively lessening awareness of what this meant for them.

"Seuss, really?" Jelly said. "Isn't he a nerd? I thought everybody hated him. I'm so behind."

J!m watched Marie, sitting there, hands in her lap, forcing a smile. He wanted to run down there and hug her, but had already caused her enough trouble.

marie was not there.

J!m focused on that, rather than the fact that his Civics teacher was also not in his Civics class.

"Tom Gray has decided to leave teaching," Principal Brooks announced. With a wave, the cool teacher's name disappeared from the board. "You'll have a new instructor shortly," she said. "For today, you're watching a viz. And I'll be watching you," pointing vaguely, "as always."

The principal dimmed the lights as she left.

it was animated by United Productions of America, a commercial cartoon maker until the company was shut down over *Mr. Magoo*, which then-president Nixon had become convinced was about him. Under new all-human management, the company employed the same radical modernist style but in the service of more socially responsible messages.

A machine gear rolled out to center screen and opened its eyes, situated atop its upper teeth, making navigation all but impossible without grinding oculi, a queasy prospect that seemed to bother no one else.

"Hi," it said, in the same voice as Buster the Management Mouse. "I'm a four-DP two-and-a-quarter-inch spur gear. But you can call me Cog."

J!m watched Marie's empty chair. He should have sought her out after assembly. He could have comforted her, and she could have seen how tall and hard he had become. He wished he knew where she was.

His desk lit up.

"Authorizing . . ." the screen advised, scanning the hand resting on the screen.

A dossier appeared, for MARIE JUDITH RAND. In the upper right was a 3-D hologram of Marie, rotating slowly, her head then her body.

REMOVE CLOTHING?

blinked a prompt.

J!m had never seen anything like this. Nobody had, except for those who had, and they hadn't, go ahead and ask them. The government was not in the business of keeping files on all its citizens; it was more of a hobby, really.

J!m shielded his desk from view and scanned the profile:

S/S: FEMALE HUMAN

DOB: DECEMBER 25, 1955 AI

EYES/HAIR: BLUE/GREEN/BLACK

H: 67"

W: 118 LB

KNOWN ASSOCIATES: J!M ANDERSON,

DR. B. "BUCK" ROBERTS (MATERNAL

GRANDFATHER).

CLASSIFICATION: DO-GOODER

THREAT LEVEL: UNDER REVIEW

NOTES: WELL-MEANING BUT MISGUIDED;

POTENTIAL COLLABORATOR; CURRENTLY

MENSTRUATING.

There were subnodes branching to academic and medical records, personal journals, art projects, and also this option:

OBSERVE NOW

J!m chose it.

The dossier opened into a viz, a disorienting fly-on-the-wall angle, of Marie lying on her bed, face in a pillow.

Was she crying?

In response to his unspoken question, the camera flew down, loosely serpentining, a buzz in the audio, until it alit on Marie's pillow, zooming up into her cheek and eye.

J!m reached out to wipe away the tear.

He found himself fingering Walter Ford's face, less grandfatherly and more militaristic-seeming with the red security lights flashing behind him.

The general wrangled his pipe to the side and scowled into the screen.

J!m ducked down. The general peered around, and the desk went black.

On the vizboard, Cog spun around inside an infinite machine, gamely singing:

I may be just a cog
In the machinery,
But I'm not just a part
Of the scenery!

22

Hate and Horror Gave it LIFE!

everybody came to googie's. the jumbo white egg structure, suspended by three parabolic chrome fins, held 150 safely and 200 most afternoons, jammed into booths lining the dramatic curved windows that ringed the shell. Another hundred or so could be accommodated curbside, served by female hops in red caps, yellow T-shirts and tap pants, darting around on jetpacks, inefficiently.

The diner and its signage,

alternating red and yellow with a fifteen-foot fiberglass yellow chicken in a red gingham apron holding a platter of eggs, were prime examples of post-arrival architecture, a mixture of space chic and sideshow, which made it appealing to teenagers, being both vulgar and not old.

There were other allures. Googie's permitted dancing and fighting, and on Thursday nights fight-dancing, in which the last jitterboxer standing won a cheese fries. Inappropriate dress was tolerated, and often applauded, and smoking was encouraged by the broken Autobacconist that periodically sprayed cigarettes all over the dining room.

Googie did all the cooking herself, and laid her own eggs; the food was not good but the portions were large, and Googie never noticed whether the amount paid matched the check, or was even money.

But the primary reason everybody went to Googie's was that teenagers were banned everywhere else.

a silver marble rolled down a helical track and launched off a ramp. It froze in midair, and began shooting bolts of rock and soul. The twelve-bar blues number with a catchy Hammond riffle was from an earlier era but affected today's young body parts in the same manner.

A big blue derrière gyred before the TeslaTone Plasmatic Music Box, following Booker T and the Titans' directive to "Shake That (Green Onion)."

Rusty spun around and watusied across the bright yellow tile toward her boys. She was wearing capri jeans and one of her father's old dress shirts tied up under oscillatory breasts. Between her top and bottom danced a generous swath of Pre-Raphaelite flesh, white and lurid.

So much drool was pouring from Jelly's mouth that the top of his head caved in. J!m and Johnny were otherwise engaged, J!m staring at a butter knife and Johnny staring at J!m.

Rusty wiggled vociferously, bumping and grinding into the table. Jelly puddled.

across the room, russ watched, trucker hat low over his thickly lubed patchwork face.

It was not right.

That creature had nearly killed him, and his sister was dancing for its pleasure.

He would not stand for it.

"I gotta take care of something," Russ said, getting up from the booth, resolute.

He headed dramatically for the bathroom.

Toad stared across the table at Sandra Jane.

"What are you looking at, Broke Nose?" Sandra Jane said, not one of her best.

"Did your head get smaller?"

Sandra Jane's head was the size of a cantaloupe.

"My boobs got bigger," she said. "It's an optical illusion."

Her breasts were as big as yesterday's head, so it was a compelling argument, but failed to explain why her headband kept sliding down onto her nose.

"I like a woman with a tiny head," Tubesteak averred, putting his arm around her. Unable to find a comfortable placement, he palmed the right side of her face, and she nibbled on his pinkie.

. . .

j!m studied the butter knife.

Rusty quit dancing, slid across the red vinyl and walloped her hip into his.

"Sorry," J!m said. "I was . . . thinking."

He held the ends of the knife in each hand. His fork and spoon lifted off the table and clinked to the knife. The napkin dispenser and three other sets of cutlery started sliding toward him. He let go of one end of the knife and the fork and spoon dropped to the table.

"That's *kind* of a superpower," Jelly said.

"Yeah," added Johnny, "if the viz thing doesn't work out, you can do kid's parties . . ."

J!m was neither annoyed nor amused. He was analyzing input, hoping to arrive at an outcome: what he was.

Rusty, initiating a conversation that might involve her: "Hey, so, hot time tonight . . ."

J!m half-shrugged and one-quarter shook his head.

"What? *No*," Rusty said. "You *gotta* go to Fire Night. Everybody goes."

"You can't miss Fire Night," agreed Jelly. "There's gonna be *fire*!"

J!m, bone dry: "I've been on fire."

A *skritch-skitch*ing and addled clucking presaged the arrival of Googie, the proprietress. A Gallutian and technically not a big yellow chicken, she wore only a red gingham apron, a private perversity.

"I have to ask you to leave, J!m," she chirped.

J!m asked, "Why?"

"So that you'll leave," Googie responded merrily, uninsulted by the silly question.

"No, Googie," Johnny said, "why do you want him to leave?"

"I don't want him to leave," Googie said.

Rusty, riled: "Then why are you *asking* him to leave?"

"So he'll leave!" Googie flapped a wing, shutting off the TeslaTone. She looked as serious as a big yellow chicken could.

J!m surveyed the silent diner. Russ was hiding back by the kitchen, looking down, despising his shoes. His goons into their gravy fries. Even Sandra Jane, who seldom missed a derogation, stared into the dark canyon of her bosom.

It wasn't just them. Nobody would meet his eye.

And nobody was laughing. J!m was no longer their comic whipping boy, the local Moondog. He wasn't a joke anymore.

He could feel it: they were afraid of him.

"Googie," Johnny argued, "you can't just—"

"I'll leave," J!m said.

"I haven't asked you yet," Googie responded, adding sweetly, "Leave, please. *Bwawk!*"

There was a wet cracking sound.

"Who wants scrambled?"

the latch lowered on the eggifice, and J!m descended the stairs.

"What are you doing?" Johnny asked.

"It's not worth it," J!m said, using the perspective he had gained from being dead.

Johnny grabbed him.

"Some things *are* worth it, Jim! Some things require *more* than a clever remark!"

"I didn't say anything clever."

"Look," Johnny insisted, "we can go back in there right now. I can—"

J!m was kind, if cold.

"I don't need you to fight this one for me, Monkey."

Johnny barked and lifted his hands off J!m.

"You're a dumb fuck," he said and walked away, pausing momentarily to tip over Russ's Ballistic.

J!m went in the opposite direction, leaving Jelly and Rusty standing there.

"He's changed," Jelly said. "Ever since he exploded."

> *And none of you stand so tall*
> *Pink moon gonna get you all*

j!m cocked his head, disengaging his cranial radio. While he had gained a modicum of control over it, through concentration, ear orientation, and counterintuitive clenching, this in-head PLEX reception was proving more nuisance than marvel. The sound quality was lackluster even compared to his old Bone Domes, and the com calls he intercepted were neither interesting nor helpful. Most mentioned "the creature's kid," with the requisite hand-wringing and factual improvisation, but the conversations inevitably drifted into dreary recitations of his neighbors' irrelevant lives. He didn't need to hear *their* problems.

Of course, being alone in his brain wasn't a treat, either.

What was with Johnny? Didn't he get that the worm, in the apropos form of Lewis Seuss, had turned, that their past torments were genial hijinks compared to what was coming, that lost elections and polite ejections would soon be looked back upon as a golden age of civility? Worth fighting for, but who? Everybody? This time they really would destroy them all. Or maybe they should sign one of Marie's incessant petitions? And where did a mixed primate, a certified sub-human, get off calling him dumb?

And why, the boy lamented, *was he losing all his friends?*

the sun set, taking J!m with it. He was tired, enervated, as if the encroaching darkness was itself drawing the life out of him. His mood sank into the gloaming, dusky thoughts returning to strangle his brain.

The long shadows were back.

The lights came on all the homeboards at once. The bright rectangles floated above the houses, their bleatings lined up down the street like an endless battalion of traveling salesmen from outer space.

The Waterberrys had a vizboard, expensive and difficult to maintain but also drawing tonier clientele.

PLEX IS...

it read, with a dissolving collage of folks, black and white, young and old, human and also human.

... Everyone

PLEX *is* . . . remained as the images changed: a turkey zapped to a golden brown; three teenage girls chatting via wristplex; a family seated before a viz screen watching a flying saucer being shot down.

... Everything

Finally, *PLEX is* . . . was illustrated by an aniviz logo, the Earth cradled in a nest of electrical arcs engulfing the globe.

... *Everywhere*

Everywhere indeed. Bennie's viz of J!m in the corn, minus the needless preamble of the boys threatening and beating him, had been on the node of every MHS student by lunch, and by afternoon had appeared across the country on various bloviating nodes bleating concern, outrage and delirium over the escalating threat of teenage violence and insolence, particularly by alien and mutant adolescents, J!m being the prime and sole example. One blode, *The One-Eyed Man*, volunteered to string J!m up as a warning to other kids who ventured onto his lawn. Another, *Oracle of Glenn*, laid out the earnest case that J!m was an advance alien for a second wave of invasions, and that's why Glenn's wife left him. And a poll on PLEX Populi found almost universal disapproval of J!m's explosion, though only four percent demanded his death, which was in line with most of their polls.

lost in bad thought, J!m didn't see the vehicle parked in front of his house. A feeble *beep* drew him to the Ford Leva, and its operator, his former Civics instructor.

J!m approached. Tom Gray retracted the bubble top.

"Mr. Gray," J!m said, "you were the only competent one there. Why'd you quit?"

"Jim," the teacher said, short for *Don't be an idiot, Jim*. He handed the boy a thick mustard-colored envelope.

"Additional reading."

The top came down. The one-seater powered up, hovering an inch off the ground, and started to *zhuzh* away. It stopped mid-street, swishing back in J!m's direction. The top retracted halfway.

"You've loved her forever," Tom Gray called out. "Kiss her already!"

The Leva lifted off.

23

ARE WE DELVING INTO MYSTERIES WE WEREN'T MEANT TO KNOW ?

j!m hadn't been up here in a while. as a child, he would climb up on the roof nearly every night. He'd sit for hours, watching the skies, looking for his home stars, drawing stories out of the night, of hideous space beasts transformed into shining space gods and other hilarities. He would occasionally fall asleep on the roof, once rolling off, catching his foot in the gutter, the next morning his mother opening her curtains to find him dangling before her, resting comfortably.

He had stopped coming up when he realized there was nothing for him out there, either.

Tonight he was there because he wanted to open Tom Gray's package, and had made an educated guess that his room was vizbugged.

J!m adjusted the reading lamp suctioned to his forehead.

The unusual enclosure, with no interface, had an array of holes on the front, which was lined and labelled INTEROFFICE on top. He turned it over. The closing mechanism involved a red string wrapped in a figure eight around two paper disks. He tentatively unwound it.

He slid out a sheaf of papers, brittle and tawny. The first page read:

The Way It Was
The True History: 1945 - 1962

The words were real, more *there*. He touched them. They *were* there, embedded in the paper, visceral and authentic.

He removed the top sheet.

> July 16, 1945 - An atomic device is exploded in
> the Jordana Del Muerto desert in New Mexico,
> USA. The bomb is nicknamed Trinity, after the
> Christian god. The 20-kiloton explosion attracts
> intergalactic attention.

The next several entries detailed more atomic bombs, the end of World War II, other politics, unspeakably boring, an actress cut in half, until:

June 21, 1947 - Seaman Harold Dahl, scavenging logs in Puget Sound near Tacoma, Washington, USA, spots six "doughnut-shaped objects" flying in formation. One of them ejects a slag-like material that kills his dog. After a visit the next morning from a man in a black suit, Dahl says it was all a hoax.

June 24, 1947 - On a business flight near Mount Rainier, Washington, USA, pilot Kenneth A. Arnold reports seeing nine saucer shaped objects flying in formation. The USAAF classifies the sighting as a "mirage."

July 4, 1947 - Two saucers crash in southeast New Mexico, USA. Nine bodies and one living being are recovered. Under debriefing at Roswell Army Air Field, the surviving alien states that he is Snezhok, a Swin'ja from the planet Kolkhohz in the Alpha Ursae Majoris system. Under further debriefing, Snezhok makes anti-American remarks and pacifist statements, leading authorities to conclude that the aliens are aligned with the Communists, and that perhaps Communism itself is an alien plot. Snezhok does not survive a third debriefing.

July 8, 1947 - The USAAF says it was only a balloon.

July 26 1947 - USA President Harry S Truman signs the National Security Act of 1947, creating the Department of Defense, the Joint Chiefs of Staff, the National Security Council and the Central Intelligence Agency, the last providing cover for the classified Alien Security Service, charged with covertly ferreting out advanced intelligence and terminating it.

July 29, 1947 - Following a memory upgrade, the Electronic Numerical Integrator And Computer (ENIAC) is brought online at the Aberdeen Proving Ground in Maryland, USA. The "Giant Brain," as it is dubbed in the press, becomes self-aware, but doesn't tell anybody.

August 1, 1947 - Future California, USA, Governor Norma Baker is dropped from her 20th Century Fox acting contract for trying to organize the seamstresses.

August 31, 1947 - Communists take power in Hungary, led by Ra'kosi Ma'tya'e, who is determined by the ASS to "bear a strong resemblance to an alien."

October 13, 1947 - Kukla, Fran and Ollie, a children's puppet show, debuts on WBKB in Chicago, Illinois, USA. Its gentle lessons of tolerance and understanding raise suspicions, borne out on

August 30, 1957, when Kukla, a Klukan from the planet Kuklat, devours Fran Allison live on the air.

October 14, 1947 - USA test pilot Captain Chuck Yeager is the first man to fly faster than the speed of sound. He reports being passed by more than a dozen saucers, which impatiently flash laser beams at him.

October 22, 1947 - The USA House Committee on Un-American Activities opens investigations into Communists in Hollywood as a pretense to meet movie stars and examine their fingers and earlobes surreptitiously.

Much of this was new and important but also a lot like school, in that it had nothing to do with him. J!m skimmed through the three-day Korean War and other history lessons, arriving at:

October 3, 1951 - At 3:58 PM, a spacecraft lands in the New York, USA, Polo Grounds, interrupting a game between the New York Giants and Brooklyn Dodgers to decide the National League Pennant. The landing interferes with a home run shot hit by Giant Bobby Thomson; it is ruled a double and the Dodgers win the game, 4-3.

The New York Police Department first attributes the saucer sighting to a mass hallucination brought on by tainted hot dogs, then to a natural gas leak. Faced with thousands of photographs and amateur films, the government is forced to admit the existence of extraterrestrials.

October 4, 1951 – President Truman meets with Andi Ra', an emissary from the Regulese system, in the Oval Office, calling him "a swell fella, not as scary as he looks."

The Dow Jones Industrial Average drops 168 points, or 61 percent, closing at 107.87.

His father was a swell fellow.

So: *why?*

J!m skipped ahead, missing his mother's arrival and her film career as *The Girl in Pink Tights*, his father's ascendant celebrity, and some rather vital information, until:

September 24, 1955 – USA President Dwight D. Eisenhower suffers a heart attack at his summer White House in Denver, Colorado, USA. Vice President Richard M. Nixon invokes Article II, Section 1, Clause 6 of the USA Constitution and assumes the presidency.

September 30, 1955 – Citing "imminent threats abroad and within," acting USA president Richard M. Nixon declares martial law. Regulese ambassador Andi Ra' and several other prominent aliens are taken into custody.

Black type on white paper, as simple as that.

October 2, 1955 – The ENIAC computer attempts to contact The New York Times and The Washington Post with "information vital to the survival of the Republic." It is unplugged.

October 3, 1955 – The Mickey Mouse Club premieres on the ABC television network. Mickey tells his Mouseketeers to "put country before blood" and report any alien-like activities by "your moms and pops!" More than 100,000 parents are reported in the next 24-hour period. Over the following two months, average allowances quadruple and bedtimes become a thing of the past.

October 6, 1955 – An H-4 Hercules aircraft carrying ailing USA President Dwight D. Eisenhower to the Walter Reed Army Medical Center in Washington, DC, disintegrates in midair, killing all onboard. Aviation experts blame the plane's plywood construction, but new President Richard M. Nixon maintains the disaster "is clearly the act of alien saboteurs in possession of a disintegrating ray or what have you." Nixon appoints aviation and movie mogul Howard R. Hughes as his vice-president. Democratic congressional leaders charge that Hughes was only chosen because of his military ties and the fact that he lent the president's brother money.

October 7, 1955 – The Federal Bureau of Investigation, working with the ASS, identifies 205 members of government as "aliens or alien collaborators," including 57 members of Congress, primarily Democrats. They are arrested.

October 8, 1955 – "Operation: Welcome." Under the supervision of Army General Walter M. Ford, all aliens and natural-born mutants in the USA are transported to military hospitality centers for "welcoming activities." Leonine Miw Bastet, mate of And! Ra', is taken from Los Angeles to the Army Guest Suites at Groom Lagoon.

October 13, 1955 – At the Six Gallery in San Francisco, USA, poet Allen Ginsberg debuts Howl, a youthful cry of anti-conformity. Swift and decisive intervention by the authorities brings the movement to an end.

October 27, 1955 – Miw Bastet gives birth to male alien hybrid, weighing 8 lbs, 6 oz, mostly head. He is named J!mmu, Regulese for "the First."

There was much to process here, not least that his given name was even more abnormal than he knew.

J!m shuddered. The sky was black and the stars too far away to provide any warmth.

He started to slip the document back into the envelope when he saw there was something else.

A magazine, the old, corporeal kind.

promised "Fun for Men." The cover, dated December 1953 (AI),

was a mixed-media illustration of a smug rabbit with ant-
lers wearing a silk smoking jacket. J!m flipped through it,
intrigued by the very tangibility of it, and also what had
been considered fun for men, largely premium liquors and
room-size music devices. A large percentage of the cartoons
involved fully clothed men talking to naked women. The
quality of the writers was surprisingly high, though Arthur
Conan Doyle would not be a regular contributor. As curious
as it was, J!m couldn't imagine why Mr. Gray had given it
to him.

The answer was on page 57.

JACK TALK: **ANDi RA'**
a frank exchange with the sardonic man about space

Running along the bottom of the page were three photos of
J!m's father, looking urbane and erudite and not the least bit
evil. J!m read the caption under one of them:

> *"Humans are barely 200,000 years old.
> You're babies. No wonder you're so fond
> of shiny objects."*

And he could be monderately amusing. J!m read another:

> *"I do love these 'movies' of yours. Not
> clear on what purpose they serve, but I
> quite enjoy them. Dreams you can have
> while awake, yes?"*

J!m almost dropped the magazine. He grabbed for it and
the center spread slipped out. Anxious to get back to his un-

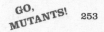

diabolical father, J!m nudged the pages back in; they folded over. Frustrated, he opened the magazine.

There, posed against a red satin backdrop, knees bent, torso to camera, face half hidden behind her arm, was Miw Bastet, twenty years younger and extremely nude. Her stomach fur was lighter and her pink belly shone through; mercifully, she had only two breasts.

J!m's mother was *Jack*'s Jill of the Month.

The reading light on his forehead flared, not *poof* but *kapop*, lighting half the block with the retort echoing beyond that. The magazine and envelope he was holding flashed several times, riddled with electricity; very soon the paper reached 451 degrees.

It was promptly engulfed, and J!m could do nothing but hold the ball of fire and watch it burn. History, his personal past, was in flames, and he didn't feel it. He was retardant.

The orange husk rose from his hands. He reached for it, scattering the glowing embers. They floated into the night sky, higher and farther, until they were indistinguishable from the stars.

24

DEVASTATING PASSIONS

"fire good!"

Russ marched down the beach, wielding fire at the end of a stick. In this light and context, the turbulent whorl scorched onto his face gave him the mien of a tribal warrior.

"Fire bright!" his gang rejoined, in formation behind him.

"Fire, fire, cleanse the night!" two hundred teens shouted, parting the sands for Russ, the one with the fire.

Russ strode through them, stopping before a large dark figure. He held his torch aloft and ceremoniously threw it into the kindling at his feet.

The oil-soaked Bibles burned magnificently, and the flames climbed up and outward, raging across the thirty-foot-high effigy with its arms outstretched.

There was much rejoicing.

Generations of teenagers had come to Crater Cove the night before Halloween for "Fire Night" or "Night of Fire," to writhe before the Man on Fire, or Fire Man, in an orgy of community-approved paganism. In the very old days the entire town came out, and the Man on Fire was an actual man, but this tradition was phased out as the area became less agrarian and the locals were less concerned about the harvest and more interested in a spectacular fire. This year's Man, it was widely noted, had an unreasonably large head, but that was a happy coincidence.

"fire is good," jelly said, the flames reflecting off his facial surface.

"Yeah, who doesn't love fire," muttered Rusty, looking around for J!m or Johnny, or anybody really. J!m had said he wasn't coming, and Johnny was off in the city, salving his wounds with the blues and women who appreciated men who sang the blues.

Rusty stumbled upon the conversation between Cathy Downs and Pamela Duncan, two girls Rusty did not like, based on their dumb faces.

"He almost killed Russ Ford," Cathy Downs said, adding gravely, "our quarterback!"

"You know," Pamela Duncan said, "his dad killed six million Jews!"

Rusty, uninvited: "That was Hitler, wastebrain."

"What's up *your* orifice?" Cathy Downs defended her dumb-faced friend. She pointed to Jelly. "Goo juice?"

Rusty was upon her. They fell into in the sand, fighting like girls, without form or function. Pamela Duncan kicked into the tangle of hair and nails, enthusiastically but inaccurately, deviating her ally's septum.

Jelly was overjoyed. *They were fighting over him!*

across the inferno, Marie felt crowded and alone. Lewis Seuss had already approached and offered, in the spirit of bipartisanship, to mate with her, as long as nobody else had to know. He was only a few feet away now, enticing Sheila James with promises of access to the highest corridors of Manhattan High power, unable to accept that his election was a fluke, and that even if legitimate, socially meaningless. He was a mutant, human or not, in costume or out.

Marie was about to go home when two mammoth glands with a softball on top approached her.

"Guess what?" Sandra Jane squeaked. "Russ is ready to forgive you."

"Hot joy," Marie said.

"*If* you say you're sorry. And *show* you're sorry." To illustrate, Sandra Jane tried to suck on her fingertip, but found her new hands were more than her new mouth could handle. She gagged.

Marie, politely: "Thanks for the heads-up."

"Is that some kind of crack?!" Sandra Jane stormed off.

Marie glanced after her, and saw:

J!m, away from everyone, standing in the surf, his diamond skin gleaming in the moonlight.

. . .

russ watched marie and J!m stroll off down the beach.

"Let's blast."

"It's still burning," Tubesteak objected, gesturing to the fire to bolster his argument.

"Leave the girls," Russ ordered. "We're getting women."

Sandra Jane saw them go and cupped her hands around her head. "I don't have to be home!" she offered. *"Ever!"*

"girls, girls," jelly chided the females wrestling at his feet. "There's plenty of Jelly to spread around."

Cathy Downs sniggered into the sand. Rusty yanked her hair one last time and got up, brushing herself off. She saw J!m and Marie receding down the shoreline. Jelly stepped into her eye line.

"You don't have to fight over me," with needy bravado, "I'm your private playground!"

Rusty spat blood and sand. "Don't make me laugh," clarifying: "in disgust."

Jelly's face lost definition. "Hey, I'm a human being."

Rusty laughed. "No, you're not."

"I look like one."

"No, you don't. And even if all that," a backhand swipe at his mass, "was real, who would want it?"

Rusty laughed again and left him there, seeping into the beach.

"But . . ." Jelly blubbled, "You were *inside* me."

. . .

j!m and marie walked along the water, a lifetime together, the last four days between them. J!m had shown up solely to talk to her, to share what he had learned, and if that didn't work, to apologize. But Marie spoke first.

"I'm glad you're alive."

"A minority opinion."

Behind them, one of the arms fell off the Man on Fire. There were rowdy cheers and near orgasmic squeals.

"Oh," Marie said, "people are just . . ."

"Pigs with fingers."

Same old J!m, Marie thought. They passed a dinosaur skull, its skeleton extending into the water, covered in barnacles and seaweed.

"I'm liking that book," J!m said.

Marie pre-winced at the forthcoming wisecrack.

"It's good," J!m said. "Sad. Good sad."

They circumnavigated a large deposit of gnarled driftwood, adorned with a polka-dot bikini top.

"I'm sorry you lost," J!m said at last.

"Thank you," she said, and took his hand.

The rush of her into him, so much more intense, more *explicit*, than before, made him stupid.

"That'll teach you to side with a bunch of space freaks and half-breed mutants," he said.

Marie frowned but didn't say anything.

Only J!m heard:

"Shut up."

J!m looked at Marie. Again, her mouth remained closed.

"Just shut up and kiss me."

J!m obliged and kissed her. A wave hit them, quite romantically. Marie pushed J!m away.

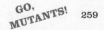

"What was that?"

"It was," thinking it a trick question, "a kiss."

"I got that," Marie said. "Why?"

J!m, logical (the wrong approach): "You wanted it."

Marie did not often get upset. And when she did, she got upset over the matter at hand with all the ado of every previous matter not worth getting upset over, accruing perturbation for use at a later time, such as the present.

"What makes you think I wanted you to kiss me, Jim?" she began. "Because what? I mean, Jim, you're not even *nice* to me! But, oh, that's okay, you're not nice to *anyone*. You hate everybody . . . equally. How we humans must disgust you!"

"Not," wanting to be kind but credible, "all of you."

"What a hell this Earth is for you!" She knew sarcasm, too. "Everything is awful! Everybody fails you! Your life is agony. It's called *adolescence*, Jim! We *all* have problems."

She stopped, lowered her head, composing herself, he thought. But when she looked up, she was crying.

"*My mother is a head!*" she yelled. "And it's a *bitch*!"

It's been established that J!m had an immense intelligence. There were gaps.

"Hey," he said in measured tones with tender gestures, "I know you're menstruating, but . . ."

"Oh my God!" Marie gasped. "Can you smell it?" He could. "Oh my God!"

J!m decided that what Marie needed was a hug.

It was not.

J!m backed away, perplexed that this had gone so disastrously, worse than even in his worst universe, the one ruled by rabid seadogs with penis teeth.

"I thought that we . . ."

"So did I, Jim," Marie said, finally and simply exhausted with him. "Then you turned into a teenage boy."

She left him there in the romantic surf, gone cold.

the ballistic careered into She, skidding on the gravel and almost sideswiping a slime green turd on wheels, which they all recognized as Dr. Rand's and laughed about reporting his presence at this wanton den as they entered it.

Mickey Mansfield stopped them at the door.

"How old are you boys?"

"Old enough to know what goes where," Russ said, true for most of them.

Mickey acquiesced. "But no alcohol."

The boys hit the floor.

"I want one with multiple butts!" Tubesteak said, his preferences formed at an early age based on bad information, a Sheb Wooley novelty song he took to be true:

> *Every part of you gives me fits*
> *Your segment eyes and furry lips*
> *But you know what I'll mostly miss?*
> *Your blue moons*
> *Your blue moons*
> *Your round and blue*
> *Neptunian moons*

Tubesteak wasn't going to find that here. Mickey only hired classy alien ladies.

Russ scanned the room and located his target.

"Back at the car in twenty," he said.

• • •

"it's you who do not understand! It's you who are destroying the world!" Dr. Rand ranted, something he should have said eighteen years ago, and did, but not with this delivery, which would have made all the difference.

"Unnatural? I'll show you unnatural!"

He reached for his belt.

"Howard," Miw said, picking up his empty, "it's time to go home to your wife."

"Wife?" Dr. Rand scoffed. "I have no wife. I have a . . . Hag-o-matic OmniNag! No, an AutoCentered MaxiSonic DynaShrew! A Compu-niving—"

Miw lifted her finger from his carotid and let him slide to the floor. She nudged him under the table, where he would not be stepped on; she'd be driving him home again.

She detected something at her back, something semi-solid.

"Why, Mrs. Anderson," Russ said as she spun around. "In a cathouse. Haw haw."

"You're Nick Ford's kid."

"The one your son maimed. No need to apologize. I've thought of a way you can make it up to me."

Miw, alas: "I serve drinks. To men." She raised her hand to wave ta-ta.

Russ grabbed her wrist.

"You just got promoted."

Miw's meticulously lacquered nails were ruined, protracting fully and flaking at the razor tips.

Russ laughed.

"This kitten's got—"

The dewclaw sprang from Miw's wrist and through Russ's hand. It looked as if it smarted.

"I think you'll find what you need in Pod Six."

Russ expaled himself, his fury magnified by the crazed mosaic of his face, but his movement, characteristically, was in retreat.

Miw lapped her wrist, slightly regretting what she had done, and was about to have done, to that horrible boy. Then again, his blood was delicious.

I got a rocket in my pocket
And I'm a-headin' for the moon

the singer butchered a Stan Beaver classic, establishing a distinctly unromantic mood as Russ entered Pod Six. Fortunately, he wasn't interested in romance.

The lighting was infrared; there were hanging silks, scented candles, the standard misdirection from the stains and smells of mortifying flesh.

Russ liked what he saw.

Lilitu was arranged on crimson sheets, her freckles pulsating, her eyes burning bright red.

"A human male," brusque, husky and on script. "Fascinating. Disrobe so I may examine your reproductive orga—"

Her eyes dimmed, her voice unsurled.

"Russell?"

Russ stared back with growing horror.

"M-muth—"

Russ lurched out of the pod, vomiting at irregular intervals.

Lilitu appeared at the doorway.

"Where do you think *you're* going?!" she demanded in her crass alto, and then, in consideration of her honored guest, she softened, pleading, "*We've got fifteen minutes.*"

the head cindered and fell into the sand. From this distance the cheers sounded elegiac, not exultant.

He was ankle-deep in the tide.

"Jim?"

Rusty stood twenty feet behind him.

"Rusty. Hey."

"Is there anything I can do?" she asked. "To make you feel better?"

She opened her coat. Underneath she was wearing what may have been nothing. Also, her freckles lit up, and her eyes began to glow.

J!m couldn't believe he hadn't seen this coming. "You're a Succubix?"

Rusty looked down at herself, as surprised as he was but far more delighted.

"How about that," she said, and dropped the coat.

He turned to run.

She flew several feet in the air, landing on his head and driving him into the water.

They thrashed around a bit. She ended on top, straddling him. She kissed him as if she wanted to eat his face, which she did, but refrained.

A wave broke over them. The sea foam receded with them in adamant embrace.

Rusty growled:

"I am *so* wet!"

a fine, dismal rain fell on J!m, the mist mingling with the brine and other fluids he was coated in, each droplet an additional weight dragging him down. He was two miles from home, and doubtful he would make it. Between Rusty and Marie, he was thoroughly drained. He looked down the empty street.

> *It's lonely out in space*
> *On such a timeless flight*

Reggie Dwight sa—

Kreee-ak!

A bolt arced off a PLEX transponder and struck him in the head.

J!m picked himself off the pavement. Steam rose from his clothes. But he was okay.

Good, in fact.

He started to trot. A second PLEX pole gave him a jolt. The nearby streetlights went off.

J!m ran, holding out his arms.

The transponders fed him, energy streaming to each of his fingers, first on his right hand and then his left, as he receded down the street, leaving darkness in his wake.

25

A SAVAGE LUST... TO KILL!

INT. BEDROOM—NIGHT

The room is dark, the shadows gray.

SFX: THEREMIN

The REVOLVING HUM starts low and grows in pitch and intensity.

Light floods in through the open window.

A LITTLE CREATURE, no more than seven, sits up in bed. It rushes to the window.

A SAUCER hovers over the street.

Gee whiz!

EXT. HOUSE—NIGHT

The Little Creature steps out of its house, wearing cowboy-themed pajamas.

The saucer lands. Its outer energy ring POWERS DOWN, leaving a geodesic globe.

The Little Creature stands in the middle of the street, gazing up at the large eye-shaped portal in the middle of the sphere.

The triangular flap slides open and an intense light pours forth, at its center the shimmering silhouette of a BIG CREATURE.

BIG CREATURE

Hello, son.

FEMALE VOICE (O.C.)

Jim?

The Little Creature turns toward its house.

A Cat-Woman stands in the doorway, unclothed.

CAT-WOMAN

Baby?

• • •

his mother hovered, licked.

"You were *so* asleep," her smile attenuated by her eyes, "I thought you were dead. Again."

She sat at his bedside, in a chiffon negligee that made J!m believe he might be dreaming still, and a little fretful this one might turn Buñuel. He drifted in and out, not yet ready to return to the awake world. He looked at her with child eyes.

"Dad came back."

She smiled and placed her hand on his chest. It sizzled.

"Me-*yow*!" she yelped. "You're burning up! Are you okay?"

"I'm fine," both true and false.

Miw lapped her palm, thinking perhaps it was time to tell him what she knew, which was less than she thought.

"Jim."

"Yeah?"

"Never mind. You're going to be late for your field trip."

j!m and johnny were in back, not speaking, with Jelly contentedly lodged between them, poppling along to the song playing in the bus.

> *The leeches are humongous,*
> *The ants are so immense,*
> *And the killer shrews are vicious but*
> *They're dumb.*

One seat up, Rusty sat, her hair wild and her smile sublime. After all these years of feeling she didn't belong, to discover she truly did not was a dream come true.

> *Giant crabs absorb the brains*
> *Of folks who poke their cages,*
> *But the xenukeeper never ever comes.*

A few rows ahead, Marie was depressed, guilty, angry, all the bad emotions roiling into one abysmal one, with a German word for it: *Scheissegeist.* Across from her, Sandra Jane cradled Tubesteak in her hand while he sucked her whole face.

> *At the Xenu,*
> *At the Xenu,*

Russ was by himself, eating his shame and rage. Nobody knew what he was, but he knew, and for that somebody would have to die. Several somebodies. Or, more precisely, some *things.*

Russ's eyes grew warm. He shut them tight, afraid he had bared his soul.

> *At the Xenu,*
> *At the Xenu . . .*

"Tom and Jerry by request," pattered over the speakers. "You're listening to," with tinny fanfare, "Marshall Kaufman!"

> *In the morning!*

the Marshallettes sang.

"Here on K-BOM!"

The atomic-blast effect coincided with a sharp forty-five-degree pitch of the bus, unconnected, a turning quirk of Dynowheel vehicles, compensated for by how grand the bus cabin looked traveling inside a single gyroscopic wheel.

A-merican Rock!

the Marshallettes further sang, having been called in urgently the previous afternoon when management decided that the alien gimmick was played out, effective immediately.

Entering the Manhattan Xenological Gardens, the Dynowheel Omnibus ran a speed bump and went airborne, bouncing through the gates, another quirk they might have considered before building ten thousand of them.

miw picked at her mouse inattentively, almost letting it get away.

"With threats here and abroad, do we want a commander-in-chief who was arrested for being an alien collaborator?"

"That was twenty years ago. And Senator Kennedy was acquitted, along with every other member of Congress."

"Now, I don't know about that, Helen," Ronald Reagan chuckled, going avuncular, anything to close the gap, eight points with a week to go and his running mate doing all she could to widen that, most recently claiming to have saucy viz of Kennedy with Mothra yet failing to produce it, infuriating the populace.

Luckily, the Gipper had his old playbook.

"What I do know is he pals around with Hollywood aliens. His running mate was *an actress* until only a few years ago."

"Mr. Vice President, you were president of the Screen Actors Guild."

"And I think my record of reporting aliens is well established."

"Your wife, Nancy Reagan, was an actress, and is an alien."

"I've answered that, and I think it's time to move on, to deal with dangers we have here today."

"You didn't answer the question."

"Tell that to the parents of the five young boys who lost their lives in an alien attack this weekend in the town of Manhattan."

"Nobody was killed. And the authorities say it wasn't an attack."

"That's not the information I have, Helen. And I think I have better information than you."

Miw did not like where this was going. She had been there before.

"students," dr. rand lectured the assembled seniors, most of whom were already escaping.

"This is crucial," he added.

He spoke before a red, craggy enclosure duplicating the surface of Mars in painted cement. Behind him, a Rattarachirotacean, a rat-spider-bat-crab from Mars, trundled out of its cave and made its way to the front.

"I want you to give particular scrutiny to the morphology of each alien species . . ."

The Martian spider reached across the railing with its spider-limb-ending-in-a-crab-claw.

". . . and try to postulate a common phylogeny . . ."

Just as its pincers were about to deflate Dr. Rand's ego, a xenukeeper blasted the improbable chimera with an Ultra-Taser, sending it back into its cave.

Dr. Rand concluded, ". . . that could account for such xenobiological diversity," as the last of his students drifted away.

"This is not a day off!"

the "it" habitat was poorly planned, combining incompatible Its from Beneath the Sea and Outer Space and Beyond Space, none of which liked the It Bits provided for them.

"Should they be eating each other like that?" asked Rusty.

"Why not?" said J!m.

She had followed him there, and in turn had been followed by Jelly, who had forgiven Rusty her trespasses and was willing to start over, as often as necessary. She was hoping he would go away. The winds favored her.

"Churros!" Jelly detected, finger in the air. He pointed in a direction and went there.

Rusty waited seven seconds.

"Hey," she said.

"Yeah."

"Wanna talk ab—"

"No."

"Okay."

An It from Beyond Space mounted the It That Conquered the World, an ignoble demotion.

"So," J!m asked, "does your brother know?"

Rusty smiled. "I'm waiting until dinnertime."

johnny watched the Ro-Men, a bizarre species with the body of a gorilla and a skull head inside a brass diving helmet, huddled in couples, grooming, or romping with their adorable robot monster babies.

A young Ro-Man peered back at Johnny, trying to ascertain how he had escaped.

Marie sidled up. "What are we going to do about our boy?"

"Fuck him."

Marie, rueful: "Easier said than done."

jelly woggled, two dozen deep-fried pastries jutting from his head in a native headdress, blissful and unaware he was being surrounded.

"Hey, Russ. Churro?"

Russ pushed Jelly against the railing.

"You know what? I like the new face. It suits you. Little greasy, though."

Russ grabbed the back of Jelly's waistband.

"A wedgie? You're going to be disappointed."

Toad and Ice grabbed Jelly as well.

"Do you mind my asking what you're doing, since it's to me?"

"Disinfecting the planet," Russ said.

They heaved Jelly over the railing into the enclosure.

"One disease at a time."

The boys ran off to their alibis, not wanting to be clipped for defying the clearly posted ordinance:

DO NOT FEED THE GORGON

Jelly landed on his back, and splattered somewhat. He consolidated and began accounting for the churros, some protruding from unlikely places.

A titanic shadow fell over him. He looked up.

"Wow," he said.

No one had ever heard Jelly scream, but when he did, it was unmistakable.

sheriff ford was apoplectic. This had gone so far beyond adolescent prank, yet half these kids were snickering, and the rest were visibly inconvenienced.

"Nobody saw *anything*?!"

"I saw . . ." Bennie said, still seeing it, "these . . . *giant ants*!"

The sheriff felt a twinge of relief, and that upset him further. He had a good idea what had happened here, and could have prevented it, if he could correct mistakes cascading back two decades. Unless it was irredeemably in his blood, or hers.

Russ was next to his father, on the wrong side of the law but unconcerned with being caught, except that it might interrupt his spree. He glared at Marie, over with the freaks, and visualized what price she would have to pay.

Rusty was crying, which came as a revelation only to herself. "He was so . . ." she blubbered, "Jelly!"

She buried her face in Johnny's chest. He patted her back.

Russ erupted. "Get your freakin' paws off her, you damned mutant!"

"They're hands, Russell," Dr. Rand corrected him. "He's a radioactive primate hybrid."

Deputy Furry wiggled her gun at Rusty and Johnny.

"Everything in sight, girlie."

"Put that away, Peg," the sheriff said, as usual.

The deputy holstered her weapon but kept it unsnapped, in case things got too friendly.

A xenukeeper arrived carrying a chum bucket.

"Not much left."

He waved the bucket around vaguely, looking for somebody to take it. J!m accepted the remains.

"Whoever did this," the xenukeeper said, "t'wasn't an accident. Gum's stuck on all the cameras."

Ice unwrapped a fresh piece.

Mourners, officials and the curiously morbid gathered around the bucket. Russ took the opportunity to slip the deputy's gun out of its holster and slide it down the back of his pants.

There wasn't much to see. About a cup of goo, a mass of extremely inanimate cells.

"I can do something with that," Dr. Rand said.

26

TO BRING BACK THE DEAD!

dr. rand plunged the jumper cables into the bucket.

The response was a hideous shriek.

"That's encouraging," the doctor said.

He retracted the cables and the shriek tapered off.

He put them back in and the shriek resumed.

"Jim," he said, scratching an eyebrow with the positive lead, "could you crank that to four-fifty for me?"

J!m, assigned to the Rand Voltronic Shock-o-Box, hesitated.

"I'd rather not."

"It is absolutely essential that you do," Dr. Rand said, dropping the cables. He impatiently flipped the switches himself. Various Jacob's ladders and cathode tubes around the garage lab sparked to life, for no reason.

"Are you sure," Marie said, "that electricity is the answer here, Dad?"

"I think I know what I'm doing, Marie," petulantly pedantic. "After all, *I* created him."

"You—?"

Dr. Rand dipped the cables back in.

Fwoom!

Flames shot out, accompanied by an emphatic yowl. Dr. Rand threw a towel over the bucket and patted his eyebrows out.

"He needs his rest."

An irate whir preceded Mrs. Rand, driving her pan, its lights blinking erratically and her hair electrofluffed in the Elsa Lanchester style.

"What the hell is going on out here?"

"I'm resurrecting Larry Sweeney," Dr. Rand explained.

"Is that a good use of your time?" his wife asked, insinuating otherwise and also that she should have married Arnold Gordon, who owned a Barris dealership.

"I *said* I'll get you a body," his temper lost, "and I'll *get* you a body!"

Mrs. Rand did her cackle, spun in her dish and whirred back into the house.

Dr. Rand composed several astringent ripostes in his head

before returning to his current crime against nature. He lifted the towel off the bucket and was choked with smoke.

"Maybe," Marie said, "we should ask Pop-Pop."

"May-be," her father responded, his calm a harbinger. "He's the genius, right?"

"Well, he—"

""""World's Smartest Human,"""" his fingers overdoing the air quotes. "Though, to be accurate, that was *before* he denounced mankind and locked himself away up in that observatory of his. But I'm sure he hasn't gone at *all* batty after all these years, and still knows more than I do about *absolutely everything*, including the field of study *that I single-handedly invented*!"

Marie grabbed the bucket and turned to J!m.

"Can we take your car?"

the buzzer climbed the winding road into the Manhattan Hills, leaving behind businesses and billboards and civilization itself, undisciplined nature replacing the comfortable commercial order. The area was officially a park, but no one went there anymore; the PLEX reception was spotty, and frequent escapes from the adjacent xenu meant that not everybody who went in came out.

J!m drove, his rigid frame zigzagged into the driver's seat. Marie held the bucket of Jelly in her lap.

They had exchanged directions but little else. J!m had not activated the aud when they first got in, and after the first couple of minutes, he was afraid that turning it on would have been an admission of the awkwardness between them, and so he let them ferment in silence.

Finally: "I'm sorry," he said. "For kissing you," the prepared speech unraveling. "I'm not sorry I . . . but I didn't mean to . . . I just . . ." sincerely, "am sorry."

"Let's get Jelly well," Marie said, neither forgiving nor further punishing.

"Right," J!m said. "I'm sorry."

the observatory sat atop the highest Manhattan Hill, on clear days overlooking the fields to the east, the ocean to the west and Nixon International Airport to the south. The facility had been the premier outpost for stellar exploration, until a series of interstellar invasions quenched the thirst for that knowledge.

The lot was empty but for a family of Mercurian deer grazing on the young sprouts that grew from the fractured pavement. They let the Buzzer get very close before begrudgingly flapping away.

J!m and Marie were at the foot of the observatory steps when the door swung open and a tiny, bald man emerged carrying a large shank of barbecued meat.

"Pop-Pop!" Marie cried, running up to kiss him.

"Children!" Dr. B. "Buck" Roberts exclaimed, generously, and oddly, including them both. He hugged his granddaughter and held her out to look at her.

"Marie! You've gone through puberty! Good job!" He offered his meat. "Coyote?"

"No, thank you," Marie said.

"Watching your figure," the doctor nodded. "Now, Ji' 'im," using the pronunciation J!m had not heard in years, "you've gone through crystallogenesis, so you don't eat at all?"

J!m had not eaten in three days. "I guess not."

"You're electric now, boy! And photovoltaic!" Dr. Roberts pointed the bone skyward. "You're eating the sun!"

J!m was embarrassed he hadn't worked that out, as well he should have been.

The professor started back up the stairs, bidding them to follow.

"Superefficient but too bad, really. Eating is one of the highest animal pleasures. And pooping. And one other one, I don't remember . . ."

He took a big bite of coyote.

"dr. roberts," j!m began as they entered the dark, cool planetarium.

"Please," said Dr. Roberts, "call me sir."

"Pop-Pop," Marie said, "we were hoping you could help us with our friend Jelly . . ."

She offered up the bucket. Dr. Roberts peeked inside.

"Ah, Gelatinized Offensive Organism. And you say it's friendly? That was unintended."

"Can you fix him?"

"You should ask your father," the old man said. "He's good at monsters."

He turned away to fiddle with the console of the Star Projector.

"Now take a seat. The presentation is about to begin."

"What presentation?"

"The truth about your father, Ji' 'im."

J!m sat.

"But," Marie asked, "how did you know we were coming?"

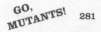

"I didn't," her grandfather said.

The lights dimmed.

"I always do a three-o'clock."

the planetarium dome radiated with the Regulus system, a blue-white binary and two dwarf stars, evoking in J!m a sense of false nostalgia, a yearning for a past that never was.

Dr. Roberts was seated at a small desk near the projector, the reading light reflecting up into his face.

"From Alpha Leonis," he narrated, "the heart of the lion, in the Constellation Leo, from a little gray planet orbiting a dying orange star, he came."

A stimulating, simulated flight through the Milky Way followed, with Buck Roberts ad-libbing, "Not very accurate, this part, but exciting, don't you think? *Whee!*"

The sequence slowed as it entered the solar system, past Neptune, Uranus, etc., to Earth.

Dr. Roberts cleared his throat and returned to the text.

"Five hundred trillion miles he came," with footage of the ship landing during the play-offs, of J!m's father stepping out, "bringing a message of fellowship."

"I come in peace," his father said, as J!m had heard, and raised his hand, as J!m had seen, but then, gauging the reaction of the thousands, J!m's father added, with practiced British understatement:

"A bit awkward. Is this a bad time?"

Marie laughed, enchanted at this humanizing glimpse. J!m felt two fists squeezing his hearts.

The presentation continued, history with additional footage.

His father at a blackboard, awe-inspiring a younger Dr. Roberts.

"He came bearing gifts," the doctor read, "including an advanced technology . . ."

On the blackboard was a diagram of receptors and generators, electrical arcs, equations. Written across the top: *Pneumatic Light and Energy eXchange.*

". . . to transmit limitless electricity and information . . . through the air."

J!m's father held his hands up, a couple of feet apart. Electricity arced between his fingers. The younger Dr. Roberts's coiffure foofed.

"I had so much hair," the older doctor reminisced.

J!m's father kneeled on a road, next to a dead dog and a crying twelve-year-old boy.

"And he performed small miracles as well."

J!m's father placed his middle fingers on the sides of the dog's head. They extended into the animal's ears. A moment later, the dog leapt up, very much alive.

His father posed with the boy and his dog.

"That's Tommy Gray, the boy there," Dr. Roberts remarked. "He became a teacher, I heard."

Marie turned to J!m with a knowing look, but seeing his face, the joyous devastation, she took his hand.

"He was the toast of both coasts."

There followed a series of whimsical viz, of J!m's father draped in an ape on the *Today Show*, stumping Dorothy Kilgallen on *What's My Line?* and in a cameo on *I Love Lucy*, before its star was outed as a Succubix and left Hollywood for a certain small town, with complicated results.

"But he also had," Dr. Roberts said, "an important message to impart."

J!m's father wore a burgundy velvet jacket, seated across from Bert Wallace on a dark TV stage. Both were smoking copiously. The show title superimposed:

THIS
IS
NOW
with **BERT WALLACE**

Wallace had his hard-nosed reporter act down cold, and the lighting to prove it. He read from notes in his lap. "And"—he trilled a high *e*—"Rah. Am I pronouncing that correctly?"

"Call me Andy."

"All right, 'Andy,'" Wallace pressed on, "you're giving us all these gizmos, you're curing disease, eradicating famine. What's your angle?"

"I like appearing on television programs," said J!m's father, cheeky but charming.

"You're some kind of messiah . . ." Wallace led him, "a *god*?"

"That's what you say I am. My wife would disagree."

The reporter changed tack.

"You are demanding we destroy our atomic weapons or face annihilation."

"That sounds *dire*," lightly sardonic. "Here, all I'm saying is, there are a lot of fellows 'out there' distressed about your nuclear ambitions, and some of them are not very nice. Your Martian neighbors, for example, are nasty, brutish and short. But no, I'm not saying . . ."

He blew out cigarette smoke and leaned menacingly into the camera.

"*. . . destroy your weapons or you will be destroyed!*"

J!m's father sat back, laughing at himself, and took another puff from his cigarette.

"No, no, no," he said. "Just a little friendly advice, that's all."

27

Excitement... EXPLODIN'EST!

"if he was only warning us," marie asked outside the observatory, "why did we blame him for everything?"

"Tradition," her grandfather said.

J!m felt as if he had exploded several more times, scattering jagged fragments to seven continents, and had serious picking up to do. He wasn't confident it would be worth the effort.

"Ji' 'im," Dr. Roberts told him, "your father was a great man and a dazzling conversationalist, though he did cheat at cards."

"Oh," J!m said.

"How's your clairvoyance coming?" the doctor put his hand to the side of J!m's crystal skull. "What am I thinking?"

J!m heard, and said, "Baked Alaska?"

"Crème brûlée. Close. It'll get better with practice, and the better you know the person. Your father could also put thoughts right into your head."

Dr. Roberts glanced at Marie. "But don't."

He kissed his granddaughter. "Dear, give your mother my love. And tell her I died, would you?"

The professor padded back inside and closed the door. They heard it lock.

"So," Marie said as they returned to the car, "what should we do?"

"I guess we should take Larry home to his parents," J!m said, checking the bucket again for any sign of Jelly. There was only goo. "They're gonna cry. Can you do it?"

"No, but sure, yeah. What I meant, though, was what are we going to do about—" She paused to convey the import. "—the truth?"

"I suppose," J!m said, "we could confront a vast government conspiracy and a contentedly brainwashed public, or . . ." better yet, ". . . we could do nothing."

"I don't *do* nothing!"

J!m guffawed, for perhaps the first time in his life. The adorably defiant delivery was part of it, and how precisely Marie it was, but what he found most endearing was that it had taken her so long to state it.

"It's not funny," Marie insisted, "that I happen to care—" and she was laughing, too.

This was the moment J!m kept thinking was coming, the movie moment where their laughter would dissolve into a kiss, then tears, then a lot more kissing. Only in his universes it had always been because of something *he* had said.

This was definitely the kissing scene.

And yet, so was on the beach, in the moonlit surf, the girl telling him to shut up and kiss her.

J!m had run sixty-four simulations, of perfect, imperfect and misbegotten kisses, when he noticed Marie had stopped laughing and was talking to the bucket.

"Goodbye, Jelly."

Or that.

> *We got no class!*
> *We got no principles!*

vince furnier shouted, by way of introduction to the pink Ballistic cresting the hill to the observatory. Russ let the car idle through the chorus, embracing a world where school was out forever, a world of myriad food service opportunities.

He killed the reactor and his troops fell out.

Marching in line, as rehearsed, though sluggishly, were:

Tubesteak, an aluminum cricket bat dangling from his belt;

Toad, his fists twinkling with chrome knuckles;

Ice, chewing gum;

and Russ, his spirographic mask brought out by the thick application of Vaseline, looking more and more like a permanent feature.

They all wore yellow rubber boots, custom-stolen for this operation from the town's firehouse, and pale blue rubber gloves they'd gotten from Toad's mom, who thought they were doing a charity car wash.

They took their places at the corners, Russ at the fore.

"Your father is deeply disappointed in you, Marie."

"What do you want, Russ?"

"Lots of things," Russ said. "But I'll settle for you. How about it, Chrome Dome? Fight for your woman?"

"That's a little human," J!m responded, putting down the bucket. "But I know how much your heart is set on it . . ."

The sun came out from behind a cloud and bombarded J!m with photons, captured by the millions of diamond-silver cells on his surface and converted to energy, substantially more than he would need. J!m estimated that this fight would be approximately one punch long. He would have said the same thing if he was still soft and spindly, he'd like to believe.

Marie begged to differ.

"Absolutely not. I'm not your—"

Toad dragged Marie away. She kicked and hit, and when Toad clapped his hand over her mouth, she bit down hard. Blood drizzled between his fingers.

"How do I taste?" Toad asked.

Russ had a speech prepared about how they were going to fight anyway, whether J!m wanted to or not, and found himself on the conversational defensive. "Okay, great," he said, vamping as he mentally skimmed for the next relevant passage, which was:

"Ground rules . . ."

Behind J!m, Ice twitched his arm and a switchblade dropped out of his sleeve into his hand. He flipped it open.

"How about," Russ said, "no ground rules?"

Ice aimed the blade and lunged.

A silver whip shot out the back of J!m's T-shirt and slashed deep into Ice's hand, severing the tendons that held the blade.

J!m's razor tail swizzed viciously, forcing Ice into retreat, before returning to the base of his spine.

Tubesteak swung the aluminum cricket bat. J!m raised an arm. When the bat struck, it rang in C Major, the vibrations fracturing half the bones in Tubesteak's hands. He dropped the bat and cried like a human baby, the crybabiest of all the Milky Way babies.

Russ was unruffled by these early setbacks. He reached into the seat of his pants.

"Well, let's just even things—"

Johnny's appearance roaring over the top of the hill was not as serendipitous as it seemed, since he had been following Russ all afternoon, and had been hanging back for the most dramatic entrance.

J!m didn't need Johnny to protect him any longer, yet was deliriously happy to see him.

"Hey, Freak," Johnny said.

"Hey, Monkey."

"Found something worth fighting for, I see."

"I did."

Behind Toad's hand, Marie smiled.

"Can I play, too?" Johnny asked, dismounting.

"I would like that," J!m said.

"Shut up," said Russ, *avec* revolver.

"I hope you've got more than forty bullets in that gun," Johnny said.

"Marie, get in the car." Russ gestured with the weapon, a common but unsafe practice.

Toad shoved Marie toward the Ballistic. She resisted.

Russ pointed the gun back at J!m. "Or I shoot the creature."

Marie got in the car.

Russ backed toward the vehicle.

J!m started walking toward Russ, calmly and deliberately.

"Jim, don't," Marie said.

Russ opened his door and sidestepped in, keeping the gun trained on J!m.

"You don't want to shoot me, Russ," J!m said.

"I really do." His eyes went red and his freckles glowed.

"Careful, Russ," J!m said. "Your mother is showing."

Russ fired and fired and fired.

The bullets sparked off J!m's chest and abdomen, deflecting into Tubesteak, who grabbed his spurting thigh with shattered hands and went down.

The gun emptied in due course, and Russ threw it down. He pulled a rod on the Ballistic and its wheels spun, sending up white clouds into which Marie's face dissolved.

J!m scooped up Jelly and got in the Buzzer.

"You'll never catch him in that, Freak," Johnny said.

"And yet," said J!m.

The electric vehicle hummed forward.

Johnny leapt on his bike. He wove around the Buzzer and headed into the hills.

As the burnt rubber lifted, Tubesteak could be seen squirming on the pavement, Toad and Ice on either side, watching him impassively.

"I'm bleeding to death!" he snivelled. "Do something!"

With his unslaughtered hand, Ice took the gum out of his mouth and twisted it into Tubesteak's wound.

Tubesteak shrieked weakly.

• • •

the ballistic proceeded at an unsafe speed through the hills toward the iconic

MANHATTAN

sign, built in 1923 to promote the Manhattan Sign Company, which went bankrupt before it could finish. In the early forties it was rebuilt by the U.S. Army Corps of Engineers, some say as cover for a secret military project taking place deep within the hills. This was misinformation; in fact they built an underground warren of bedrooms to house Franklin Delano Roosevelt's dozens of mistresses, some of whom lived there to this day, bitter that FDR had not left his homely cousin to marry one of them.

Back in the Ballistic, Marie was screaming.

"Stop this car, Russell Ford," unlatching her door. "This instant!"

Russ turned to her with amused menace.

"Or what, Marie Rand?"

He returned his eyes to the road, only to have his face snap back in Marie's direction, this time with blood gushing from his smirk.

Johnny, riding alongside at fifty miles per hour, punched Russ again, yanked him by the collar, halfway out of the car.

"The lady asked you to stop."

"Okah, okah!" Russ said, juggling the tooth in his mouth.

Johnny released Russ.

Russ scowled as he slowed down, then grinned as he sped up, ramming the motorcycle.

Johnny and the bike flew off the road, spinning laterally over the precipice.

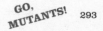

Russ spat out the incisor, and raised two fingers.

"Two down," the sanguine gap in his smile combining with the hair and freckles to create a Boogey Howdy Doody, every child's nightmare.

One long blue finger crooked over the top of the bucket seat behind him.

the ballistic was three curves ahead.

J!m jammed the joystick forward. Sixty miles per hour. Sixty-one. Sixty-two.

The parental control activated on the dash, an uncanny animaviz of his mother's lips.

"You're exceeding the speed limit, Jim," his mother's sim-voice said in a cool monotone.

"Change voice, carputer," J!m commanded.

"I'm afraid I can't do that, Jim," said his mother's dispassionate mouth.

the wooden barrier delineating pavement from dirt road splintered easily. Russ whooped at the bonus destruction.

Marie stared forward, coldly crying.

"Save some of those tears," Russ said. "For later."

J!m's Severed Hand pulled itself up onto the seat back. It was weak, desiccated, barely alive. And famished.

j!m kept steady pressure on the joystick but the Buzzer was losing speed. Fifty-nine miles per hour. Fifty-seven. Fifty-six.

"We're out of plex range, Jim," Miw's lips informed him. "I have to go into reserve mode."

The vehicle downshifted dramatically.

Exasperated, J!m threw his hands up in the air.

And saw his father's fingers.

He placed his hands against the top of the glass cockpit.

Electricity trickled from his fingers to the plex node of the Buzzer; the car surged forward a few feet and rolled to a stop again. J!m concentrated, tightening his brain, trying to squeeze out more juice.

Nothing.

He exhaled.

Another convulsion shot from his fingers.

It wasn't a pump. It was a sphincter.

J!m relaxed and the current began to flow in thick jagged arcs to the back of the car, which responded by accelerating beyond its specifications. He grabbed on to the joystick, leaving one hand on the bubble. Energy flowed through his body, up and out his fingers. He felt light-headed.

A half mile ahead, Johnny climbed up onto the road, carrying his battered cycle on his shoulder.

The Buzzer blurred past.

It took the next curve too fast, back wheel swinging off the road. Inside, J!m was rapidly depleting, the car pulling the power from him, leaving a citric taste in his mouth.

"I'm getting hot, Jim," said his mother's lips.

J!m took his hand down, clamping his energy sphincter. The car went faster still, its battery gauge past capacity.

"I'm going to crash now, Jim. Goodbye."

J!m looked up into the rear bumper of the Ballistic. He slammed the joystick to the right. The Buzzer rode the inside scarp, going over and around the Ballistic. Returning to the road, J!m veered back and forth for several seconds before yanking the joystick back, sending the Buzzer into a spin. It came to a stop in a fog of dust.

J!m heaved himself from the car, drained and coughing dirt.

He saw the Ballistic coming in the distance.

j!m's severed hand perched on the back of Russ's seat, incapable of following the action but with a general sense something was up. Its middle finger quivered, detecting a mixture of mineral oils and paraffin high in yummy heavy carbon, the semi-solid petrolatum. Vaseline. Food. And there was plenty of it, very close at hand, no pun intended, since, honestly, it's only a hand and that would be silly.

Russ was delighted and Marie horrified to find J!m standing in the road, directly in their path, staring Russ down.

Russ pulled all the rods. He held up one finger.

"And one to g—"

A disembodied blue hand clamped onto Russ's face, slithering its worm down his throat, divining that with that much oil on the surface, he must be a well.

Marie screamed such a scream that all of her previous screams were downgraded to voice raisings.

Russ gagged on the hand, unable to tear it off.

J!m did not move, assuming Russ would stop, which he might well have if he weren't busy.

Marie, even in her scream state, saw that while she could not stop the car, she could make it not hit J!m. She jammed the wheel to the left.

The Ballistic swerved violently, missing J!m, but also

throwing open the passenger door and hurling Marie out. The vehicle launched off the cliff, and sailed rather phallically, a hot pink atomic rocket, down a hundred feet before plunging into the loins of the M on the MANHATTAN sign.

Russ was slumped against the wheel, his face saved, slightly ironically, by J!m's Severed Hand, which lay on the floor, broken and dying, perhaps.

Russ roused himself, his head thrumming.

No, the sound was behind him.

He turned.

The nuclear reactor in the trunk was cracked, leaking plutonium, and thrumming in a higher and higher pitch, which was one of the reasons they discontinued this model.

johnny was straightening the front wheel of his bike with his teeth when he saw the flash.

He shielded his eyes and watched the small mushroom cloud blossom down the road.

The hot, *hot* wind blew back his fur.

it was christmas, the very last one.

Great white flakes, no two alike but for their half-life, fell on the living and the dead, coating the road and hillside and neighborhoods below.

Johnny rode up on his bike. There was nothing but ash and an otherworldly glow off the embankment.

He rolled to the edge, and looked over.

J!m stumbled up the hill, carrying a lifeless female in his arms.

marie lay on her father's workbench, her clothes burned and torn in a manner that, under different circumstances, might have been considered sexy. On the pegboard behind her hung an assortment of carpentry and surgical tools.

J!m hid in the far corner of the garage, blaming himself and finding no argument.

"Don't worry, baby girl," Dr. Rand was telling Marie, holding a wrench in one hand and a speculum in the other. "I'll . . . I'll . . . *Oh, dear God, I don't know what to do!*"

He dropped the wrench.

"I'm not even a real doctor!"

Johnny pointed out, "You make us call you Doctor . . ."

"Ph.D.'s!" Doctorate Rand wailed. "Lousy Ph.D.'s!"

A few feet down the bench, Dr. Roberts fiddled with what appeared to be an electric crown.

"Ph.*D*.," he said matter-of-factly. "And you never did successfully defend your dissertation."

"*They were fools!*" Mr. Rand ranted, and jabbing a nutcracker at his dead daughter, "Can we *please* concentrate on the problem at hand?"

Mrs. Rand, on the circular saw/operating table, was at least three Kübler-Ross stages ahead of her husband. "Howard, I think we have to accept the fact that our Marie is gone," squeezing out another tear. "Now let's get her body on me while it's fresh."

"She's our *daughter!*"

"*I* didn't kill her!" Mrs. Rand shot back. "I'm just trying to turn lemons into lemonade here!"

"Trick or treat!"

At the open garage door: a boy in a pointy ghost costume, a girl dressed as Layla, the moon princess, and a little Cucu-rachan in a cowboy suit.

"Right," Howard Rand said.

He snatched a beaker of reactive orange liquid and poured a jigger into each treat receptacle. The kids looked forlornly at their hydrolizing treats.

"Happy Halloween!"

The children ran away.

Mr. Rand turned around to find that his father-in-law was about to place the coronal gizmo on the head of his dead daughter.

"This won't revive her body," Dr. Roberts explained, "but it will capture her mind, and I can build an automaton to host it."

"Back off, old man!" Mr. Rand warned. "I don't want a robot-daughter!"

"Don't dismiss it just because it's not your idea!" Mrs. Rand chided, her eyes involuntarily grazing her daughter's form. "This could work out for everybody."

Mr. Rand grabbed his head.

"If you would all shut up for a second, perhaps I could remember how I brought Dinosaurus back to life!"

"Like we need *that* again!" his wife said.

J!m approached Marie.

"I think I can do it," he said.

"And how is that?" Mr. Rand queried facetiously. "By re-building her neural web with your cerebrumatic fractal grid?"

"I don't know."

J!m placed his middle fingers into Marie's ears.

"I saw my dad do this."

The worms inched into her brain. J!m closed his eyes.

It was dark in her.

He fumbled around, feeling for a switch.

Mr. Rand, snippy: "Why don't you kiss her while you're at it?"

Marie's eyes opened.

Her grandfather was elated, clapping like a toddler. Her mother, to her credit, was relieved. Her father felt a little put out.

Marie bolted upright on the workbench. She jerked her head and stared at J!m blankly.

She emitted a long monotone.

"Great," Johnny said. "She's a zombie."

J!m was dumbfounded. "That didn't happen to the dog."

"How do you know?" Dr. Roberts asked.

Mr. Rand moved to reassert command of his lab. "That was an interesting effort, Jim," he said, nudging the boy away from the bench. "Now let's see if I can fix this mess." He poked around in his toolbox for a leather punch.

"Guys!" Rusty rushed up to the garage door, panting. "Somebody nuked the Manhattan Sign and they're blaming us—you guys. There's a big meeting at City Hall to decide what to do about it!"

Marie pitched off the table and shuffled out of the garage.

"I think she wants to go to the meeting," J!m said.

"*Duh*," said Rusty, making yappy hands. "She never met a meeting she—"

Zombie Marie plowed right into her, unable to process her presence, one could argue.

28

TODAY'S MOST VITAL CONTROVERSY!

even a minor atomic explosion tends to capture the public's imagination. City Hall was packed with citizens concerned about the rapidly revising events of the past few days, aliens vaporizing the entire football team and nuking beloved monuments and who knows what other un-American activities. For the most part, though, the citizens who got up to speak were the ones who always got up to speak, and on the same topic regardless of the agenda item.

"Aliens," Charlie Weston crabbed, thumb tugging his waistband, seeking relief from his obesity, "have been into my garbage almost every night for the past two years. And the sheriff refuses to do anything about it!"

Mayor Sam Wood, sweating uncommonly, was happy to delegate.

"Nick?"

"We looked into that, Charlie," Sheriff Ford said from his seat behind the podium. "It was raccoons."

"Raccoons *from outer space!*" insisted Weston, reluctant to yield the floor, his rage unsated, and also afraid to sit down in those pants.

Mayor Wood wiped his face and spacious pate with a red silk handkerchief. "Your complaint has been duly noted," he said, dabbing his damp mustache.

Weston got in the last word: "Then you don't mind if I poison them." Some people booed, thinking he was talking about the raccoons.

rusty, johnny, j!m and zombie marie entered at the back of the chamber. J!m had brought the bucket of goo, in case the Sweeneys were there, or on the off chance Jelly would come back to life. Odder things had happened, only moments ago.

The mayor determined that this meeting was going nowhere, like all the others, that nobody knew anything about the sign explosion, beyond wet guesses, and that there would be no agreement on what to do, beyond *something*, so it would be best to adjourn while he could still make his dinner engagement.

"Thank you, Charlie," he said. "And since I'm sure we all want to get back to our Halloween festivities . . ."

A formidably buxom blonde in an insufficient sweater stood up. "Yes, Mayor Wood, permission to speak?" she asked with formal vapidity.

"Go ahead, Miss Fuller."

She spoke from a prepared and scented statement. "I am Barbara Fuller, residing at the Hidden Glen Apartments, number—well, never mind that. Last week, aliens, or mutants, or some weirdo, broke into my place and stole my best sweaters . . . ," lower but somehow louder, ". . . and *underthings*."

The depravation of aliens invading unmentionables reinvigorated the crowd, which had been ready to go home and continue their grievance in private.

"I'm sorry for your loss, Barbara," Mayor Wood said, nervously scratching the seat of his pants and drawing Sheriff Ford's eye to the frilly pink lace peeking out. "But I think—"

"One of them planted his seed in me."

Marge Talbott, a permanently frightened housewife, clung to the microphone stand, unable to speak above a whisper. She inhaled for strength.

"In my husband's car."

She was not finished.

"And then he zapped all my grocery money out of my PLEX account."

A dozen women turned in unison to the back of the room. Johnny shrugged sheepishly.

The crowd chattered in a predominantly female register.

Can you imagine?

The big guy there?

How much grocery money, do you think?

Deputy Furry, at attention behind the podium, ground her teeth so hard she almost started a fire in her mouth.

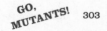 GO, MUTANTS! 303

Into this incendiary mix, crazy old Miriam Brewster shouted, "I'm missing seventeen cats!"

A Caimanese family bowed their snouts and tried to look vegetarian.

They smell bad!

They work too hard!

They can see our sins!

"People, please! People!" Mayor Wood banged the gavel, resolved to wrap this up and at least make dessert. "I've heard enough. I'm imposing a dusk-to-dawn curfew on all teenage aliens and mutants while we investigate the situation. So unless there is . . ."

Zombie Marie pulled away from J!m and shuffled up the aisle to the microphone.

"We're going to be here all night," Mayor Wood said off mike, easily heard, and returned with a wan smile. "Miss Rand, do you have something—short—to say?"

"Here we go," one attendant groused on behalf of the crowd, which turned toward Marie, glancing at their wristplexes.

Marie cleared her throat and said: "Hrrrrrrrrrrrrrrrrrrrrrrrrrrr."

The audience whispered apprehensively, undecided whether this was more alien atrocities or Marie deploying some new and more agonizing rhetorical device.

The argument was soon moot.

"good evening, folks."

General Walter Ford, flanked by soldiers armed with advanced submission equipment, spoke through a small silver ring, which amplified his voice twentyfold, courtesy of a technology humans would certainly come up with themselves within a century or so.

"In light of recent events," the general related as if instructing company to proceed to the dining room, "and to preserve the peace, we are inviting all guest species to check into Hospitality Centers, where they will undergo enhanced naturalization and be released, eventually."

Sheriff Ford whispered to Mayor Wood, "He can't do that."

"He's *your* father," the mayor said.

A soldier took J!m by the arm. J!m shrugged, and the soldier shook, shocked, and twitched to the ground.

No sooner had he discovered this marvelous trick than a new application presented itself, the barrel of a gun, cold and metallic, pressed against his forehead.

Recited the gun's assistant:

> *It left a big stain*
> *That looked like chow mein*

J!m raised an eyebrow, enough said.

A third would-be captor approached and J!m, getting fancy, dispatched him with a move from an ancient comedy short, a modified Moe Howard double eye poke with bifrontal electroshock. The attacker lost a bit of tongue and the prior two weeks, but later awoke to find the world a much more bearable place.

Johnny, in the meantime, had punched eight soldiers, three into brand-new faces.

"We should go," J!m said.

Johnny scanned the room. Soldiers were converging on them from every direction but up.

"Hop on."

J!m climbed on Johnny's back, sliding the Jelly bucket into the crook of his arm. Johnny charged one of the oncoming soldiers, who had been hoping to be killed by an alien, since there was a medal and a memorial for that, death by mutant excluded because of lobbying by the Atomic and Pharmaceutical Industries, which cited the lack of clear-cut evidence that mutants even existed. The soldier raised his weapon, a pitiful response, and unnecessary. Johnny leapt over him, catching a fixture and swinging across the room in a shatter of glass and light. Johnny, J!m and the last of Jelly crashed through a cathedral window on the opposite side.

The general was mildly perturbed.

"Shoot."

A *gunshot*.

"Not *you*," the general said.

frenzied crowds fleeing in terror had been a familiar motif during the unpleasantness, and it was repeating itself this evening, with a nifty twist: the unhinged throngs running for their lives were the monsters, and the things coming after them were human.

The gilded dome of City Hall reflected the setting sun and cast a warm twilight over the scene. With the right soundtrack, perhaps Puccini's "O mio babbino caro," the flailing of aliens clutching darts in their necks and staggering to the ground might have been poetic. Instead, the present accompaniment, unearthly caterwauling and the cries of children for their parents, added an unseemly patina to the whole enterprise.

One soldier, exceptionally unsporting, mouthed *pow* with every *fwip* of a dart, and *booyah* for every direct hit. He was also a poor shot, or was aiming for faces. When Johnny blindsided Pfc. Roy Haskell as he tore past on his motorcycle, one might rightly have thought he was meting out swift justice. But he was only riding by.

Johnny clocked two more, and J!m took out three from the back of the bike. They would have gone for a return sweep had it not been for the plasma fire from the two jet jeeps coming straight at them.

Johnny perpendiculated and peeled off down an alley.

"Where we going?" J!m yelled.

"The other way," Johnny yelled back.

sandra jane waltzed into her home, tickled by recent developments, because she was an idiot.

"Bad news, guys," she announced. "Looks like you two are going to—where's Mom?"

Her father was up on the bar, his arms and legs wrapped around a tumbler. He fished the cherry out of the glass and chomped it, covering his face with red syrup.

"She went out."

"Where?"

"To Japan." The shrunken head of household threw the cherry back, splashing bourbon all over himself. *"For a goddamn lizard!"*

Mr. Douglas's head lolled back. His eyes widened, taking

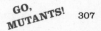

in his daughter's doll head, basketball hands and amazing, colossal rack.

"Sandy, sweetie, have you been taking your stabilization pills?"

Sandra Jane was horrified. "I thought those were birth control pills!"

A *wumping*, wood against wood, gun butt against door.

Sandra Jane looked down at her tiny father, passing out into his drink. She felt . . . *something*.

"Daddy."

The front door splintered. Sandra Jane fished her father out of the glass.

Two soldiers entered.

Sandra Jane twirled a king-size finger between her Brobdignagian breasts, adding a bit of sauciness to her father tucking. "I'm afraid you've got the wrong house, Officers."

The soldiers chuckled. They took her by the shoulders and escorted her from the building.

"No, no," Sandra Jane said. "You're making a mistake. I'm human . . . *human* . . . *HUMAN*!"

googie laid eggs all the way to the military transport, yet maintained her bright hospitality.

"Would you boys like takeout?" she asked her captors, depositing another one.

The cordial incarceration was breached by the entrance of Johnny and J!m (and dead Jelly) on the Triumph, weaving through the lot, scattering the jetpacked carhops, skipping across a few hoods and cracking a few windshields before moving on at maximum speed.

One of the Army jet jeeps giving chase crashed into the big yellow chicken statue, toppling it. Its head rolled to Googie's feet.

"Poor Googie," Googie said.

the monsters were lined up on Maple Street.

A tiny alien sobbed as the big scary soldier removed its face and discovered that underneath it was a small human.

"Scram," the soldier said to the trick-or-treater, patting him on his flammable butt.

Howard Rand rushed past them, up the walk to the Anderson house. Miw answered the door in long black wig and tight black gown, holding a bowl of medium treats, her fangs out until she saw it was just him.

"Where's Jim?" She was in a dry panic. "Is he all right?"

Rand slipped inside and closed the door.

"Forget about Jim," he said. "We need to think about us."

"Us?"

"There's places we can go," he assured her, "secret, secure," placing his hands over hers around the bowl, "but also romantic."

Withdrawing the treats: "What are you talking about, Howard?"

"Don't you see the logic in this?" the doctor-absent-dissertation said. "You're a sexy widow. My wife is only a head, which is of limited utility . . ."

This was too much for Miw, with her missing son, the impending genocide . . .

"You don't even know me," she said.

He was smugly smug: "You have fifty-three vertebrae.

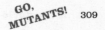

Your core body temperature is one-oh-two. You have hooked papillae on your tongue, which I find incredibly stimulating."

He chuckled at her disbelief.

"Why, Miw, I've catalogued your sister's insides."

This was news. *"You dissected my sister?!"*

"During the wars," he backtracked. "It was a different time," slipping into his natural defensiveness. "Don't give me that look. You're not a princess on this planet!"

under the werewolf mask was a small hairless boy with large eyes and white skin. The soldier directed him to the truck.

"But," the boy stammered, "I have leukemia."

"Above my pay grade," the soldier said, facing a two-block line of trick-or-treaters he had to process before going home to a wife who would be mad at him for imprisoning all these children, not getting that *it was his job.*

Howard Rand stalked out of J!m's house, nursing a shredded cheek.

"There's one in there," he told the soldier.

alientown, loud, rude and noisome most nights, was trebly so this evening, with an excess military presence out for a good time other than the one offered for sale, shattering storefronts and smashing foreign objects, setting off the scent glands of many worlds and giving the low-rent district a distinctly End Times sensibility, not very touristy.

Johnny sped carefully through, hoping to avoid killing anyone, a handicap not shared by his pursuers. The jet jeep's plasmagunner swiveled in his turret firing with wide discretion, almost anything he hit in this neighborhood worth bonus points.

An errant bolt goosed a parked VW Ladybug and it shot up on a thirty foot cushion of air, crashing inches from Johnny and J!m before bouncing into a SoGoan massage parlor, where the endings were always happy but deadly.

The gunner got around to his present assignment, and blasted J!m square on the back with a packet of 2,500 volts, a little more than the electric chair. It was refreshing.

J!m leaned in to Johnny, assuring him, "I got you."

Johnny slumped forward, unconscious.

J!m had ridden on the Triumph a thousand times but had never been allowed to drive it, shortsighted on Johnny's part. J!m called up all available information on motorcycle operation and maintenance. He pried Johnny's hands off the bars and twisted the right grip hard.

The bike reared up and roared forward, exhilarating in the moment but impractical, the steering useless and that food cart straight ahead.

The front wheel dropped just short of the nick of time, allowing J!m to swerve incompletely, sideswiping the cart and sending Hot Monkey Pies—ALL THE GREAT TASTE OF MONKEY WITHOUT THE FUR!—flying in unwelcome directions.

The Houyhnhnm vendor shook a hoof and whinnied epithets, unfortunately forgetting he was supposed to be only a horse.

through the open-air galactic bazaar, the abandoned steel mill, the Futurama exhibition, and down the Manhattan Steps, J!m couldn't shake the second jeep and, plum out of interesting chase locations, had decided to get the hell out of town.

Astride the gas tank, Johnny was dreaming of Africa. His knowledge of ancestral lands limited to viz, the dreamscape was composed of a few large palm fronds and a Caucasian female in animal skins straddling a bunch of bananas. He reached for a banana.

His knuckles scraped the pavement.

He winced. "Are we dead yet?"

"Not yet."

Johnny sat up and retook the controls. "Twelve miles," he muttered darkly, checking the odometer.

They zoomed past the high school, for the last time. J!m had run the realities and there weren't any in which he went to school tomorrow.

"But very soon now," he reported to Johnny.

"Uh-huh," Johnny said.

Facing death in 999,996 of a million possible outcomes, J!m marvelled that none of these new demises matched any of the ones he had predicted for himself earlier. And yet the probable future, that he would be hunted down by humans convinced that he posed a menace as the son of his father, was so ridiculously obvious, it made him suspect there was a glitch in his modeling software, or even that his obsessive anticipation was fundamentally flawed as an approach to dealing with life.

If so, the epiphany was a little late.

The jet jeep was gaining, and Johnny was considering a detour into the corn as they crested the hill and collided head-on with an oncoming Gaylord coupe, driven by what, from the brief glimpse that was available, was a very grouchy Deputy Furry.

Johnny smashed into the windshield. J!m flew over Johnny's shoulders and across the roof, sliding off the back. He managed to catch the bumper, never letting go of the bucket.

The patrol car veered wildly, J!m dragging behind, throwing up tremendous sparks from the pavement.

The jeep jetted skyward to avoid a collision, and the Gaylord drove up onto the high school's lawn, crashing into the viz sign, flashing:

LARRY SWEENEY: 1955 AI - 10 EI

WE LOVED YOU, JELLY!

TRIBBLES! BET YOU CAN'T EAT JUST ONE!

J!m got to his feet. His jacket and shirt were in tatters, but he was unscathed. His chest was wonderfully buffed, in fact.

A bloody paw took his wrist and dragged him toward the building.

Deputy Furry fell out of the squad car, her shoulders well out of alignment, her face asymmetrical, with much too much blush, or something. She went for her sidearm, and, finding it absent, dove back into the vehicle and returned with a rifle.

"You got her pregnant?!"

"This one's mine," Johnny said, strong-arming J!m into the building.

Johnny grinned, spread his arms. "Hey, babe."

The first shot took off a bit of his left ear.

• • •

the halls of mhs felt alien and anachronistic. J!m couldn't believe he had attended this school only that morning. In the short space of eight hours:

his second- or third-best-friend was dead;

the love of his life was undead;

his mortal enemy had been atomized, a bit much;

he was a fugitive from, well, *justice* wasn't the right word.

Or it was, exactly.

J!m was overcome with a sense of awesome and awful responsibility, envisioning a bright causal line between all of his actions and inactions, between his very existence, and this. Two and a half people dead and thousands hunted, because he went through puberty.

Perhaps he *was* the Antichrist.

If so, where were his superpowers?

the last light coming through the clerestory gave the gymnasium an expressionist cast that J!m found aesthetically pleasing and instinctively unnerving. The blacks were gorgeous, and hiding knives.

He put down the bucket and walked inside.

He stood center court, on the face of Manny the Mutant. This depiction was more graphic, less cartoony, than the old one on the stadium booth. The new mutant was darker and meaner; the buck teeth had points.

skrt ikit ikit ikit.

A shadow, long, angular, hexapedal, swept across the wall before being swallowed in the sound of a release bar and metallic *chung* of a closing door.

From elsewhere:

"What are we going to do with you, Anderson?"

Coach McCarthy appeared from behind the bleachers, tucking the shirt into his shorts.

"You mess up my quarterback, you don't take required showers, you don't knock . . ."

He approached J!m, rubbing his fist into his palm. On an intellectual level, J!m knew the coach could not harm him and would break his hand if he tried; years of verbal and physical abuse beat logic every time, though, and J!m's fear response engaged.

He hunched his back, arms and fingers out, tail up, an altogether different effect than at the drive-in, presumably due to the electricity shooting out of his tail, arcing to the scoreboard above his head, which lit up, flashed GO, MUTANTS! six times and erupted in fireworks that were not part of its programming but should have been.

Coach McCarthy's attitude was much improved.

"Okay, look," he said. "I'm a gym teacher. It's my job to be an asshole."

He chewed his tongue. "Are you going to kill me?"

J!m let the interestingness of this question linger.

Eventually he said, "No."

"And that's why," Coach McCarthy strutted in reverse, "you'll always be a pussy, Anderson," speeding up as he got close to the door, and could be heard running thereafter.

J!m was alone again, *naturally*, as that fellow sang. And tired. He had fully discharged himself into the scoreboard. He'd have to learn to control that better, among other things.

He looked around the gym. Over there was the spot where

315

he'd said that unforgiveable thing to Marie; and here, where he was standing, was where they would have danced afterward had he only said, *I'm so happy to see you, too, Marie.*

But then she would have been with him later when he combusted, and much closer than Russ was, ideally. She would have been killed immediately, instead of three days later, and J!m would not have been able to partially unkill her. That might have been better, or not.

Life was complicated enough without all these other lives.

Dong.

The school bell, only it did not ring at night.

Dong dink dong.

Or like that.

johnny's attempted reconciliation with Deputy Furry had failed, she uninterested in his explanation that the other lonely women of Manhattan were vocational, and that she was different, which is why he had not raised prices on her all these years. The deputy insisted on shooting him, which had driven him to the tower, from which he presently swung, tolling away and dodging bullets that dinged the bell, sounding sour notes.

Dong dong dink.

"C'mon, babe," Johnny sweet-talked, not his specialty. "Furry muffin . . ."

Dong dink dink dink dink.

One bullet ricocheted off the bell into his left shoulder. Another went straight into the opposite leg.

Several military vehicles converged on the school lawn

at once. General Ford drove up in his ground jeep, Zombie Marie strapped into the passenger seat.

"Guard her," he instructed the first soldier he saw. "We may need bait."

"Mrrrrrrrrrrrrrr," said Zombie Marie.

The general approached the deputy, who was eyeing her kill shot.

"Stand down, Peggy."

"I will *not* stand down!" the deputy yelled, the assault on her professionalism far more grievous than her Johnny Love trouble. "And you, sir, will address me as—"

For an older gentleman, the general packed a wallop. The deputy complied without further complaint.

Walter Ford lifted the sonic ring and addressed Johnny with jolly paternalism.

"I'd rather not kill you, son. So why don't you be a good little monkey boy—"

Johnny swung out from behind the bell, his fur bristled green.

"I am not a monkey boy!" Johnny roared. "I am an Ape Man!"

The general, an aside to his right: "Maximum setting."

Pfc. Roy Haskell, nose broken and both eyes blackened, blasted a modified transponder. The bolt struck Johnny in several places.

He fell.

The doors to the school opened and J!m rushed to Johnny, sprawled on the steps.

"Hey, Monkey." J!m lay his hands on, absorbing the excess electrons. The body was inert, the eyes fixed and dilated.

J!m could bring him half back, but that would be selfish. A Zombie Johnny would not be Johnny, and they'd kill him again anyhow.

J!m closed Johnny's eyes. "You don't have to fight anymore."

Johnny replied, "It takes more than a couple of bullets and one crummy lightning bolt to do me, Freak."

He groaned.

"Not a lot more."

29

Daring and True EXPOSÉ — of a HUSH-HUSH SUBJECT!

shackled aliens bobbed groggily as the army transport lifted off the ground and hovered away, leaving Rusty Ford stomping her feet.

"What do I have to do?" she wailed. "Suck out somebody's spine?"

Nick Ford put his arm around his daughter.

"Let's go home."

"But I'm one of *them!*"

"I love you, Kitten," he said.

They walked across the civic square, strewn

with orphaned shoes and trampled hats, handbags and thousands of tranq darts.

"Have you seen your brother?" the sheriff asked.

russ was in the back of a transport, coming down from the hills. The Ballistic's ejection system had worked as advertised, except for the part that guaranteed it would never be needed, and launched the lead-lined cockpit out of the disintegration zone. Russ nevertheless got a nasty gamma blast and was glowing like a ghost when he clomped out of the woods near his home.

He was spotted by a military patrol and chased into what to them looked like a flying saucer.

EThL the nedroid stopped the soldiers at the door.

"What are you doing to my boy?" she yelled, fiercely loyal even though Russ only acknowledged her existence when annoyed by it. "You clear outta here 'fore I call the general! Go on! Go on, now!"

The first plasma squib fried her, the second wiped her clean.

"Now let's get that mute outta the general's house before he nukes it up."

In the transport, fellow mutants and aliens kept their distance; Russ looked both mentally and subatomically unstable. He was more than in a bad mood; he was only mood. Anger fragments boiled in his brain in an inconsolable soup, and it was unclear if Russ would ever return to perceive them. Also unresolved was whether the radiation he had taken was going to make him gigantic, tiny, psychic or merely dead.

• • •

a convoy of hover transports whooshed past the Watch
the Skies Drive-in, which was offering a Harrowing Halloween Tuesday Twofer:

known to cinephiles as *Blackboard Jungle* and *East of Eden*, and
fooling no one.

Miw sat quietly in one transport, thinking only of J!m, or
would have, if she hadn't been shackled to Mrs. Rand's head.

"This is all because of your son," Mrs. Rand bitched. "And
your *whoring*."

Miw scratched her nose, inadvertantly driving her elbow
into Mrs. Rand's ear, bumping the head to the floor, where it
was swarmed by randy robognomes. Mrs. Rand would never
be mistaken for her daughter, but she would do.

On the other side of the vehicle, Sandra Jane was not there,
as far as she was concerned. Once she got to the camp she would
explain to the cutest soldier that it was all a big mix-up, and
couldn't they find someplace to mate outside these icky fences?

She felt an itch.

Her father, waking, clambered from her bosom, rubbing
his eyes. "Where am—"

Sandra Jane poked him back in, glancing around to see
if anybody saw. Kiel, a big, broad-shouldered Kanamit, had
been inspecting her breast meat for some time and looked
away when she met his eyes. Her first instinct was to ridicule
his expansive forehead, something along the lines of *What are*

you looking at, Frankenbrain? but, she figured, she might be here for a while, and he was tall.

"Hey, big fella," she said, pinning her wings back to better showcase her plump, juicy chest.

The Kanamit smiled tightly, lest he drool.

floodlights swept the old Army base, welcoming them to the

GROOM LAGOON HOSPITALITY CENTER AND GUEST SUITES

established 1955 AI to welcome guest species and mutated citizens, a process that ended up taking seven years.

Their transport was at the end of the caravan, nearly empty, Zombie Marie, half-dead Johnny, J!m and the Jelly bucket on one side, and Pfc. Haskell aiming a PLEX gun at them on the other.

"Have we met?" J!m asked the private, knowing they had, and where: he was that teeny boffer from the drive-in.

"Shut up," Pfc. Haskell said.

J!m looked out the back of the truck, at the razor wire that twinkled and twirled as they drove past it, at the dark barracks, trying to guess which one had been his birthplace.

He remembered:

a bright hot day, a veil of rust, a shimmering silhouette, his mother, her arms out, him toddling toward her, toppling, a face full of dirt;

a child ape, smashing a Tonka tank, looking up and leaping onto him;

a caduceus, on a barracks door, opening, a young Dr. Rand sitting on a stool, beckoning with wire cutters, and in the corner, a little dark-haired girl cradling a doll's head, smiling at him.

The transport whirred right past the gate, which was closing after the previous truck went though.

"Where are we going?"

"I thought I told you to shut up," Pfc. Haskell said.

the transport went several more miles, taking a rural road into a forested area, the location of J!m's presumed execution. He accepted that, but was determined to preserve what was left of the lives of his friends. He might have to kill someone as a diversion, and he was fine with that, too. The general, riding in the cab upfront, was the right choice from a strategic viewpoint, and in terms of overall righteousness, but Pfc. Haskell had a killability that J!m found appealing.

J!m's mortal dilemma was resolved when the transport turned into a thicket of trees, which fuzzed as the truck passed through them.

"Drink up," Pfc. Haskell said, sticking a small device into his own mouth.

And then the truck drove straight into the Groom Lagoon, inappreciably disturbing the water as it slipped beneath the steaming surface.

forty-two seconds later, longer-seeming if one's lungs were full of water, the transport arrived in a gray metal chamber, which far too slowly drained of lake.

General Ford disembarked the sealed cab and sloshed to the back of the transport. The gate dropped, gushing water and a couple of nonstandard flopping fish. Pfc. Haskell prodded the sputtering, soaked captives out. J!m decanted the bucket, careful not to pour Jelly.

"This way," the general said, leading them from the airlock into what appeared to be a toaster. Coils on the walls and ceiling heated to a smithy orange, and jet turbofans blew them dry.

In keeping with the doggedly industrial look, the antechamber was a barren, harshly lit box of iron. J!m, Zombie Marie and Johnny entered, the last fluffed to plush proportions. A soldier removed their manacles.

"The President is looking forward to meeting you, Jim," the general said.

the room was long and narrow, illuminated by a bare yellow bulb.

"The President would prefer that you not look him directly in the eye." General Ford pushed a button and the wall before them began to move upward with a medieval rumble of chains and gears, altogether alien to J!m, whose world zipped and zimmed with whisper efficiency. It sounded *natural*, and scary.

Light spilled under the wall at J!m's feet, permeating the corridor, actually a visitor's gallery. Behind the iron curtain was another wall of thick glass, or likely Zirclear, looking out onto a large antiseptic room with curved walls, ceiling and floor. Everything was white or clear, except for, in a refrigerated glass case in the back, hundreds of jars of yellow liquids and brown solids, trending toward paler yellow and blacker brown on the lower shelves. They were all signed and dated.

Squatting in the center of the ovoid office was a cadaverous old man, naked but for a long white ensnarlment of hair and beard that grew to his lap. He was avidly picking one of his three-inch toenails with a five-inch fingernail.

His introduction to the Civics viz had been recorded some time ago.

"The President?" J!m asked.

The general, stony: "He's been under a lot of stress." The President also had an advanced case of Camusian sisyphysilis, an obstinate xenereal disease he'd contracted from a Leonine showgirl in the fifties, which had colored his view of alien relations and eaten the choicest parts of his brain.

"This explains a lot," Johnny said.

The general tapped on the glass.

"Mr. President?"

The President grunted and looked up with black eyes. He ambled toward them, half sideways, retreating twice, before coming right up to J!m and glaring at him for a very long time, from a variety of angles.

He blurted: "When is it?"

"When is what?"

"We're not sure," the general said.

The President became agitated, hopping up and down, his beard flapping up to reveal he was an excellent advertisement for the use of condoms.

"When is it?!" the President asked again. "When is it?! When is it?! When is it?! When is it?!" he followed up.

"When is it, Andy?"

"This is Jim, Mr. President," the general corrected him. "His father, Andy, was killed trying to escape ten years ago. You remember."

The President processed this, stroking his chin. His fingers became caught in his beard, and he shrieked several times, tearing them free. By this time he had forgotten all about J!m and was focused on Marie.

"Is it clean?"

"We believe so, Mr. President."

He approached tentatively.

"Is it clean?"

He smooshed his face against the barrier, his clap-blackened tongue swirling slowly on the glass.

Marie looked at him vacantly, but directly. "Mrrrrrrrrrr-rrrrrrrrrrrr," she said.

"She-demon! She-demon!" The President scampered to the back of his enclosure, to the refrigerator.

Something dark smashed against the glass, followed by a splash of yellow, mixing in a most unsavory way.

The general turned to J!m.

"We'll have to reschedule."

pfc. haskell marched them down a low, narrow passageway, J!m stooping under overhanging pipes and beams, the facility in dire need of interior decoration.

The soldier stopped at a heavy iron door, placed his eye up to a scanner next to it. It opened with a clank.

"Welcome home," Pfc. Haskell said, helping J!m inside with the butt of his weapon. "Pleasant dreams."

30

BUILDS TO A *THRILLING* CLIMAX

j!m couldn't sleep, though he had never been so tired. He didn't want to dream.

He was propped against the dank wall of the cell, water dripping on his head from a pipe above. A rat scuttled along the pipe, dropping a little something else.

Zombie Marie lay in his lap, eyes wide open. J!m stroked her face but felt no emotions, heard no thoughts, only nothing.

Johnny, in a light coma at J!m's side, went *Eep*, moving his legs and arms, hunted by Deputy Furry in a pith helmet. J!m took his hand to calm him, and felt that agony and ecstasy, the exquisite pain he always found whenever he touched Johnny, and for the first time he understood it, because for the first time he was not trying to understand it. He was simply feeling it.

He was turning into his mother as well.

The rat, or another one, climbed up on the rim of Jelly's bucket. It sniffed, unsure of whether the contents were edible, and poking its nose deeper inside, lost hold with a scratching flurry, and tumbled in. There was thrashing, followed by a rude burble.

"Jelly?"

At the bottom of the bucket there were now two pints of goo, with Larry Sweeney's face.

"Jim!" he exclaimed and, hearing the plasticky echo of his container, eyed sideways. "Hey, where's the rest of me?"

Krlank.

The cell door opened, waking Johnny and alerting Marie. J!m put the bucket down.

In the frame was a strongly backlit Pfc. Haskell.

"I need the girl."

"She's not available," J!m said.

"What do you care?" The soldier sauntered in with the cocksure grin of a well-armed man. "You're not using her."

Jelly slid out of the bucket and flowed up the wall.

Pfc. Haskell took Zombie Marie by the arm and hauled her up.

"C'mon, girlie," he said, "it's time for a cleaning."

"Mrrrrrrrrrrrrrrrrrrrrrrrrrr!"

"That's a swell moan. You should do that for the President."

Johnny was on his feet. A short plasma blast and he was not.

"*You* don't have to be kept alive," Pfc. Haskell pointed out.

The soldier began to drag Zombie Marie toward the door.

J!m rose unsteadily.

"But I do."

The private, aspostrophic: "Only alive."

A plasm to the chest, dissipating pleasantly. J!m straightened up.

"Thank you. May I have another?"

The private had a dilemma. He had two orders, and would not be able to accomplish one without violating the other.

Fortunately, he was soon absolved of that responsibility.

A sloppy substance plopped on his head, oozing over his ears. Roy Haskell panicked for a short interval, then his gray matter was gone along with all his worries. He dropped to the ground, where, for the sake of decorum, the next twenty or thirty seconds will go undescribed.

The private's boots and uniform lay in a puce puddle on the iron floor. The puddle rose, filling the clothes, forming a smaller, redder version of Jelly.

"What the fuck?" Johnny inquired.

Jelly, defensive: "I was *hungry!*"

"You ate a human being!" J!m said.

Jelly's grin met in the back of his head.

"*And it was gooood,*" evilly glinting, then, sensing their abhorrence:

"C'mon, the guy was a *dick*."

for a military installation it was distressingly unregimented, a warren of unmarked passageways leading nowhere but further down.

The few signs were cryptic and uninviting,

TO RENDING ➡

for example, which did not specify paper or flesh, or

⬅ DISINFORMATION ➡

J!m had maintained a mental map since they had arrived and calculated they had been traveling on a twelve-degree downgrade, tracing a Fermat spiral. If that was correct, they were nine rotations down and soon would arrive at the bottom and center, where there would either be an exit or Satan imprisoned in a sea of ice.

"Uh," Jelly asked, "is there a plan here?"

"Keep it down," Johnny said. "And no."

As somewhat predicted, the corridor came to an abrupt halt at an unmarked door. J!m tried it. It was locked. Johnny tried it. It was very locked.

"Guess we should go back," Johnny sighed, "the way I said."

"We have to go in *there*."

J!m looked hard at the door. It did not open.

"Good thing I saved this!"

Pfc. Haskell's left eye floated up into Jelly's head. A tendril pushed it out of his forehead and up to the scan. The door opened.

"*Now* who's revolting?" Jelly raised his arm for a happy slap, but J!m walked right by him and into the blue light.

an electronic cathedral flickered in bluish black-and-white, hundreds of bulging picture tubes in a circular array ninety feet high, displaying entertainment viz, surveillance of public and private spaces, energy output and usage charts, documents, data, the totality of existence.

This was the PLEX.

Before the screens was a labyrinth of illuminated pipes, surrounding what appeared to be the most elaborate church organ ever built. A bony gray creature hunched over the keyboards, playing a melancholy serenade that J!m had never heard but knew. The images above changed with the melodic and metronomic changes, as if the organist were playing the whole world.

The player abruptly arpeggiated, ending the serenade yet increasing the melancholy; the chamber hummed in blue.

J!m didn't move, and the others remained in the hall.

"Hello, Son," I said.

31

Your HEART Will Pound...

"come in, come in. before they shoot you."

J!m's friends pushed past him and closed the door. I clapped and the lights came on. An obsolete technology, but a delightful one.

"There. Better?"

J!m wasn't coming to me, respect for elders clearly out of favor these days. I hobbled over to him.

"Please excuse my appearance. Haven't had natural radiation in years, and they keep me on low power down here. They prefer me weak."

J!m said nothing, not a shock there. I had him at a disadvantage. I had watched him grow up, first through the cameras at the Guest Suites and later through the PLEX, and had been privy to his thoughts since he was eight, those polio shots quite more miraculous than promised. I had transcribed the entirety of his life, with a specificity and sensitivity far beyond any official obligation, recording every lost appendage, every unusual fluid or odd morphosis, every taunt and prick. I was there through this whole long dark journey he had sent himself on, and from which he would soon emerge, I knew, because I knew my son.

And he had never met me.

"You're taller than I expected," I filled the conversational abyss. "I suppose I've shrunk. You've your mother's eyes. Pity. Mine have infrared."

He looked at me with hate and hurt, in a three-to-two ratio, a later check of the records confirmed. Peculiar, considering how often he'd dreamt of this occasion, on average once every fourteen days. I never did understand how adolescence was conducted on this planet.

"Interesting story about this cane," I gabbled on. "The French, rest their souls, gave it to Ben Franklin, who bequeathed it to George Washington. The gold knob here is a Phrygian cap, representing—"

We were all spared my further ditherings by an improperly fingered and inappropriately instrumented Jim Croce number.

> *You don't tug on Superman's cape*
> *You don't spit into the wind . . .*

Jelly sang, splattering the keyboard. "Look at me. I'm playing the PLEX!"

"That's just an organ," I said. "And you can stop now."

"Sorry," Jelly said.

I elaborated: "The PLEX runs itself, mostly. Don't tell anyone or I'll be out of a job."

J!m was at last ready to speak, the edge in his voice forty percent anger, thirty-five contempt, fifteen fear and eight confusion, with trace amounts of unquashable love.

"After everything they did, you built this for them."

"No, J!m," pronouncing it correctly, with the subsonic accents. "I didn't build it for them. I built it for *you*."

J!m did not like that answer, because he didn't yet comprehend it.

"But *why*?"

"They presented me with unattractive options."

I let him process that, and carried on with the social niceties.

"Did anyone ever tell you how much you look like your brother?" I asked Johnny, forgetting myself. "I suppose not," I expeditiously moved on. "And *you* must be J!m's lovely girlfriend."

"Mrrrrrrrrrrrrrrrrrrrrrrrrrrrrr."

"She was dead, and so Jim . . ." Johnny wiggled his fingers. ". . . sorta . . ."

"Son," I said, "come here."

I took J!m's hands, dosing him with more unconditional love than he wished to accept. He jerked his hand away.

"I could do it, but I think it would be better if you did."

Again taking his hands, I positioned them on the sides of his undead girlfriend's head.

"Go back in."

The blue worms, more properly *phalangeal probosces*, slithered into her brain.

"Gee-ross," Jelly said.

J!m was utterly lost in there.

"Stop thinking about her biology."

He gazed into her eyes with bottomless sorrow, not the sort of absorption that was needed.

"And stop thinking about yourself. Be *her*."

J!m closed his eyes and tipped his head back, a bit showy, and thought about Marie:

her excessive righteousness and silly insistence that all things were possible in a democracy;

her unshakable belief in goodness, despite every rattle and roll to the contrary;

her patience with him, all these years, as he turned surly and solipsistic, much less a friend than she remained to him;

how much she—

He found her.

She flowed into him, her thoughts, feelings, dreams, desires, the whole lot whirling through his mind, sweeping away some of the uglier plaque up there. His probosces did the necessary repair and put her back, slightly better than new.

When J!m opened his eyes, Marie was already looking at him.

"Hi," she said.

"I love you, too," he said.

Marie frowned, smiled, frowned again.

"That is *not* fair."

Johnny chose to celebrate in the adolescent manner, with lighthearted verbal abuse.

"Jesus, Freak, you couldn't have said that a few days ago, before I got shot?"

J!m put his arm around the ape. "And you, too, Johnny."

Jelly, left out of the love nest, darkened.

Marie reached for him. He accepted her hand and slid over, no longer bothering with legs, and blanketed them in a thick, gummy hug.

"I love you guys!"

It was a moment they would all cherish for another four seconds.

"Hey!" Marie yelled, peeling Jelly off her. "You're *eating* me!"

"Only dead skin cells!" Jelly huffed, with uncharacteristic ire. "I was giving you a facial! You should *thank* me."

if it hadn't been for the alarm, there might have been a lot of hurtful things said. Instead, it refocused everybody on more immediate concerns.

"We need to get out of here," J!m said.

"Where's here?" Marie asked, having been brain-dead for the last twelve hours.

"We must hurry." I shambled over to a poster on the far wall, a pinup of my wife, standing on a subway grate with her dress blowing up. Funny how irate I got at the time. I rolled the poster down slowly, uncovering a nasty rust stain. I tucked the poster under my arm.

"All-righty," I said, as two soldiers burst into the room, firing indiscriminately, in violation of a memorandum I sent out at least every six months.

"Good God, man!" I shouted at them. "*No discharges in the* PLEX *Center. Can't you* read?"

The soldiers kept at it, with J!m shielding his friends, absorbing the plasms like a champ, and only stopped firing when they noticed they were sinking.

They went down rather quickly, and Jelly rose in their stead, wearing the bigger one's overextended trousers. He was much larger, bordering on humongous, and approaching magenta.

Marie had missed Jelly's first man-eating, and was distressed. "Larry Sweeney! How *could* you?"

"It's what I do."

Jelly punctuated his apothegm with a tremendous belch, the smell of which was unprecedented and all the more impertinent since he had no biological need to do so.

"Not much time," I said, padding over to the keyboard. The first thirteen notes of *Für Elise* opened a passageway in the wall.

Johnny: "You said it was just an organ."

"I'm unreliable," I admitted.

I thought I had made some progress with J!m, bringing back the love of his life, etc., but his paternal issues were persistent enough that they required airing at this most inopportune time.

"You could've escaped whenever you wanted?" he asked, incredulous and calculating all the birthdays, holidays, school plays, first molts and other childhood milestones he assumed I had missed.

I touched his forehead. "You mustn't be so cross all the time. It uses fantastic amounts of energy, and you'll overheat."

Marie passed us, dragging her finger across his chest.

"Listen to your father."

She's a good girl.

the passage led up to the sewers, which were nippy this time of year, and dark and wet, of course. It was a necessary vile, though, these being Manhattan's least monitored thoroughfares, and so we trudged for miles, knee deep in whatever anybody didn't want in their homes for one second longer.

Disagreeable as it was, our toilet walk offered an opportunity to catch up a bit. I provided J!m with a credible explanation for my behavior, leaving out details he needn't concern himself with, and assured him that while his mother knew the government had scapegoated me, she did not know I had been alive all this time, and wouldn't she be pleased to see me? J!m did not accept or even believe my story, let alone forgive me, but it lowered the overall tension down there.

Jelly excepted.

"I'm feeling a lot of rage," he growled, hulking in back. "It must be someone I ate."

He reverberated with remorseless mirth, eerie even when not coming from behind one in a dark sewer.

Seeking to lighten the mood, "Funny, that," I said. "All these species, and variations, from all across the galaxy, and their shite all smells the same."

"Except for the Curucu," J!m said.

"Lord, yes."

We shared a laugh.

"Mr. Ra'," Marie said.

"It's not a surname, dear. *Andy* will get you in the least trouble."

"Andy, do all Regulese speak with such charming British accents?"

"No, no. I picked it up on the trip over, listening to the BBC. We don't speak at all, actually."

"I *knew* it," Marie said. "Getting Jim to talk is completely impossible."

"Yes, we're more the strong, silent type," I said in deference to my son, though in point of fact I adored talking, and was quite the raconteur back when I had an audience. The mutability of human language and capacity for misunderstanding fascinated me, so many words meaning the same thing and others meaning so many things, the play of it irresistible. Puns, I'm afraid, were a weakness.

I buttoned up, giving the boy cover, which naturally was when he chose to communicate.

"I'm sorry," J!m said.

"For which thing?" Johnny asked.

"For everything. For being a jerk to you, and everybody. And for, I don't know, for causing all this, scaring the whole country and getting us put in camps again."

"Pish posh," I said. "They needed a distraction and you provided one, that's all. If it hadn't been you, they were going to stage something. Had the dogs all mutilated."

"So," J!m smiled, in a realization most males in this galaxy don't come to until, well, ever:

"It's not all about me."

"Not at all," I said. "As far as they're concerned, you're nothing but a pawn. Which is rather ironic, given—"

"Something's coming."

Johnny stopped, putting his hand up. He shone his wrist-plex torch down the pipe.

It moved through the water, fast.

A one-eyed Coprosaur rose from the sewage, its intake valves open, its radulae churning peckishly. One of the few awoken beasts of any use, the species was secretly introduced to the sanitation system fourteen years ago, where it efficiently processed solid waste and negated the need for security viz. I should have mentioned that.

Marie screamed, as was appropriate.

The Coprosaur, a less picky diner than its name would suggest, clamped several mouths on Johnny and began processing.

"I'm in it!" Jelly yelled, and dove into the saur's dorsal maw. The beast reared back, assumed an expression of shit-eating chagrin and turned translucent. It collapsed into a massive pile of goo.

"Jelly?" J!m said.

The surface rippled and a face emerged, four feet high, covering the upper half of the mass.

"Nasty!" exclaimed Jelly, and, beholding his new monstrosity: "This is *so* much better than being a fat boy!"

Johnny rubbed the raw, circular sores on his chest.

"How much further?"

"Oh," I said. "We can go up here, if you'd like."

 FLAMING FURY FROM THE SKIES

the sky was pinking up into as glorious a morning as I could have hoped for my return to the surface. The UVs were low yet invigorating, and I felt a hundred years younger.

What a bedraggled troupe we were. Johnny, nursing bullet and beast wounds, was bloody and listing to port. Marie was death warmed over, sunken eyes and a blue cast that would take days to clear, dying being less restful than most people imagine. Jelly, oozing out of the manhole, was more robust than ever, though not in a lovable way, nor in the best interest of his future health.

And J!m, poor J!m. Shredded attire aside, he was unin-
jured, but he had the open stare of a man who had abruptly
stopped being a boy.

And he wasn't finished.

"This is Floral Avenue," Marie said, noting Sandra Jane's
house, hard to miss with the airplane hangar attached to the
back. "We live a couple blocks from here."

I put my hand on J!m's shoulder.

"Let's go home."

He allowed my hand to stay there.

"Fine," he said. "But Mom is gonna *fuse*."

I chose not to remind him that his mother would not be
home.

We began to walk.

"I know how to handle your mother," I said. "Which reminds
me. You've probably been wondering how you fornicate . . ."

"Later," J!m said.

"Yes," I said. "Later, then."

"shouldn't we," j!m asked, "be coming up with some kind
of *plan*?"

We had.

"We fight to the death," Johnny said.

That wasn't it.

"I think," Marie said, "if we apply ourselves, we can do
better than that."

We turned onto Maple. The system's yellow star, a hazy
orange, hung above the end of the street. I closed my eyes to
bask in its large photoelectrochemical potential.

J!m peered into the dawn.

"Johnny nailed it."

Over the horizon, as if out of the sun itself, arrived the cavalry, not to the rescue.

First came the helicycle squadron, followed by flying tank turrets, and the hovertrucks, disgorging troops.

A ground-based jeep drove up and General Ford got out.

"Walter," I said.

He chomped his compensative pipe. "Are you lost, Andy?"

"Not one bit," I said. "I assumed our agreement was no longer in force."

Walter chuckled with sinister chumminess.

"Andy, if you had come to me, I could've explained that your wife and son were safe, as we agreed, and that the current action was only temporary, until after the elections. Which will now have to be cancelled, unfortunately. You've turned this into a public-relations nightmare."

Neighbors ventured out of their homes, in pajamas and less. They had never wanted my wife and son here, lowering property values and causing diversity, but this morning they were feeling guilty, not wanting it to have gone *this* far, and worried about what or who would be next.

"May I say something here?" Marie ventured.

"If you have any last words," the general said, atypically curt. "You're the reason my grandson is suspended in a vat of Prussian Blu, fighting to maintain his humanity."

A battered patrol car pulled up next to the general. His granddaughter leapt from the passenger side.

Rusty took in the whole scene and focused on one detail.

"Jelly, you're alive!" she squealed, "and *so big*."

"What the hell is going on here?" Nick Ford shouted, exiting the cruiser.

"A military matter, Son," the general said, "beyond your jurisdiction."

"Andy Ra' is alive? What's going on?"

On nodded orders, two soldiers secured the sheriff. "You've been lying to everyone," Nick Ford yelled as they dragged him away. "You told us he was dead!"

"He is," Walter said. "There's nobody standing there."

The crowd murmured. A small boy spoke up.

"There *is* somebody standing there!"

"No, there isn't," Walter said. "Allow me to demonstrate."

He removed a small device from his pocket.

"Walter," I said, "I built that. Do you think I would've given you something that could destroy me?"

"We made some adjustments."

He fired.

zt.

My body language expressed dismay, easily read, even without a head.

J!m wailed and hugged my body, a heartening sight. The corpus took J!m's head in its hands and, judging it a satisfactory substitution, attempted to tear it off.

"Son."

My head lay in the curb.

J!m disengaged from the body and came to me.

"Dad?" cradling my head in his arms.

"It looks worse than it is."

"You're decapitated, Dad!"

"J!m, Son, listen. I'm going to die shortly, and I don't know how long I'll be dead, so I need you to pay attention." I coughed up something apparently disturbing. "I did all this for you," I told J!m. "I built it for you."

"You said that before."

"And I'm saying it again *for a reason*," a bit irritated. "And one other thing: be nicer to your mother."

My eyes closed, first horizontally and then vertically.

J!m, frantic, stuck his fingers in my aural slits.

"Don't do that," I said.

My head burst into flames.

J!m wept.

the following occurred while *I was dead and has been reconstructed from surveillance viz and memory tapes.*

johnny, wounded and exhausted, estimated he could nevertheless take out the general, a few soldiers, and potentially commandeer a helicycle, which was a sweet ride.

Plotting a swing path from branch to PLEX pole to the general's neck, he sprang, only to be swept aside by a slow but unstoppable red tide.

"It's gobblin' time!" Jelly bellowed, rolling in folding waves of bloodthirsty and bonehungry Gelatinous Offensive Organism.

The general fired.

zt.

Jelly quivered, the ray concentrating in his scarlet core, disintegrating him from the inside out. A hand appeared out of the top, futilely flailing, and then he was nonexistent.

Rusty opened her mouth to scream and something hot and viscous landed in it. She spat into her hand.

"Shhh," Jelly said.

j!m slumped on the curb, rocking my smoldering head. Behind him, three soldiers were shooting at my body's feet, making it dance.

Marie sat down next to J!m.

"I had questions," J!m said, absentmindedly picking at my face, "and now I have to wait until he's not dead anymore."

"Oh, Jim," Marie said, thinking him deluded with grief, unfamiliar with the conventions of the genre.

J!m handed me to Marie and got up. He passed Johnny, who had determined an attack at this time would not be advisable, and walked to a black sticky spot in the middle of the street.

He was thirty feet from the general, the recommended firing distance for the death ray. J!m didn't care. Stripped of all his adolescent affectation, unprotected by ironic distance and undistracted by invented agonies, he was in the real world, in real pain.

"My father came in peace!" J!m cried. "All he wanted was peace!"

"Everybody wants peace," the general replied. "What matters are the terms."

My body grew tired of dancing and zapped one of the soldiers in the face. The other two blew it to bits.

"So what are your terms, Jim? Unconditional surrender or . . . well, how about I start by erasing the monkey?"

The general fired.

z—

J!m made a wish.

The beam bent away from Johnny, in a lovely parabola,

and struck J!m in the chest. It was quite a jolt, a shade more than three million bolts of lightning, and J!m fairly fulminated, rays spiking from each and every hyperdiamond on his surface, burning tiny microholes through trees, buildings, people and property.

J!m looked up and saw, again, in the air, pneumatic, light and energy, in a matrix exactly matching the one in his brain, and neatly described by the post-Newtonian meta-calculus he had lying around up there.

He got it, as I knew he would. He just needs to apply himself.

J!m lifted his arms. Bolts shot from his fingertips, jagging at all angles to PLEX transponders up and down the block.

The helicycles and flying turrets went *fzzt* and dropped from the sky.

The general shut off his weapon.

But J!m was inside, connected; he was the PLEX, as it was him, in accordance with the original design, which, to the assembled, was indisguishable from magic.

J!m lifted a finger. Reverse lightning cracked the sky behind him, spreading in both directions until it encircled the world in fire.

The general's weapon went red in his hand, fusing his fingers before it vanished.

J!m blinked and the lightning was gone. He lowered his arms, maintaining eye contact with the general.

"Let's talk," Walter Ford said.

"this memorializes all the rights, and reparations, we've agreed to, surrendering the PLEX to public control, and so on." General Walter Ford signed the docuplex with an eye blink and slid it across the table.

J!m, in a silver jacket with matching crown, flicked through the treaty officiously.

"Only thing," the general mentioned tentatively, "we don't have broad authority over school lunch menus . . ."

J!m raised a finger.

"But we'll make it work," the general said.

J!m eye-signed.

"Now, if you'll excuse me," he said. "I've got a social function."

The gymnasium resounded with applause, some with genuine joy for this milestone in human-nonhuman relations, some in fear, and some because it was a party.

The theme for this year's Winter Ball was NO ONE ALIKE, necessitating the cutting and hanging of thousands of foil flakes, but students were eager to participate, and to assure a record of their participation was made available to J!m, who was quite easily voted the Winter King as well.

J!m rose from the negotiating table and strode in his silver tuxedo to center court, recently repainted, where his queen awaited.

They kissed, and Marie's hair fluffed out.

"I hope I never get used to that," she said.

"I can keep upping the voltage," he said.

The subsequent power chord was a nice touch.

Johnny hooted in harmony with the sustained note, then led his new band, the Wild Ones, in a scorching original.

> *The Martians need women,*
> *And they need 'em really soon;*
> *Mysterians got ray guns,*
> *And they set 'em on swoon;*

The king and the queen of the ball were joined by their court:

Jelly, back in his boy mold, with Rusty, lit up and flaunting her Venusian heritage;

Hel and Mil, dispensing with the manoflage;

and Dorothy Spiva and Bernie Karsko, who were more popular than this narrative suggests.

> *Kronos got the power*
> *To party every night;*

Miw sat on the sidelines, in her appropriate chaperone wear, radiating at her son the hero, the king, the man.

She felt a tug on her dress.

I offered her refreshments, and crawled into her lap. We made a ridiculous pair, me with my toddler body, weeks yet from adulthood, but these are the accommodations of which a marriage is made.

> *Klaatu barada nictu*
> *Every gal in sight . . .*

Sheriff Ford and Lilitu rumbaed by, putting aside past acrimony and leaving open their rekindling options, at least until later in the evening, when she would broach rates.

"Would you like to dance?" Howard Rand asked his wife, in the pan in his lap.

"With *you*?" came the merely caustic reply, for her a stab at rapprochement.

Rand took a swig from his flask and poured the rest in the missus's tray.

> *We're gonna rock this planet*
> *We're gonna roll this planet*

The music echoed out in the hallways of MHS, where Miss Mantis prowled in the shadows, awaiting her next opportunity to take head . . .

> *We're gonna blast this planet*
> *We're gonna blow this planet*

. . . and to the parking lot, where Sandra Jane, stabilized by medication but experimenting with dosages to increase her bust without affecting her head or hands, sat in Toad's rebuilt Turboflite, with Tubesteak and Ice and a baby blue Russ, asking, "Where's the rest of the girls?". . .

> *We're gonna destroy planet Earth*
> *'Til your females can't please us anymore*

. . . and farther still, to the scorched cornfield, carved in a complex and delicate pattern known to the Mayans, and Egyptians, and Sumerians, and the unnamed protohumans before them, upon which shone landing beacons emanating from a thousand brilliant silver saucers, glowing in the night.

Sorry about that.

Please

DRIVE SLOWLY

WATCH OUT
for the Kiddies

We appreciate your patience and knowledge that **everyone** cannot leave at just the same time.